The man was as dirty as a cop could get. He was also dangerous and hated my guts…

Jones noticed and grinned wider. "Where'd you put the body, Bo?"

"Be a little clearer."

"You know what I mean. I left that bruno as a warning to Johnny Cutter. Thanks to you, Cutter didn't get the message. Now it's too late to warn him."

"Didn't think a cake-eater like Johnny Cutter would scare you that much. You're slipping, Jonesy."

Jones stood away from the door, balancing himself on the balls of both feet. He dropped the cigarette on the floor and ground it with his heel, his eyes not leaving mine. His right hand dipped into his coat pocket. "That body shows up, Bo, I'm gonna tag it to you. Should've thought of that in the first place. But I didn't come here to your cage to talk about a dead torpedo who only thought he was tough. I come to see a walkin' corpse that knows he ain't tough. Little Bo Peep. I just wanted to see your pan to tell you that what you got the other night is comin' back to you, Bo, and you ain't walkin' away again."

"You could have phoned that in and not brought your stink."

His right hand came out of his coat pocket holding a snub-nosed .38 Special. He squeezed off a shot that shattered the glass in the window behind me, the slug tearing into the Stage One wall. He grinned at me, slipped the gat back into his pocket, and pointed his right index finger at me. "Tick…tick…tick."

Neil Brand is a former World War I soldier and disgraced ex-cop, now running security for Harry York at York Brothers Studio in 1931 Hollywood. York has a problem with bad boy actor Johnny Cutter, who failed to show up on the set to finish his latest picture, and Brand is sent to find the star. In doing so, Brand uncovers a trail of white slavery, drugs, and murder, involving famous actors and wealthy businessmen—and a dirty cop who was once Brand's partner on the force. As the body count mounts, Brand tries desperately to discover the truth—before he becomes one of the victims.

KUDOS for *Ice Cream Blonde*

In *The Ice Cream Blonde* by Ray Dyson, Neil Brand is a former cop turned private detective/security specialist for a Hollywood studio in the 1930s. His job is to protect the studio from bad publicity—at any cost. When one of the studio's most famous actors fails to show up on the set of his latest picture, Brand is sent to investigate. What he uncovers is a lot more than either he or the studio had bargained for, including murder, missing women, and organized crime. Sometimes it's hard to tell who the good guys and the bad guys are. *The Ice Cream Blonde* is reminiscent of an old black and white movie, taking you back to a simpler time of gumshoes and the great depression. The author's voice is fresh and, for the time period, very authentic. I felt as if I had stepped back in time. It's a great book for a rainy afternoon when life is just too stressful and you need to escape into a great story. ~ *Taylor Jones, Reviewer*

The Ice Cream Blonde by Ray Dyson is the story of 1930s Hollywood, its actors, their indiscretions, and what the studios did to keep those indiscretions from becoming public knowledge. Our hero, Neil Brand, is a former disgraced cop who now works for a Hollywood studio, and whose job it is to keep the studio from getting any bad publicity. To accomplish this, he dives into the underworld of organized crime, murder, drug addicts, and those who think their money and fame make them above the law. *The Ice Cream Blonde* is told in a blunt, honest, and gritty voice that fits the story to a tee. The character development is superb, the plot strong, fast-paced, and tension-filled. It held my interest from the very first word. ~ *Regan Murphy, Reviewer*

ACKNOWLEDGEMENTS

I would like to express my deepest thanks to all the wonderful folks at Black Opal Books, and especially to editor Lauri Wellington, who gave *Ice Cream Blonde* the green light, to editors Faith Caminski and Reyana Blondin, who kept the work on track, and to cover artist Jack Jackson, who is filled with creative ideas.

And to Dash and Ray, who paved the way.

THE ICE CREAM BLONDE

Ray Dyson

A Black Opal Books Publication

Black Opal Books

BECAUSE SOME STORIES JUST HAVE TO BE TOLD

GENRE: MYSTERY-DETECTIVE/SUSPENSE

ICE CREAM BLONDE
Copyright © 2015 by Ray Dyson
Cover Design by Jackson Cover Designs
All cover art copyright © 2015
All Rights Reserved
Print ISBN: 978-1-626942-95-0

First Publication: JULY 2015

Published by Black Opal Books **http://www.blackopalbooks.com**

DEDICATION

For Cheryl, the mystery lady

For Pamela, always

CHAPTER 1

Wednesday, September 16, 1931:

The day he died, Johnny Cutter was the most popular motion picture star in Hollywood. Tall and athletic, charming and urbane, dashing and magnetic—his flashing dark eyes could pierce any woman's soul right down to where she lived.

But just now those dreamy eyes were as cold as yesterday's breakfast.

It was just past four o'clock. The hot day cooled quickly this high in the hills. The sun balanced awkwardly on the top of dark mountains, apparently undecided on its next move. A breeze carried the faint perfume of the lilac bushes forming a perfect line twenty yards west of the dark red flagstones circling the L-shaped swimming pool. Long shadows danced across the pool and across a man's body gently bobbing face down like a discarded sack of bleached flour. Slamming car doors set off a Chinese gong inside my head. A gleaming red and black Rolls Royce Tourer hummed down the long, winding drive shaded by groomed Coulter pines. A similarly painted Packard roadster tucked in close behind the Rolls.

The cars faded into the pines. The gong rupturing my

head turned into cannon fire. Monday night, a thug cop
with a homicidal grudge had tried to split open my melon
with a crowbar, or maybe something harder. He'd never
know how close he came to cracking my egg. Even so, I
was still upright and still thinking—if that's what you
want to call it—while a dogged Hun tirelessly fired off
the Big Bertha inside my head.

I squeezed my eyes shut against the torture and went
inside the sprawling ranch house to find the blower. The
proper call would have been to the sheriff, but Harry
York did not want the county boys mixing in. When Harry York bought somebody, he expected them to stay
bought. The county boys sometimes had a problem with
that.

The LA buttons burned their tires getting to Johnny
Cutter's gated estate at the edge of the Santa Monica
foothills. The bulls showed up in four black and white
radio cars, the dull black meat wagon tagging behind.
Short, rotund Detective Sergeant Harvey Pelz slid off the
shotgun seat of the lead car and began barking orders. He
eased his overloaded frame onto a wicker patio chair
painted soft yellow, lit a smoke, and coldly eyed the scene while a rubber-faced scarecrow with a shiny buzzer
pinned to his sunken chest fished the late picture star out
of the water. Occasionally, Pelz turned his head to where
I sat in a light blue Adirondack chair under the shade of a
purple jacaranda, his dark eyes burning through me. His
body had the vague shape of a Christmas tree and looked
like five pounds of unpeeled potatoes in a four-pound
bag. His nose resembled a plump prune painted bright red
and plopped in the middle of a pie face set off by heavy
jowls and a thick neck. His chocolate fedora was pushed
back to expose a long, shiny forehead. I had no beef with
Harvey Pelz. The only beef he had with me was that I got
kicked off the force for taking a bribe.

Pelz watched the coroner's boys stretch out Cutter's body along the side of the pool. A man I knew as the assistant medical examiner bent briefly over the body, and then the scarecrow covered Cutter with a black sheet. Pelz fished another cigarette out of his vest pocket, stuck a wooden match to it, tossed the match into the pool, and ambled my way. I didn't get up to greet him. My head hurt too much to stand.

"You found the body?"

I did not expect a friendly greeting. I didn't need one. I shook my damaged head just enough for Pelz to understand the answer and waited.

"Who then?"

"Jimmy Gallen."

"Who?"

"He runs publicity for York Studio."

"Where is he?"

"Just left."

"Where'd he go? You should know better than to let him leave."

"He went to see the coroner."

"The cor—why?"

"That's what Harry York wanted."

The name Jimmy Gallen meant no more than an empty bottle to Pelz, but he knew about Harry York.

"York here?"

I shook my head again. "He left just ahead of Gallen."

"Leaving you to handle his business?"

"Harry handles his own business."

"I want to talk to him."

"You'll get a call from the DA before Cutter's body dries."

"That where York went?"

"Right now, he's holding the DA's hand. Maybe the mayor's, too, and the police chief's."

Pelz swore and threw down his gasper. He ground it out with the heel of his little brogan and jerked a thumb toward the distant front gate.

"You're okay to leave."

"Sorry. Harry wants me to stay and keep an eye on the silverware. Newspaper boys will be here soon. I expect the DA to show up and get his picture taken."

"I could have you thrown out."

I grinned and shook my head. A uniformed cop yelled at Pelz, who swore again and waddled back to the pool. The uniform said a couple of words to Pelz and the sergeant climbed into the lead radio car. He spent a few minutes on the two-way, got out of the car, and nodded at the scarecrow.

Four cops lifted Cutter's sheet-draped body and loaded it into the meat wagon. Pelz walked back to the jacaranda and eyed me bitterly while he lit a Pall Mall. The meat wagon fired up and headed down the drive.

"Your boss did his work. Coroner already ruled it accidental drowning without taking his feet off his desk. DA's on his way and the vultures won't be far behind."

"Sounds like you're okay to leave."

"Don't push it, Brand. I got no use for you."

A woodpecker lit into a nearby tree trunk off to my right. I must have moved my head too quickly at the sudden noise. A hard throb hit me and I flinched. Pelz stood slightly to my left and the jerking of my head must have given him a good look. He stepped closer and to my left.

"Damn!" A hard look crossed his face, followed quickly by a grin. "Who did that? I'd like to shake his hand."

"I expect you have."

"What?"

"The uniform wants you."

I motioned behind Pelz. The sergeant turned to see the uniform waving for him again.

"Too bad whoever did that wasn't stronger," Pelz said over his shoulder. He muttered a couple of words I didn't understand. I was clenching my teeth against the roaring in my head.

I stared blankly at the reddening sky and let the cool breeze caress my face. Pelz and his boys got comfortable by the pool and a few of them wandered into Cutter's house. The woodpecker kept at it awhile then fell silent. Not much stirred until the newspaper boys—some bristling with pen and paper, others fiddling with bulky Speed Graphic press cameras—fetched the circus. The DA showed, with Gallen in tow but not Harry. The DA could glom a photo opportunity as easy as he could smell ripe money. The newspaper boys would climb all over Cutter's death, but the stuff that would get printed would only be sweet and sycophantic, no matter how deep into that muck they trundled. I could have wired them and might have if somebody had only asked. Pelz should have, but he was never much of a thinker.

The truth was plain and simple. Just a few hours before the coroner's boys dragged Cutter from his pool, the late heartthrob took his final fade-out in his big, round bed—cold and naked and as dry as Dorothy Parker's wit.

I had a front row seat to the whole sweet deal.

CHAPTER 2

Thursday, September 17, 1931:

Seventeen hours after the meat wagon claimed Cutter, Harry York summoned me to his inner sanctum. It did not shake out to be a pleasant visit. Time spent with Harry was never pleasant. I cooled my heels for nearly an hour in Betsy Hammerlin's cozy office. I stared at a bunch of movie pictures and flirted halfheartedly with Harry's lovely but unconquerable executive secretary outside the doors of the mausoleum Harry called his office. I was in no mood to talk about Cutter or anybody else. I was still upright and probably still rational, but an overripe watermelon had replaced my head. All I really wanted to do was sleep.

Betsy Hammerlin's defenses were slowly crumbling against my woozy-headed charms when she at last got the cue to open the doors to the York kingdom. Betsy unfolded her long, slender frame from the chair and crossed to the massive mahogany double doors that kept the heathens from Harry. She tugged the left door to Harry's mammoth office and held it open for me. She never opened the door on the right. The sudden twinkle in her green eyes suggested a hangman gleefully waiting at the bottom of the gallows steps. I walked in and the heavy door closed solidly behind me.

Harry's raspy growl angrily spit out a rush of words into the black mouthpiece of one of his telephones. His tongue flapped like an overworked beagle. His left hand jerked in short, rapid convulsions, making the ice cube that passed for a diamond flash like a lighthouse beacon on his little finger. Curling smoke from a Cuban cigar the size of a baseball bat hung heavy around his dark, scowling face.

"I'm on it. I'm on it," he yelled into the receiver clutched tightly in his right hand. "I said it was all fixed, didn't I? Whaddya think I'm doing out here, anyway? Itching my nose and waiting for you to do something illustrated? I got my end nailed down. Tight as a rock. You got nothing to worry about here. I don't care what you heard. You take care of your business and spend less time worrying about my end, we'll get through this mess. My ducks are rowed up. See about yours."

Harry slammed the blower down with a loud curse. His dark eyes stalked me while I made the long haul from his office door to the elevated barge he called a desk. His face, oddly pallid for someone who lived in sunny California, flushed deep red. The puffy bags under his black eyes would have dammed the St. Francis flood. Most people had to miss a week's sleep to look that decayed.

"Pissant."

I leaned against one of three overstuffed, low-back oxblood chairs immediately in front of his hand-carved, mahogany desk and said nothing. Harry York, the big wheel behind York Brothers Studio, one of the major players in Hollywood, hardly ever smiled and never looked happy when he did. The dollar signs in his windowless eyes cracked open at the news of his top box-office draw taking the big express without his permission.

Harry York's soul feasted on the bottom line and his blood ran pure green.

"Miserable bastard," Harry said to one of the picture windows to his right. The window stretched floor to ceiling, the dense, dark red drapes opened to the noonday light entering cautiously over Sunset Boulevard. Everything that entered Harry's office did so with great care.

He leaned back in his mammoth leather swivel rocker and took a long pull on the stogie. He looked at me through the wafting smoke the way a big game hunter coldly eyes a trophy head mounted on the wall of his den.

"Not you. Not you. My brother, the—"

Harry coughed and balanced the cigar on the edge of a hefty crystal ashtray big enough to hold my hat. He dug a bottle of aspirin out of his desk drawer and popped a handful of little white pills, washing them down with sand-colored joe from a bone chinaware cup. Brilliant blue, flowery designs stood out starkly against the intense white of the cup and saucer. A large, silver coffee pot rested gracefully on a fancy silver tray on the corner of the barge, along with a silver spoon, a bone china cup of sugar, and another matching cup half-full of cream.

"Come to think of it, I am not very happy with you, anyway." He motioned to the center chair. "Sit down. I'm too tired to have you stand there."

I sat. I needed to. Big Bertha kept pounding inside my skull.

Harry looked at me tartly and a long silence overpowered the room while he dragged on his cigar. He blew the smoke upward. The white alabaster curlicues on his ceiling might have changed color.

"Johnny Cutter's dead," he said at last.

"I heard."

"That's the trouble with bums like him. They go and do something stupid and it's hard to keep it out of the papers." His cold eyes struck me like darts. "You are supposed to protect my people."

"I can't sleep with them."

"You'd like to sleep with some of them."

I could not deny that. A couple hundred of the most beautiful and unattached women in the world worked for Harry. York's Pudding, one of Harry's writers called them.

"Okay, okay. That's water under the dam. We got to be caustic with this. We are skating on thin ground here. Cops talk to you?"

I shook my head.

"Well, they won't. It's taken care of. The bigwigs will say Cutter's death was accidental drowning. The papers'll print that and, if everybody knows what's good for him, he won't go raising up a stink about it. That should protect our box office when that lousy picture opens. And it wasn't cheap, the damn crooks. Used to be you could deal with those greedy bastards."

I didn't say anything. The water was under the dam. The ground was thin under our skates. If we couldn't be careful, we'd be caustic. I was just waiting to hear more of Harry's mangled metaphors, or whatever they were, since it appeared I still had a job.

"What I need you to do is look into this on the cutie so's not to stir up the hash. Know what I mean?"

I could have told him the expression was QT, but a fella could waste a lot of time correcting Harry's prose. "You want me to find out who killed Cutter," I said instead. "And you don't want anybody to know I'm even digging."

"I don't care who killed that lousy bum. He's dead. He ain't coming back like...like that guy in the Bible." Harry stopped abruptly and looked into space. His lips pursed and he got a faraway look in his eye. His head bobbed as he mulled an idea. "I wonder if anybody's made that story."

He was talking to himself, not me.

"Lazarus," I said.

"Lazarus?"

"The guy in the Bible."

"Yeah. Him. I betcha even DeMille hasn't made that story. Gotta check on it. Good story. Big box." Harry waved his cigar around in the air. "Maybe make Lazarus a woman."

He looked at me. "Where were we?"

"Johnny Cutter." I was happy to change the topic, even if it was back to recently packed ham.

"Yeah, yeah. Cutter." Harry practically spit out his late star's name. "I got an investment to protect. I gotta know what that bum was up to. Why he was killed. I can even let the newspaper boys print that he was killed and he didn't drown if he wasn't killed over some trolley—"

I think Harry meant trollop. You could never be certain the way he mangled his words.

"—or was being blackmailed or something just as bad. But if it gets out he was murdered, I got to know why so I can deal with it. Understand? We can't be stumbling around in the darkness, y'know?"

"I don't know if I can find out why without knowing who."

Harry slammed the palm of his hand on his desk. The sound echoed off the alabaster. It hurt, you could see that by the fleeting brightness in Harry's eyes, but he tried hard not to let on. He dropped his hand beside his chair and the motion of his shoulder told me he was rubbing his hand along his leg.

"I don't care who. Just why. Well, find out both. Get the pacifics, but keep it quiet. I'm the only one you talk to. You don't tell nobody. Not the cops. Not your lady.

Not anybody. Not any director. Not any producer. Not anybody who works for me. Or doesn't work for me, for that matter. Got that? Nobody. And especially not a writer. Hell, I'd have a screen treatment on my desk the next day."

"Gallen?"

"Nobody." He banged his hand again, this time a lot easier. "How hard a word is that to not understand?"

"Anyone doing an autopsy? Being an accidental drowning and all."

"No official autopsy. Are you kidding? All the payoffs in the world wouldn't keep autopsy results on the cutie. The body is being released to my personal physical. He'll do the autopsy right away, and I'll give it to you. Verbally. Nobody is going to see anything in writing. Not even that rat brother of mine." Harry thought about that a second. "'Specially him."

"He coming for the funeral?"

Harry's lips curved downward. The bitterness flared again in his dark brown eyes. He swiveled his chair so he was facing the long windows. His stubby fingers drummed the desk. "That miserable bastard. Know how long I've been running this studio? Since 1916. A year before we got into the war. Fifteen years. I've built it up to where it is through hard work, good planning and, yeah, some luck. I got more than a thousand people working for me and we're turning out ten pictures every week. Good pictures. Pictures people want to see. Know how easy it could all come crashing down? You wanna end up on Poverty Row?"

Harry's fingers stopped drumming. Somehow, he seemed suddenly at peace. "I always admired you boys was in the war. That's guts I do not understand, but guts just the same. God knows I don't have anybody else working for me with any guts. You boys saved the world for democrats."

He looked at me. It was not a warm look, but it had defrosted at the edges. "For a while, anyway."

The window had his attention again. The cigar, back in his hand, had gone cold.

"York isn't my real name. Guess you know that. I have never tried to keep it a secret. My brother's idea to shorten it, the bum. Said it looked better painted on walls. Like he was ashamed of it. Like York is a better, more elegant name than Yorkapich. Why should I be ashamed? Know where I come from ordinarily?"

"Eastern Europe, I believe."

"Galicia. Parents went first to Germany. Last name got changed to Yorkapich when we came to this country. We got herded off the boat and through the station, and a man in a uniform wanted to know our names. My father spoke a little broken English and somehow Czorczopicz turned into Yorkapich. We were all a little scared and excited, and our parents had no wish to stir up trouble. They'd had plenty of that back in the old country. Papa figured a name change was no big deal. New home, new name. They put Yorkapich on the official papers and that's who we became. I was eight. Louie was ten. Had two younger brothers, but they both died of a fever right after we got here. Got three sisters but none of them are in the business. They all married well, though. Two doctors and a lawyer. Lawyer works the New York office with Louie. We come over with nothing but the clothes on our backs and a few bundles. My parents worked hard. All their children worked hard, too. Louie and me, we Ameranized our first names—Lazar to Louie, Hirsch to Harry—and started peddling on the street. Got into the nickels when they started thirty years ago. I figured why not get us a camera and make our own product. Money on both ends.

Came out here in '16 and started this studio in a cow pastor. And look where I am now. Married. Two kids. Three grandkids. I'm respected. I'm on a first name base with the chief of police, the district attorney, the mayor, the governor, all kinds of senators and important men who wouldn't give bums like you the time of day. I have been to the White House as a guest. Me, a bum from the old country. Lots of people scrape and bow and call me mister. And it could all come down just like that."

He snapped his short, thick fingers. It was a sharp crack. Harry excelled at snapping his fingers. "So I want to make sure we handle this thing right. Cutter's picture bombs and Louie will cut my legs right out from under me like I was that dummy...you know, Charlie Bergen. He'll use the bottom line sheet for an axe. He thinks I don't run the studio sufficiently. He comes out here once a year and waves those damned expense sheets under my nose like he's Moses come off the mountain. Wants to tell me where I could be more sufficient. He don't know shinola about making pictures, but he thinks he can tell me how to do 'em better. When we were starting out, I was the one who made up the stories and cranked the camera and found the meat to prance around in front of it. Louie stood by counting the shekels. That's all he's good for. Not a creative bone in his whole worthless body."

He waved his arms to show off his office. "Know what Louie gave me for a birthday present once? For this office. A lousy cocoa clock. Ugliest thing you ever saw. For this office. All the mazuma I spent to make it classy and the bum gives me a lousy cocoa clock for my wall. Imagine that? Had an owl that came out and hooted on the hour. Hooted. In this office. Ridiculous. He's still mad at me 'cause I wouldn't hang it. I told him hanging was too good for it."

He turned from the window and stared at me. "You

know, that's not a bad idea. Picture based on Johnny Cutter's life. Might make some money in a couple years. We could re-release some of his other stuff to go with it. Shame a lot of it was silents."

Harry waved the cold cigar in front of his face. "We could add some sound. You know, for effect. Turn that bum into a real hero. Got to think about that. Got to put a writer on it, get a treatment done. Maybe that new kid I hired. He's...naw, that bum's only making two-fifty. If he's only making two-fifty, how good can he be? Gotta be one of my best writers. The expensive guys. Those dopes making two-fifty can't write their way out of a paper bag. Gotta be one of those fifteen hundred a week bums."

His head bobbed up and down like a butterfly in a breeze. "Gotta think on that. Gotta find somebody to play Cutter. Got a new mug I just signed might work out." He leaned back in his rocker and rubbernecked the alabaster curlicues. "You know. I might have made a mistake with a couple of bums I had in here. Made a Western a few years ago with a kid named Cooper. He was good in that, but I don't make many Westerns. Too hard, what with all those horses and extras and locations. Anyway, I let Cooper sign with Paramount because I didn't know what to do with him if it wasn't a Western. Might have been a mistake.

"Same with that fella Gable. Ears stuck out like the doors on my Rolls. I let him go to Mayer. That might have been a mistake. See, I can make mistakes just like everybody else in this rotten business. I mean, every once in a while."

He straightened and tapped a manicured forefinger on his desk. "So back to the point in hand. I will give you the autopsy soon's I get it, which won't be long. Right now that's my doctor's only perjury."

I tried to figure what word Harry meant. I settled on priority.

"You get on it. Do what you can without making waves. Keep it on the cutie."

"I'll do what I can."

"You were a good soldier. You were a good cop." He waved his hand and puffed hard, relighting the stogie. He almost disappeared in the smoke. "I never believed that bribery stuff, just so's you know. You did good work for me and I asked around. It was all good. All good from the people I trusted. I've got a lot of contacts around this town. A lot of people give me the straight goods. That's what I got on you. Now I need the straight goods from you. I think I can count on you."

Sometimes it was hard to understand Harry. Sometimes not.

"I hear you got a twin brother in the old soldiers' home. Like I said, I lost two brothers so I know what that's like. If you ever want to talk about it—"

My face turned into a death mask. I had a fraternal twin, Nelson, dying slowly but surely in a lonely hospital bed in Sawtelle, but I was not going to talk to Harry York about it. Ever.

"Well, I've got work to do," he said, scratching his right ear. A neat trick with that smoldering log he called a cigar in his hand. "I've got a funeral to plan. Some writers are coming up and we're gonna work out one of the biggest shows this town's ever seen. Gonna write the best...the best...Yule logs...no, that isn't right."

He stared at me, searching his mind for the word he wanted. "What are those things they say over people who died? You know."

"Eulogies," I ventured, trying not to choke.

"Yeah, yeah. Eulogies. Gonna write the best eulogies you ever heard. When this is over all the goombahs in this lousy town will know they've seen a funeral."

I could see it plainly. Flashing neon lights over the casket in the cathedral. The Johnny Cutter Funeral. A Harry York Production. Starring a completely washed-up ham. Drum roll, maestro.

"By the way, the answer is yes."

I gave Harry a blank look.

"My brother's coming here. For the funeral. To put me on the spot. Right after we premiere *Doorway to Heaven* in New York. Let's hope for big numbers. Make it easier to deal with that bum if we got a good box."

"That's a pretty quick premiere."

"Gotta rush it. Gotta take advantage of bad news."

"When's the funeral?"

"Next week. Monday, Tuesday. Got a lot of planning to do." Harry looked at his watch. "Where are those writers, anyway?"

"We done, Harry?"

He nodded. I headed for the door.

"Remember what I told you. Do a good job for me, I won't forget." Harry's mind had tuned me out. He was ogling the alabaster curlicues. They had not changed color. Not yet. "*Doorway to Heaven*," he muttered. "Might have to change that title."

CHAPTER 3

The cubbyhole I called an office took up a tiny piece of the ground floor of the studio's main building, tucked in the back corner. You would not mistake it for a broom closet. It wasn't big enough. A small wooden desk, a straight-back wooden chair for the occasional lost visitor, and a couple of light gray steel filing cabinets about shoulder high crammed the room. The filing cabinets were empty except for a few things in the top drawer of the one closest to the desk.

The little desk, a battered refugee from the Leland Stanford administration, faced the door, with just enough space between it and the wall for a thin lad like me to slide through, but you had better watch your shins.

A small casement window behind the desk looked directly at the white, stucco wall of Stage One. The open window and the whirring, four-blade GE fan on my desk stirred up a little air in the close room. A three-hook coat rack filled the area between the window and the wall. The plaster walls, once white, needed a serious paint job. A ritzy room, all right, just like its inhabitant.

A Philco cathedral-style wooden radio perched on the left corner of the desk beside the telephone. A little box containing pens and ink glowed under the desk lamp.

Harry's secretary had given me the lamp and the box to help brighten the decor. Inside the desk were the usual odds and ends, but by far the most important item was the bottle of genuine Canadian whiskey in the bottom right drawer. A law prohibited liquor everywhere in the country, and, even worse, a York Brothers rule barred booze on studio property, but Harry's top people laughed at that rule and made toasts to it. I was not top people, but the whiskey was there to stay. I kept paper cups in the drawer, but paper cups were optional most days. I left the office door open to allow air to circulate, settled into the squeaky reclining desk chair with lopsided padding, propped my feet on the battered desk, and sipped straight from the bottle. The whiskey eased my head and the breeze from the fan cuddled my face. It was better than aspirin.

I always did my best thinking this way, staring over my feet at the little calendar nailed to the wall while the contents of the whiskey bottle slowly faded into a comforting glow. Herbert Hoover cheapened this year's calendar, looking officious behind his Oval Office desk with a big American flag behind him. With the election a little more than a year off, the shine on the seat of my blue serge pants gleamed brighter than the beleaguered president's chances of getting elected again. If you looked at the picture on the calendar close enough, you could see hot water lapping at Hoover's chin. His political future plummeted like a box office turkey, but he would at least land on a fluffy pillow. If I toppled from my slippery ledge, no soft spot would ease the fall.

I stared at the calendar and sipped. Hoover's pained face melted away. I could drive up the coast and fall off the earth, or do a little fishing high in the mountains. Maybe drive down to Agua Caliente. Lose money on the ponies by day, crawl into the bottle at night. I truly did not need Harry York and his headaches. There were other ways to die slowly.

Thoughts of Nels hit me. A couple of minutes older than me, he looked more like our dad. In 1917, at the ripe age of nineteen we joined the Army, and crossed over to Europe side-by-side in the spring of 1918. Off on a great adventure with the American Expeditionary Force. We both got all the war we wanted about ten minutes after we landed in France. I caught a little mustard gas not worth mentioning during the Meuse-Argonne fight that September. Nels caught a lot of gas. It ate at his skin and blistered his lungs and he fought the rest of the war in a string of hospitals around battle-torn France.

By the time we got home the stuff had turned Nels to paste, but he hung tough and got well enough to join the police force. I joined and got bounced for being a crooked cop—

Eddie Cantor: "Three guys standing on a street corner in LA. How do you know who's the crooked cop?"

Straight man: "How?"

Cantor: "He's the one with the badge."

—but Nels' fading health soon forced him to retire. After that, he kept sinking into himself, wasting to nothing, spending listless days in a reclining wheelchair, mostly sleeping, with nothing to do but wait for the end.

I looked in on him almost every day. Mostly he slept, but some days I found him awake. Sometimes being awake meant he was alert. When he was alert, he always asked me that same question. The question I could not face. In my more romantic moments, I told myself Nels was getting better. Those few moments became fewer. Most of the time, I faced up to his bleak prospects. My mother, nearly eight years dead of cancer, would have smiled and been strong. She was stronger in mind than any of us were. Especially my old man. A bitter shell replaced him. Each day, he drew closer to a dying son. Each day, he pushed his other son farther away.

I capped the bottle and set it on my desk. Johnny Cutter popped into my head. Success had pumped up Cutter's ego like a hot-air balloon. The problem child showed up for work late after all-night binges, or didn't show up at all, or caused trouble on the set with rude, erratic behavior. When talkies came in, he'd forget his lines or slur his speech, or curse long and loud for the camera. But Harry tolerated Cutter because Johnny Cutter was top box office and that forgave a lot of sins in Hollywood. A week ago, he failed to show up to shoot the final scenes on a big-budget potboiler, and Harry sent me to find him. I figured he was merely strung out again on illegal hooch or shacked up with another young, willing bit player. A simple job to pry him from her arms, sober him up, get his clothes on, and get him back in front of the cameras. From that point, he was the director's problem.

But it wasn't simple. The Cutter mess opened a deep pit of quicksand and I teetered on the edge while somebody shoveled mud at me. And laughed wickedly while he was shoveling.

The smell of cigarette smoke brought me back to life.

"How you sleepin' at nights, Bo?"

The laughing in my head stopped. The cannon went silent. Wicked thoughts shoved out the morbid thoughts. The bogeyman, in the form of LAPD Detective Sergeant Elmo Jones, loomed at my door.

"How'd you get in here?"

"Man at that boat hadn't shown, Bo, you'd still be sleeping. Way down deep."

He leaned his right shoulder against the door frame. His burning gasper dangled from the side of his mouth, which twisted into a weasel grin from under the glare of rat-mean eyes. His left hand peeled back his suit coat, showing his police shield and his worn service revolver.

"This gets me places," he said, tapping his badge.

"You can't hide behind that buzzer forever. Sooner or later you'll get swept out with the garbage." I was not heeled. No need for guns inside the studio. Until now.

"I ain't hidin', Bo. I'm right out here in the open. You invited me to come check out your melon." His mouth twisted into what might have been a grin. His eyes retreated behind dark slits. "Remember?"

I reached for the bottle and took it by the neck. "You'd have to step a little closer."

Jones noticed and grinned wider. "Where'd you put the body, Bo?"

"Be a little clearer."

"You know what I mean. I left that bruno as a warning to Johnny Cutter. Thanks to you, Cutter didn't get the message. Now it's too late to warn him."

"Didn't think a cake-eater like Johnny Cutter would scare you that much. You're slipping, Jonesy."

Jones stood away from the door, balancing himself on the balls of both feet. He dropped the cigarette on the floor and ground it with his heel, his eyes not leaving mine. His right hand dipped into his coat pocket. "That body shows up, Bo, I'm gonna tag it to you. Should've thought of that in the first place. But I didn't come here to your cage to talk about a dead torpedo who only thought he was tough. I come to see a walkin' corpse that knows he ain't tough. Little Bo Peep. I just wanted to see your pan to tell you that what you got the other night is comin' back to you, Bo, and you ain't walkin' away again."

"You could have phoned that in and not brought your stink."

His right hand came out of his coat pocket holding a snub-nosed .38 Special. He squeezed off a shot that shattered the glass in the window behind me, the slug tearing into the Stage One wall. He grinned at me, slipped the gat back into his pocket, and pointed his right index finger at me. "Tick...tick...tick."

Harsh laughter trailed behind him like oil from a broken engine as he walked down the hallway. The door at the end of the hall clicked shut. I grabbed the bottle and finished it with one long pull. This deep into the bowels of York Brothers Studio, no one had heard the shot. And chasing after Detective Sergeant Elmo Jones just now was a damn fool idea. I dialed the switchboard and told Gertie to send someone to replace a broken window in my office, and keep his yap shut about it. I put my hat on my aching head and went outside.

Sunlight hit me like a scabby fist. Big Bertha fired another salvo inside my skull. Jones was gone but I could still smell him. A hellish image of rat-mean eyes scorched my baked mind. The sidewalk felt like quicksand, dirty and sluggish at my feet. I didn't know where or how this damned mess would end, only that it wouldn't go on much longer.

A week ago, Harry sent me to find a missing picture star named Johnny Cutter. But this whole business had started long before that, started with a dirty cop named Elmo Jones, and it didn't take a genius to see that's where it would finish...

∽∾∽∾

Saturday, June 21, 1924:

A middle-aged Fox contract Airedale who called himself Henderson Pettigrew loaded up on good hooch and bad ideas just before he took a dive over a second story balcony railing shortly after midnight, while trying to deprive a tasty young dish of her clothing. Pettigrew couldn't hold his booze and he couldn't hit his mark. He landed on the edge of the cold, stone patio about ten inches from the deep end of the kidney-shaped swimming pool.

A party was in full swing, but the revelry crashed to a sudden halt. A few guests dusted. Several hung around to await the second act.

It was my first call involving a death. I had been a member of the Los Angeles Police Department slightly more than three months—just off probation, still more than a little wet behind the ears. My father was a career police officer, and my brother had joined the department three years before I did. I tried my hand at various jobs, including some stunt riding as a motion picture extra in a bunch of cut-rate horse operas. The only future that of-fered was a busted-up frame and a calcified liver, and so finally, inevitably, I joined the force in early March 1924.

My training sergeant was Franklin Arthur Harless. They told me he was one of the finest cops on the force. They said he was going places and I had hit the jackpot by getting assigned to him. He was a good cop, they said, who did things the right way, and he would teach me to do things the right way. He was on the level, they said, and that was straight goods. But Franklin Arthur Harless was fast-tracked toward a detective's shield, and when that happened I got a new partner, Sergeant Elmo Law-rence Jones. Jones was the polar opposite of Frank Harless.

I got my first slant at Jones the night Pettigrew splat-tered himself. Party-goers enjoyed their particular vices behind the stone walls of a swanky Beverly Hills man-sion owned by a film director named Homan Dennes, one of the brightest lights in the motion picture heaven. Any-thing that had to do with the motion picture industry in those days was big juice and had to be trod around carefully. Jones and a dim-bulb partner of his named Hiram Strakowsky got the call that night. Harless and I were nearby, buzzing a red hot grifter in a souped-up Stutz. Harless said we had better answer the Dennes call, too. His lip curled at the notion of Jones and his thug partner alone with a bunch of high hatters. We hustled and got there just behind Jones.

The hooked-nosed Jones and the flat-faced Strakowsky were both baby grand cops with thick necks and wide shoulders, although Jones was half a head taller. Both of them were weasel mean, but Elmo at least had some brains.

There was no foul play involved as it turned out. Ribbed up on straight whiskey, Pettigrew had clumsily tried to undress a blonde skirt who closed the bank on him. Pettigrew grabbed for her. She jerked away. His wobbly stilts gave out and he chased himself over the polished cherry railing. One of the guests panicked and called the bulls, else they could have cleaned up the scene and dropped Pettigrew miles from the Dennes place.

Instead of calling the city marshal, someone goofed and called the LAPD. It was simply poor luck that Jones and his partner were first to arrive.

Most of those at the party skipped before the bulls got there, including the blonde skirt. None of the remaining guests could recall her name or what she looked like. One of those guests was an up-and-coming actress named Thiele Garsone. She had been in a back bedroom on the second floor in full undress rehearsal with a handsome young actor who called himself Johnny Cutter. They were expending a great deal of ardor on a love scene. By the time they got dressed and downstairs, it was too late to escape.

A relaxed Cutter sat down in an overstuffed chair in the Egyptian-themed living room, slung a leg over a chair arm, and nonchalantly lit a Chesterfield. Thiele Garsone, whose official studio bio said she was born about fifty miles outside Paris, entrenched herself in a Denon empire chair in the corner and dried up like a canceled stamp. She discreetly closed the door of a rosewood armoire full of illegal hooch and suddenly remembered she didn't speak English.

Another young player named Joan Banes had passed out in the master bathroom with her head in the toilet, courtesy of a quart of brown plaid. Dennes revived her and she tried to blow before the cops arrived, but she was too late. Still fried on the scotch, she tried to climb over the stone wall surrounding the mansion. It was Jones who dragged her off the wall, gleefully using more muscle than was needed. She slapped his face and tried to kick him, but Jones just grinned at her. It was not a comical grin.

Jones had launched into his standard heavy-handed tactics when Harless and I rolled in. Frank, who out-ranked the three of us, took over. He divided the director and the few guests who had not escaped our clutches into two groups, separated them, and fired up the grill. Frank and I got one group, Jones and Strakowsky the other. Frank held his one-on-one interviews in the formal dining room with the Venetian mirrors, while I kept the others in the main living room, not letting them talk to one another. We wanted to hear their stories before they could re-hearse them. Jones worked his interviews in the library, with Strakowsky keeping the rest of the guests quiet in an anteroom.

Somehow, Frank's group included most of the men at the party. Jones got the dolls, all young and pretty, with slim figures and disdainful stares. One of the tomatoes Jones grilled was the bearcat who had tried to climb the wall. Even after a half-hour with her head in the toilet,

Joan Banes was strikingly beautiful with platinum hair topping her head like a scoop of vanilla ice cream. She was sobering up and was as jumpy as a bent frog, but Elmo Jones made a lot of people nervous.

The Beverly Hills city marshal showed and put an end to us. It was his jurisdiction, and we were as welcome as a whorehouse priest. He didn't want anybody tromping on the wrong toes in his city. His lab boys examined the body, half-heartedly went through the second floor bedroom, and half-listened as the guests recited basically the same story. The evidence matched the tale told by the guests and Pettigrew's death was written off as a heart attack.

Homan Dennes was pals with a couple of mayors, the district attorney, the city marshal, and the city hall janitor. He had plenty of Hollywood pull. The papers said Henderson Pettigrew died of a heart attack while having dinner at the home of a good friend. We were four years into Prohibition. There was no mention of alcohol at the scene.

A routine case. Except for Jones. And, as it turned out, the bearcat he pulled off the wall.

Three months later the brass bounced Hiram Strakowsky from the force for a variety of naughty things. Three weeks after that Frank Harless made detective lieutenant, and I was given over to the tender care of Elmo Jones. It didn't take long until my police career was on the fast track to nowhere. Pettigrew's header had not only finished the eroding career of a rummy actor, it had derailed the future of a young picture actress, and put the skids under a rising LAPD cop.

I was that cop. Joan Banes was the actress. The skids under her were greased far slicker than mine.

CHAPTER 4

Wednesday, September 9, 1931, early morning:

I t had become a daily ritual.

Shave, shower, dress, eat breakfast—sit on the edge of the bed and stare grimly at the bottom drawer of the little black night stand. The Colt model 1911 rested in there like a sleeping ghoul, the seven-shot magazine nestled beside it. There was only one bullet in the clip, but one slug was all I needed. One slug would end the agony. One lousy pull of the trigger.

Let the gun warm my hand. Ram the magazine home. Rack the slide. That's all it took. That and the guts just to do it, even though my gut ached at the thought of it.

A daily ritual—like putting on your shoes—but it always came to the same uneasy end. The untouched .45 would remain in the drawer, cold, hard, and alone with just the clip for company. To do the thing that had been requested was to abandon all hope and, against all reason, I still clung to that hope.

Hope as faint as the quiet murmur of a distant heartbeat.

Just a faint hope.

Nothing more.

e/oe/o

Wednesday, September 9, 1931, late morning:

A short, thin man with lifts in his shoes kicked open the flimsy door and stepped into a shoddily furnished room, his white dinner jacket drooping over bony shoulders. He held a loaded, short-barreled revolver the way a bachelor would hold a loaded diaper. He banged off three shots at a man sitting at a small, round table. The man made a show of falling to the floor, and the dark brunette sitting at the table tried not to laugh.

"Cut," the director yelled.

The dead man got off the floor. The brunette yawned. A makeup lady appeared and began dusting the brunette. A prop man came from nowhere to put more blanks into the gun. The sound man fooled with the microphone hidden in the lamp on the table.

The director crawled onto the set and tried to show his clumsy actor how to hold a gun and make believe he could actually shoot it. The actor was supposed to be a gangster, not a fag teacher in a girls' school. The director tried to show his actor what he wanted. Drake Charles was a pretty good B director, but he knew a lot more about holding a bottle than holding a roscoe.

I was standing in the shadows way back behind the cameras, the script girl, the grips, and the extras, back where nobody could see me. Nobody but a little, daisy character actor named Vernon Willson, who had a scene coming up if the guy with the gun ever learned to shoot somebody. Willson had just asked about my brother. I had no interest in talking with Willson, but I had come to the set to deliver a short message for him from Harry York.

A week earlier, the indiscreet Willson had mistaken a

male pedestrian for a driveway just outside a boys only juice joint downtown. Willson's passenger had his face in Vern's lap at the time and Willson barely had time to button his pants before witnesses showed. Turns out the grifter who got hit was a double-jointed fakeloo artist the buttons called Philly the Flop, who made a living of sorts out of getting hit and settling for whatever the driver had on him instead of calling the bulls.

I had rousted Philly once when I was still on the force. That was six years ago and he was still trying to make jack with that two-bit caper. Jimmy Gallen, Harry's top publicity hack, worked his magic and kept Willson's name out of the papers. That saved Vern's career, but Harry decided to enforce the morals clause in Willson's contract and he cut the actor's $1,500 weekly salary to $500. I was there this morning to deliver the news.

Willson acted outraged, he was good at that. He sputtered, waved his arms, and called down various curses on Harry York. Didn't matter. People far more spiritual than Vern Willson soundly cussed out Harry York daily—although never to his face—and, in the end, between Willson, York, and the world, only Willson gave a damn about his contract.

"Willie boy, you're lucky to have a job. You want to kick to York, okay. Harry could snap his fingers and you'd be under glass or out of the business. A salary cut might mean one or two fewer gaycats for you, but you'll get by."

Willson took a deep breath and stared past me. I had delivered the message and the director, ready to reshoot the scene, yelled for quiet.

"Just keep your pants buttoned in public," I said and turned for the door.

I slipped through the Stage Two exit and into the bright sunlight. I stopped halfway down the eight steps when I heard my name yelled loudly. It was Merly the Mouth, Harry York's gopher. Merly almost got run over by a black knight on a black horse headed for pre-production costuming for a King Arthur picture, but he deftly avoided the collision. Merly didn't look to be the type who could avoid much, but after you'd been around him awhile, you realized avoiding things was his biggest talent. Merly said the big man wanted me in his oversized office. That was a rare thing. Even if you were getting fired, Harry York didn't call you to his office. He preferred to send memos.

"What about? He need his shoes tied?"

"I know from nothing. Boss just said find you pronto. Been lookin' for ten minutes so he's gonna be really pumped."

"On my way. You've got something else to do, I'm sure."

The top of Merly's head reached the breast pocket on my suit coat. Rail thin and just a little stooped, he could step on your toe with a cement block in his pocket, and you wouldn't feel it. The wide, spongy nose on Merly's oblong head looked like Mount Vesuvius, and if he wiggled his oversized ears you'd expect him to fly. His soft, gray eyes opened like a couple of clam shells and his long face bobbed. "Pipe that," he said. "Thanks."

Merly the Mouth hustled off like a man walking his sore dogs on hot coals.

Harry's office took up most of the top floor of the main studio building fronting Sunset. He had the long, four-story building of wood and stucco painted frosty white. It was painted frosty white twice a year. A drawing of a motion picture camera, painted black, took up the top two stories on the left of the building and, on the right, a streamer pretending to be unspooling film bore letters spelling out *York Brothers Studio*. Older brother Louis had shortened their name to York without asking his brother. Harry didn't like that, but he was in Hollywood scouting studio locations when Louis changed it. When Harry found out, it was too late. The legal papers were drawn, the publicity mill was grinding, and it was too expensive to change the name.

Harry did what he had to. He accepted the shortened name and put another black mark on a long list he was compiling of things he didn't like about his brother.

The Yorks had divided their budding enterprise into two locations. Harry stayed in Hollywood to handle the creative end of York Brothers Studios. Louis lived in New York, within arm's reach of the big banks. From there, Louis controlled the purse strings. Too late, Harry realized the money end made Louis the real studio power. It was no secret the brothers did not get along, and three thousand miles of hard ground between them might be the only thing that kept one from killing the other.

I entered the main building at the side entrance and started up the carpeted steps. I didn't like the elevator. Too many people used it. The commissary and kitchen filled most of the ground floor, with a few offices for the low-rung writers tucked in the back. Harry had a large private dining room just off the commissary for honored guests. The second and third floors were almost entirely offices for studio producers, directors and the top-paid writers, along with a couple of smaller meeting rooms and several projection rooms.

Harry's office took up most of the top floor, along with his private projection room, a large meeting room, and smaller but expensively furnished offices presided over by a collection of vice presidents who were mostly Harry's yes-men.

A long, brightly lit hallway ran the length of the top floor against the wall facing the lot. Signed photographs of York Brothers stars, wannabe stars, contract players, character actors, directors, agents and producers—close to a thousand photos in all—covered the hallway walls, all personally signed to Harry, none to Louis. Probably a black mark on the hate list Louis was compiling in New York.

Two outer rooms protected Harry's office. Polished wooden chairs for the chosen few who were called, but still had to wait, lined the first room. The receptionist filled the space to the left of the door, and to the right, behind a closed door, two switchboard operators could gossip in private.

Gertie, the receptionist—a pretty redhead with lots of freckles and lots of trouble holding her weight down— waved me into the second room, where Harry's private secretary sat behind an imposing desk covered with a Fil- ofax, three telephones, a dictograph, a typewriter, an of- fice intercom, and several loose-leaf books, bulging with all the names, addresses, phone numbers and who knew what else for everybody who worked for the York Broth- ers.

Betsy Hammerlin was a silky brunette with star-maker looks. Tall and lithe, she belonged in front of a movie camera, not behind a gaggle of telephones. At least, I kept telling her that.

"Listen, buster," she told me icily the first time I men- tioned it, "this town is full of good-looking babes with lots of talent who can't even get a career started under the sheets. Those of us with no talent, and who know we have no talent, are just fine where we are. I didn't need sheets to get me here and I don't need 'em to keep me here."

Every time I saw Betsy, I got hung up on that sheets thing. When I walked in, she gave me a tired smile and hung up the phone.

"Trying to call me?"

"Uh-huh. Harry's yelled at me three times in the last five minutes wanting to know where you are."

"He could be MGM's new lion."

"Don't mention MGM in this office," she said lightly. She crossed to the doors and turned the left knob. I think Betsy was the only person in the world allowed to touch it.

You could play a Wimbledon match in Harry's office and have plenty of room left over for a few side games of shuffleboard. The medium gray carpet wasn't too soft— you only sank in to your ankles. The ceiling was twelve feet high and the double doors to his office were each six feet wide and ten feet high, covered in oxblood leather with a giant gold-plated doorknob in the middle of each door for show. It was impossible to turn the knobs. The doors only opened from the outside, which was Harry's idea because he only used his private exit in the back right corner of his office. He wanted the hired help and honored guests shuffled in and out through the kingdom's front gates, and they could only leave when Harry buzzed Betsy.

The furniture was Queen Anne, picked by Harry because he thought the name sounded expensive and impressive. His designer—who doubled as the studio's top set designer—originally suggested Louis XV furniture, but Harry was damned if he was going to decorate with anything that had his brother's name on it. Two picture windows, each six feet wide and running floor to ceiling, graced the wall to the left, overlooking Sunset and the main entrance to the studio. Between the long windows, a white marble bust of the Roman philosopher Marcus Tullius Cicero rested on a chiseled six-foot-high white marble stand designed to look like a miniature Roman column. Harry picked a bust of Cicero for the same reason he chose Queen Anne, but everybody knew Harry couldn't pick Marcus Tullius from Slick Sid Cicero, a rumpled racetrack tout down at Agua Caliente.

Light fixtures, scattered strategically around the room, allowed Harry to close the window drapes, pull down the blinds, and darken the room for special effects. He could brighten or darken the recessed lighting to regulate the mood he wanted.

About a hundred signed photos of big-time Hollywood stars and directors littered the wall opposite the windows.

In the corner of that wall, Harry's private office door opened to the long hallway. His private bath, opposite the main doors and in the corner beside the private office door, featured a bathtub big enough for four. A mahogany platform, elegantly carved, extended from the left wall just past the last window to the corner between the two private doors, rising about four inches above the rest of the office. The platform's buffed mahogany floor had no carpeting and needed none because Harry's desk covered most of it. A basketball team could have played on his desk. Harry sat in a big overstuffed swivel chair behind the desk, which made him a good foot higher than anyone else in the room, so everyone who came in had to look up at him. It was an effect Harry liked. He needed it. He was about five-feet-six in his stocking feet.

Behind the desk, a radio five feet high and three feet wide bore more dials than a battleship's boiler room. On the wall above the radio, a four-by-six-feet oil portrait of Harry glared down on the room. A brass light fixture above the painting threw a delicate beam across the portrait. I wanted to ask Harry why he didn't surround the painting with lights that would flash on and off when the big office doors opened but I was afraid he might like the idea.

When I walked in, Harry took an unlit Havana out of

his mouth and glared at me. Without the stogie, his mouth looked like a torn pocket. "Where you been?" he said gruffly. "Sent for you ten minutes ago."

"It's a big lot."

"Yeah. Well, I make big motion pictures. Sit down."

I grabbed a space on the sofa against the right wall, under a signed photo of the always-spectacular Dolores del Rio. Jimmy Gallen, sitting at the end of the sofa, turned a light-colored straw boater around in his manicured mitts.

The three overstuffed chairs in front of Harry's desk held the overstuffed butts of producer Jerry Hilt, director Tod Markham, and Harry's attorney, Al Fein. Jerry and Tod gave me cursory glances, but no hellos. The fat lawyer just stared at the burnished wingtips covering his tiny plates.

"We got a problem, Brand," Harry said. He was talking to me but looking at the alabaster curlicues on his ceiling. "Jerry, you tell him. Be pacific."

Hilt didn't look at me, but his deep voice carried across the room. A tall man in his mid-forties, he resembled a bell with two pins for legs.

"You probably know we're making a big budget picture called *Doorway to Heaven*. Johnny Cutter is our star, only we can't find him. He hasn't been here for two days. We're about to wrap it and all we got left is his key scene. We need him here."

"Know what Cutter's problem is?" Harry moaned. "Know why he pulls this? Big head. Full of himself. That's why. This time, I'm gonna teach that bum a little humidity."

A silence fell over us while we tried not to snicker.

"We've got a schedule to make," Hilt said, thankfully breaking the silence. "And the premiere's already booked for New York."

"Send anyone to his house?" I asked.

"After several unanswered phone calls, we sent Merly up to check," Hilt said. "He says no one is home. Place is locked tight."

"Merly'd only knock on the door and come back here when he got no answer," I said. "What about Cutter's agent? Anybody call him?"

"Myron quit him a while back," Hilt said. "Irreconcilable differences."

"You and Jimmy go," Harry said. "You get in the house and Jimmy takes it from there. We find something we don't wanna find, I want Jimmy on the spot to handle it."

"Last time Cutter didn't show, he was shacked up with a case of booze and two very friendly frails from central casting."

"And I had to give both of 'em six-month contracts to keep their yaps closed. Listen, Brand, Cutter has three years left on his contract and his pictures make a lot of money. If he ain't home, you find him. Get him back here." Harry pointed his cigar at Gallen. "And, Jimmy, whatever you find better not hit the papers. And I better not hear it on the radio."

He stuck the stogie into his mouth, pulled it out immediately. "And if Lolly Parsons embarrasses me again, you're fired."

"We can keep anything out of the papers." Gallen shrugged. "How we do it just depends on who Johnny's with. And what he's doing."

"You protect this studio, you protect your job. I can count on you, Jimmy, but I want Brand with you. Might need some muscle. Now get outta here, both of you."

Betsy was magically there to hold the door open for us.

"I'll drive," Gallen said, fixing his straw boater on his

head. "That boiler of yours probably won't make it off the lot."

"Okay by me. I need to work on my muscle flex in case I need 'em."

CHAPTER 5

Jimmy Gallen owned a bright red, black-trimmed 1929 Packard roadster with an in-dash radio. The engine sprang to life with a deep-throated roar, and Eddie Cantor started singing "Now's the Time to Fall in Love." Mercifully, Gallen switched off the radio.

A light breeze blew in off the ocean, fine tuning a perfect September day. The Hollywoodland sign glistened under the dazzling sun.

"Willson wants to stay on the payroll," I said over the growl of the Packard's big engine.

Gallen laughed. "Yeah. Sure he does. Here's the thing. Actors making fifteen get much better roles than actors making five. When that saucer's deal is up, Harry will offer him a buck fifty if he wants to stay on, 'cause his name will be dead by then. If he takes the bounce, he'll be lucky to find work on Poverty Row for peanuts. Harry won't let him get higher than that."

"Tough business."

"For some."

Gallen drove easily through traffic and around street-cars, shifting smoothly and not wasting time. He didn't often bother to stop for traffic signals. He'd wave at the bulls, look left and right, gun the motor or tap the brakes as needed, and go right on through the intersections. I guess he knew every traffic cop in town, and every traffic cop in town knew Harry York's top publicity mug.

A good-looking Irishman in his mid-thirties, shaded six feet, slender, Gallen's diamond ring shimmered as he worked the gearbox. His boater covered dark brown hair. Without his hat, he bore a strong resemblance to Joel McCrea, RKO's young star, right down to the blue eyes.

A few blocks down Sunset, Gallen asked, "Neil, how's your brother? If you don't mind me prying."

"He's dying, Jimmy," I said quietly.

"Sorry, Neil. Give me the gate. I didn't mean to—"

"No, no. That's fine. He's dying and there's nothing to be done about it."

Johnny Cutter had a house on a winding road named Palmero, just off Mulholland Drive, hard against the Santa Monica Mountains in one of the endless canyons twisting through the steep hills. A wrought-iron gate blocked the driveway, but the lock was easy to pick. The short driveway curved left through tall Coulter pines and circled around a life-size statue of a naked woman holding a basket filled with water lilies while standing knee deep in a flower-strewn pool fed by sparkling blue water trickling from the basket. The naked dame seemed wholly unconcerned while a lonely robin relieved itself on her marble brow.

"Fancy that," Gallen said, eyeing the statue.

"What?"

"Last time I was up here that statue was taking a leak."

"Maybe Cutter's learning a little class."

"That'd be the miracle of the century."

The white stucco ranch house spread to the right where the driveway circled. Gallen parked in front of the three-car garage and I peeked in one of the garage's small windows. "Cadillac in there."

"See a Duesy?"

I shook my head but Gallen was already out of sight,
his heels clicking on red flagstones leading to the front
door. He began whistling again. While he was knocking
on the door, I tried to see through the windows, but the
painted chintz curtains blocked my view. After a while,
Gallen stopped knocking and wandered my way.

We walked around to the back through some neatly
trimmed waist-high hedges. A red stone patio fronted an
L-shaped swimming pool. A bunch of brightly colored
patio tables and chairs filled the stone walk that circled
the pool. A ten-foot-high cream-colored stucco wall enclosed the entire area.

The locked back door was easier to pick than the front
gate. We entered quietly and stood in the short foyer, listening to nothing. We silently moved forward. It would
not pay to go busting in on Harry's biggest picture star if
he was engaged in the horizontal two-step with a tomato
or two. We went into the kitchen and out another door
into a formal dining room. We saw no one and heard
nothing. Gallen went left and I went right. After quietly
checking every room, we met at the front door.

"Our boy isn't here," I said.

"Harry won't be happy about that."

"Cost him less to be unhappy with us than with Cutter."

"He could be on his boat. Might as well drive out
there."

"Didn't know he had a boat."

"Docks it in Laurel City."

"That could be a trip for biscuits."

"Might as well take a look, anyway. I had better call
Harry. Out to Laurel City and back to the studio is the
rest of the day. By the time we get back, Harry will be
banging Jerry Hilt's head against Cicero."

Gallen rang Betsy from a phone on a small, round table beside an overstuffed chair in the corner of the sitting room. On the chair, a romantic drawing of Cutter's handsome mug stared into space from the cover of that month's *Photoplay* magazine. A Victrola filled the corner beside the chair.

I wandered around the house. Cutter had a lot of expensive art deco crap scattered around, along with a bunch of autographed pictures from his show business cronies and several more paintings by the old masters. Copies, I supposed, but I wondered who got them for him. The only masterpiece that interested a sheik like Johnny Cutter was a straight flush. And maybe a sweet-tasting dish with firm bubs and long legs.

I rummaged through a desk beside a floor-model Philco radio at the sitting room entrance. In one of the drawers, I uncovered an autographed picture of Lena Landers, the statuesque queen of the B pictures. The world knew Lena as the Ice Cream Blonde for her startling snow-white hair and cold violet eyes. Nearly six-feet tall, with shapely gams that went the distance, she dazzled in a low-cut, tightly clinging lamé gown. At the bottom right corner of the photo very nice, delicate handwriting spelled out: *Nice to be back, Johnny. Love, Lena.*

Gallen hung up the phone. "Let's go."

CHAPTER 6

T hat's a boat?" I asked. "Looks more like *Empress of Britain.*"

Cutter's yacht—*Sea Venture*—lay several hundred yards off one of the long piers at the Laurel Bay docks, riding easily on the calm waters of the huge inlet, anchored leeward of the open ocean. We went down the pier that ended closest to the immaculate white yacht, past dozens of gently bobbing craft tied to the slips. You could have bivouacked Pershing's army aboard the steel-hulled, long-keeled *Sea Venture* and had plenty of room left over for a couple dozen mariachi bands. A high fly bridge long enough for a game of football scraped the cloudless sky. Every inch of the imposing vessel glistened grandly in the late-afternoon sunlight.

I looked around, saw no one to hassle us. We untied a dinghy from the dock and started rowing toward *Sea Venture*, my back to the yacht. The slight breeze in our faces felt good as we strained at the oars locked into their traces. A tall, wide-shouldered bruno ran down the dock and stopped at the edge, staring at us with both fists digging into his hips.

A Jacob's ladder dangled from *Sea Venture's* stern. We tied the dinghy and scrambled up the long ladder. I went topside while Gallen investigated the boat's interior. The decks, fly bridge and the pilothouse were spotless, not a trace of dust, dirt or spit.

It would have taken the entire LAPD two days to search the yacht, but it felt empty. Jimmy rustled around in the immense galley, but found nothing to eat. There was, however, enough liquor on board to float both *Sea Venture* and *Empress*.

When we started rowing back, I faced the dock again. The big man had not moved. He still stared at us with huge fists digging into his hips. We tied the dinghy to the dock and the big man started yelling before we got out of the boat. He was about forty, with a florid face, a wide nose, and thick lips. A tattered seaman's cap angled across a broad head, and his red-and-black plaid cotton shirt and weathered dungarees had faded mostly white. The end of a long toothpick stuck out between thick lips.

"Ain't nobody allowed out there. Ya follow?"

Gallen pulled a handkerchief from his breast pocket and wiped his hands. "Nobody?" he asked innocently.

"Nobody. Ya follow? Ain't nobody allowed out there on that boat. So screw."

"That boat belongs to York Brothers Studio." Gallen fixed the big man with those charming blue eyes. "I represent Mr. York. My name is Gallen." He pointed to me. "This is Mr. Brand. He is in charge of security for Mr. York."

"Mr. Cutter owns that boat," the big man said, "and he told me they ain't nobody allowed on his boat 'less he says so. So screw."

Gallen nodded. "I will take that under advisement. If you will excuse us, I must call Mr. York at York Brothers Studio."

He started past the big man. The bimbo moved slightly at Gallen, but apparently the name Harry York meant something even to him and he let Jimmy pass. He eyed me stonily.

"Don't try gettin' on that boat again," he said. "Only reason you got on it this time was I went to eat."

"A whole cow I bet," I said and slipped past him.

"Saucers," the gink growled. I think the toothpick snapped. "Don't know when to dangle."

It was nearly four and neither Gallen nor I had eaten since breakfast. We ordered two ham specials at a drugstore a couple miles from the dock. Gallen dug a nickel from his pocket for the phone booth in the corner.

"Guess we'll have to tell the old man to call out the army if he wants his boy back. Either that or wait for Cutter to show up. If the phone booth blows up, tell my wife I died on the job. Tell her I went out gallantly."

"I'm sure she'll know that."

I remembered the photo in Cutter's sitting room desk. "How about Lena Landers?"

"Other than the obvious, how about her?"

"Didn't she and Cutter hit some hot spots together a few years ago?"

"So? That affair was over in '29. Neither of those two come built for long relationships, the kind where you're supposed to care about the other person."

"I don't think that picture I saw at Cutter's was taken very long ago. The photo was a still from her latest picture. Saw it last night."

His eyes opened wide. "You saw a Lena Landers picture? As a critic once famously said about her acting, she's the nothing in *Much Ado About Nothing*."

I grinned. "Looks like hers, you don't have to act."

"She's real, all right. Every inch of her. Someone once called her the world's busiest playground. Half the mugs watching her have their hats on their laps. Bet you did, too."

"Didn't want to embarrass the young lady I was with."

Now he was grinning. "You were with a young lady? As they say, the plot thickens."

"Betsy. She wanted to see that new Crawford picture, *Laughing Sinners*. Lena's B picture was part of the show."

"Betsy? Our Betsy?"

"Don't go sending out press releases. We went as nothing but friends. Don't start any rumors."

He chuckled. "Neil, sorry to tell you this, but nobody wants to hear about a security gink and a secretary, rumors or not."

The ham specials came, along with two cups of joe.

"Ever hear the story about Lena and Johnny?" Gallen asked.

"I've heard a lot of stories about those two."

"The one where Cutter and his then-wife were at the Cocoanut Grove one night when Lena came in with a few friends?"

I shook my head around a bite of ham.

"Cutter and Lena were going at it hot-and-heavy in those days, but Cutter's wife somehow didn't know about their affair. Talk about blinders. Anyway, Cutter tried to get his wife out of the Grove without Lena seeing them, but he couldn't get past her. Lena ran to him, slapped him on the ass, and yelled loud enough for the whole room to hear, 'What's the matter, Cutter. Don't you recognize me with my clothes on?' That, my friend, was the end of Cutter's marriage. It lasted about six weeks."

He laughed. "And the end of his affair with Lena. For a while, anyway. Those two can't stay together long, but they can't stay away from each other for long, either." He turned to his plate. "You can tell me where to head in," he said, his tone somber, "but I am sorry about your brother, Neil."

I pushed back my half-eaten ham special. I had no interest in the sympathy clouding Gallen's eyes.

"I'd be just as happy you didn't bring it up again."

"Sorry." His voice was as soft as the butter on my bread. "Ready?"

"Let's get out of here."

"I'll get the bill. It's Harry's nickel."

Gallen rammed his way through evening traffic like Billy Arnold at the Indy 500. Lena Landers owned a rambling, pale yellow two-story Georgian Colonial monstrosity overlooking a steep bluff in Holmby Hills. An ornate, pale yellow iron gate blocked the driveway, set between two English-style street lamps. Gallen pulled up and pushed the call button.

Sitting at the gate, you could see all the way to nowhere across the Los Angeles Basin. Static blasting from the speaker knocked out the silence.

"*Sí?*"

"Jimmy Gallen from York Brothers Studio. I need to see Miss Landers. Tell her it is very important."

"*Sí.*"

The yellow gates swung inward.

"How'd she get this place?" I asked.

"Wharton Noble. Third husband, I think. Big star in the silents. Lost out when the talkies came, then lost all he had when the market went belly up. Except the house. Pulled a Dutch act. Took a long walk in the ocean one night. Lena married him just in time to inherit this place and cash in on his life insurance."

"Insurance wouldn't pay off on suicide."

"Couldn't prove it. Lena claimed it was accidental. Company took her to court, but you put Lena on a stand in front of twelve good men and true, and they'd find her innocent of killing the pope on Sunset Boulevard at high noon."

"I remember Noble. Did she watch him take that walk?"

"Couldn't say. But it's a thought."

We parked by the pale yellow, oak front door, blocked by a short, plump Mexican maid who looked as if two very large mice were about to invade her palace.

"We'd like to see Miss Landers, please." Gallen flashed his most charming smile.

"Let them in, Elena."

The maid reluctantly stepped aside, holding the door.

In her mid-thirties and in her considerable prime, Lena was gorgeous on the screen, and ravishing in person. She stretched her luscious six feet chassis at the foot of a long, curved staircase, and let the late evening sunlight stream through a large glass door behind her, plainly showing the contours of her stunning nude body through the flimsy white negligee she had apparently just thrown on. It was a practiced pose and it worked. She was smiling. A smile that could melt a diamond.

"Trim the grease, Jimmy. I know why you're here. Johnny's upstairs in the master bedroom."

"How long's he been here?"

Her smile widened and her tongue flicked the bottom row of perfect white teeth. Her startling violet eyes could be either ice cold or hot enough to burn Rome. At the moment, they were somewhere in between.

"Oh, two days." The eyes warmed. "And two nights."

"He coulda called the studio. Harry's poppin' his collar."

"Yes. I see he sent his shark out. And the shark's pet." Her violet eyes ran me over without emotion. "Have we met?"

"We were childhood playmates." I gave her my best smile, but she was no longer there.

She glided down the hall like summer smoke drifting

in a languid breeze, the soft sunlight oozing through that flimsy dressing gown.

"First door, boys," she said over her shoulder and turned out of sight.

We started up the curved steps.

"This the place?"

Gallen stopped and looked at me.

"Yeah, she was on this step." He pointed to the right corner of the big room below us. "I was down there, stuffed in the corner between two fat Lasky press agents. It was a big blow-out. The place was full. Lena came in late, all smiles and laughs and purring sex. Wearing a full-length fur coat. Got halfway up these steps and let the coat fall. All she had on was her heels and a little black ribbon around her neck. She stretched her arms over her head, rolled her bubs, wiggled her bare ass, told everyone to have a good time, and walked on up the steps. Nobody saw her the rest of the night. A hell of an entrance and a hell of an exit, all at the same time."

"I miss all the fun."

"All the guys and half the women were entertained." He smiled at me. "My wife included. Tell you what, after the place quieted down Carole Lombard got a laugh when she said, 'Now I know how she got this place.'"

Late afternoon light filtered through the double-wide door to the master bedroom at the top of the stairs. I went in ahead of Gallen and swore at my mistake. Black-haired Johnny Cutter lounged naked on the bed, propped against a bunch of pillows, his limp schlong looking at me like a piece of rolled up dough. I grabbed a little red velvet pillow and put it where it did some good. Cutter flashed his lopsided grin, reached for the Fatima smokes beside him, and put a match to a Turkish gasper.

"Gentlemen, a most ill-timed interruption."

Gallen cracked a smile. "You need a break, my boy."

Cutter's grin hung on. "I was very satisfied."

I crossed the room and plopped into an overstuffed chair beside a small table that held a lamp, a bottle of Tanqueray gin, and two glasses.

"You seem to be neglecting your duties," Gallen said.

"Not entirely."

"Excuse me. Your duties to Harry York, who I believe pays you a great deal of scratch to be in his pictures. He requests your presence to finish your latest *magnus opus*. Or whatever the hell the Latin word is for turkey."

"Ah. Therein, my dear Irish friend, lies—or lays, you tell me—the crux. I am in no hurry to take out the trash. *Doorway to Heaven* is more precisely *Dropoff to Hades*. To be polite."

"Regardless. Harry's pissed. You got a seven a.m. call tomorrow."

Cutter threw the velvet pillow across the room. It landed at my feet. "Shall I come dressed?"

"Just come," Gallen said, turning to the door. "If you still can. Seven a.m."

I threw the red velvet pillow into Johnny's handsome face as I followed Gallen through the door.

"You fellows are welcome to stay," Cutter called after us, although he did not sound like he meant it.

We hit the bottom of the stairs and headed for the front door. The frowning maid held it open.

"You boys come back anytime," Lena purred sweetly.

She was already halfway up the stairs.

CHAPTER 7

I parked my cobalt blue 1925 Chevrolet K roadster in Johnny Cutter's driveway the next morning long before the sun woke up. I pounded on the front door and a heavyset bruno who would have had to turn sideways to go through a hangar door answered, pasting me with the look of a man watching a cockroach. An alarm bell went off in the tiny part of me that was still a cop. The bimbo's dark blue, double breasted seersucker suit didn't quite cover the bulge under his left arm. The two-inch scar on his left cheek hadn't aged much, and the light red tie dotted with hand-painted lilies looked out of place around a short, thick neck. His black hair was oiled straight back. His wide beezer hadn't fully healed from the last time it had been broken.

Black eyes stared a hole through me. "Yeah?"

"I'm here to take Johnny Cutter to the studio."

"I'll be right out," Cutter's voice called from inside the house. "Please wait outside."

The man in the seersucker wordlessly closed the door in my face.

I went around back and peered in the kitchen window. Cutter had the phone to his face, talking excitedly to someone. He hung up, stared at the empty sink for several seconds, and left the room. I wandered over to my car and got comfortable against the front fender. Daylight was beginning to cut open the morning haze when Cutter came out, wearing wraparound cheaters, tan riding pants with long black boots, a stiff white shirt, and a bright red scarf tied around his neck. A black beret hung at a crazy angle on his head. He looked ridiculous, but he was a handsome mug and that outfit probably made the ladies' hearts flutter.

He pulled up short when he saw my Chevy roadster.

"Not in that. Take my Cadillac."

"Fine. You drive. I'll go home."

"No, you drive my Caddy." He waved a sheaf of white paper in his left hand. "Know how much I miss the old days? Before talkies, I could just show up and act. Now I got to know words. I need you to drive so I can study my lines on the way. If I don't know this drivel when the camera rolls, I'll be there all night."

Three buttons under a flap on the side of the garage opened the doors. I pushed the button on the right at Cutter's instruction and the garage door closest to me rumbled. I jumped in the Caddy, a maroon V-12 phaeton, and hit the electric starter. The engine throbbed to life and Cutter jumped into the back seat. I almost asked him if I needed a chauffeur's cap.

We went down the drive with the seersucker watching us from the front door. I could have struck a match on the hard look in his eyes. The front gate opened automatically from the driveway side when we approached. Cutter told me to get out of the Caddy, close and lock the gate. I ignored him and, luckily for him, he didn't ask a second time. I quickly picked up speed on Palmero, the Caddy's big engine purring. The rising sun painted the eastern clouds a yellow-pink tinge, promising another postcard day in paradise.

"When we get to the studio, you may drive my car back to my house and pick up yours. I will get a ride this evening."

"Keep it up, Cutter, and they'll have to do some major makeup on your puss. Great Depression or not."

Cutter laughed. "Okay, okay. We're jake. Just trying to rub you. I got no kick with you, Neil. Frankly, all I wanted to do was lie dormy awhile and stick it to Harry a little. Between you, me, and the highway, I can't wait to get out of my contract. Find a studio that cares a little bit about their talent."

"Good luck there."

"Yeah, I know."

I turned onto Mulholland and started to hit a little early morning traffic. Cutter went back to his script, reading the words aloud, while I fought my way through thickening traffic. He was right about one thing. Bill Shakespeare couldn't lift that script above drivel.

Cutter read all the way to the studio, the same scene over and over. I tried to sound him out about the baby grand who had answered his door. Cutter made it plain it was none of my business.

I let him out at his dressing room at two minutes before seven, and he actually muttered thanks. I turned the Caddy around and headed back to the hills.

My Chevy was where I left it, but something didn't feel right. Nothing you could put a finger on. Just instinct honed by war and police work. Suddenly, I got the same feeling I had leading night patrol in ravaged France in 1918, or covering a dark Los Angeles alley a few years later with a badge on my chest and a service revolver in my hand.

I pulled the Caddy into the garage, turned the engine off, and sat there, listening and watching. Nothing. I got out, closed the garage door, and waited beside it, listening to the stillness hanging heavy in the light morning air. The faint trickle of water leaking from the naked lady's basket tapped the pool. I crossed to the house, knocked on the front door, and got no answer. Where was the seersucker? Bird watching?

I walked to the back. Nothing around the sun-drenched pool area looked different. I started to go back to my Chevy when I noticed the back door to the house ajar. I looked through the screen door and knew where the seersucker had gone, and it wasn't to watch birds. He sprawled on his back, his head at a funny angle against the wall, his chin against his chest, his legs splayed in front of him. I knelt beside him. Blood from a small hole in his throat covered the front of his shirt, and powder burns singed the shirt collar.

The seersucker was not moving and he was not going to.

I unbuttoned his coat. A .45 rested in his shoulder rig, the seven-shot clip full. I wiped the clip with my hand-kerchief and shoved it back into the holster. I dug out his wallet and thumbed through it. Forty-one dollars, a New York state driver's license, and nothing else. The name on the license was Carmine Alberto Broglio. Queens, New York City. Born November 13, 1897. Height six feet, one inch. Weight 280. Brown hair, brown eyes. I wiped everything clean and put the wallet back. I went through his pockets and found a key that probably worked a door. No change, no other keys, nothing else. I pulled up the legs of his trousers and found a shiv taped above his right ankle.

I put the key in my pocket, found the horn in the living room, and called the studio switchboard. I asked for Jimmy Gallen, but he didn't answer his office phone. I got back to the girl at the switchboard and asked her if she had seen Merly that morning.

"Yes, Mr. Brand. He's sitting with Gertie."

"Get him."

Gertie was the freckled receptionist in the first and smallest of Harry York's three-room offices. Merly squatted there most of the time, waiting like a puppy dog for a pat on the head. It took him ten seconds to get on the line.

"Merly, this is Brand. You find Jimmy Gallen for me and get a wiggle on. Tell him to call me at Johnny Cutter's house. Got that?"

"Yes, sir."

"Thanks, Merly. And Merly, you never got this call."

"What call?" He hung up.

I went through the house, but everything looked the same as the day before. A petrol blue fedora hung on a hook by the back door. The tag inside said size 9, way too big for Cutter, but just about right for Carmine's massive conk. I tossed the lid onto the bimbo's substantial lap.

I found a seat outside the back door and watched the swimming pool do nothing. Almost an hour passed before the blower sounded. I held the earpiece to my ear but didn't say anything.

"Brand?"

"Get up here and be quick. Bring a studio truck."

I hung up. I wandered through the garage and found some old blankets in a cabinet. I looked for a rope, but couldn't find one. I brought the blankets out and put them on the hood of my roadster. I went through them, but nothing connected them to Cutter. I got a butcher knife from the kitchen and sliced one of the blankets into long strips.

I cleaned up the kitchen and was thumbing through a stack of fan magazines, all with Johnny Cutter on the cover, about two hours later, when I heard Gallen roaring up the drive in a dark blue Model A stake-bed pickup.

He slammed on the brakes beside my Chevy, and jumped out. "What the hell, Neil?"

"You got some work ahead of you, Jimmy. Yesterday was a picnic."

I took him through the back door. He didn't say anything, just stood and looked at the dead man, tilting his head side to side and twisting his mouth around. I could see all kinds of ideas running around in his noodle. "Know him?" he finally asked.

"No. You?"

"No."

I told him what I had found out from his wallet.

"This is a problem."

"Thought you'd think so. See Cutter this morning?"

"I did. He was hard at work. Kissed and made up with everybody. That's all down the drain. Gotta finish that picture."

We both kept looking at Carmine.

"Got plugged by something small," I said. "No bigger than a .32. No exit wound."

"A cannon ball couldn't go through that thick neck. No gun?"

"Only a .45 semi strapped under his left arm."

"We better search again."

"We can't just call the bulls."

"Body can't be found here."

"Why we got the truck."

"What can we wrap him in? Don't want blood in that truck."

"I dug up some blankets in the garage."

"Pipe that."

We spread a few blankets in the wooden truck bed, dumped Carmine on them, and covered him with the rest of the blankets. I tied it all up with the long strips I had cut, and tossed the petrol blue fedora in the truck. Gallen and I made sure nothing left behind in the house would connect Cutter to Broglio. Gallen drove the studio pickup. I locked the front gate this time and followed Jimmy to a deserted place where Mulholland turned around the high cliffs. We rolled Carmine from the truck and sent him over the cliff.

He hit hard and tumbled through the brush, finally stopping far below us. I wiped off his fedora and threw it after him. It was about noon and getting hot.

CHAPTER 8

Harry York's publicity department took over a five-room house just inside the studio lot in 1925. Gallen's secretary held down the fort in one room, unfashionably bare with just her desk, a few chairs, and copies of cover pages of fan magazines featuring Harry's players on the walls. Several tall filing cabinets, two tables piled high with assorted publicity junk, and five desks, where Gallen's assistants banged out their daily pap, cluttered another room. Lobby cards and one-sheet movie posters covered the walls.

A nondescript desk, three chairs, a loveseat, and a squadron of filing cabinets took up the available space in Gallen's office, the largest of the five rooms. Assorted products of Gallen's publicity mill littered the tops of the filing cabinets, piled almost to the ceiling. French doors to the right opened onto the back lot, revealing sound stages to the right and a line of dressing rooms to the left. When the situation demanded, Gallen could close off the patio doors by dropping wooden shades suspended from the ceiling.

He sat down heavily in his oak swivel chair and I grabbed one of the oak straight backs beside his desk. "I need your help, Neil."

"Uh-huh."

"You've got to find out about Cutter and Carmine. I need to know. I've got to be wired if this mess comes back to us."

"Cutter didn't kill him. Carmine was alive when we left this morning."

"They had some kind of relationship, and I need to know what it was."

"Who wrote the studio bio for Cutter? You or the staff?"

"I wrote that one. Harry wanted to build him up right from the start. Thought he'd be a big player. For once, Harry was right."

"Dig it out."

"Carmine Broglio isn't in it. Are you nuts?"

"Dig it out, anyway."

He let out an exasperated breath and began rummaging around in a file cabinet.

After a while, he produced his masterpiece of fiction on Johnny Cutter.

I sat in a chair and read it while Gallen ran through the manual of schemes he carried in his handsome head. "Any of this true?" I asked.

"Some. Not much."

"What's Cutter's real moniker?"

"Gerald Maurice Bonecutter. Harry didn't like it. Johnny Cutter, he liked. Thought that name up himself."

"Cutter was born in 1900?"

"Naw. Couple years before that. Harry wanted him a little younger."

"He grew up on the Upper West Side in New York?"

"Naw. Lower East Side. The slums. Hard part of town. I think that's where Cagney came from. Kids down there grow up three ways. They become trouble boys, they become priests, or they turn to hoofing and acting."

"Cagney started that way?"

"Yep. Hoofed his way right to the big time."

"Just like Johnny Cutter."

"Just like. Only Cagney is his real name."

"Cagney's whose real name?"

Gallen rolled up a paper wad and threw it at me. "Disappointed in you, old boy. That is one really bad joke."

"So our friend Carmine comes from New York. He's about Cutter's age. Reckon he was from the Lower East Side, too? Maybe knew each other there."

"Could be. So?"

"Got any friends in New York?"

"Lots of friends in New York. Worked at the *World* nearly ten years before this gig came along."

"One of 'em in with the bulls?"

"Most of 'em. All newspaper bums mix it up with the cops. Even the sports guys. Goes with the job."

"See if one of 'em can wire Carmine Broglio. Like to find out something before the bulls find his body and get on it."

"Sure, sure. Danny Tannheuser fits that bill. Solid newshawk. Been there twenty years or more. Knows every cop in town. He not only knows who's on the take, but he knows how much they're taking. I'll call him now."

"Good. I'm gonna hang around Stage Two a while. Keep an eye on Cutter. Talk to him if I get a chance."

Gallen raised an eyebrow. "Gonna tell him Carmine's dead?"

"No. I tell him we moved Carmine he might spill it to the bulls. Don't think our boy Johnny will stand up under a hard grill."

"Lord, no. He'll fold like a cheap crutch."

"If the bulls tie him to Carmine, it'll be best if he doesn't know where Carmine got shot. Cutter wasn't there and can't tell them." I started out the door but looked back at the publicity expert. "Bulls start asking questions, will you hold up?"

He smiled. "Don't be a bunny. Even if the cops find out what we did, it's all silk. Harry won't let anything happen to us. He knows we can gum up the works. He's wise to us protecting his biggest box office and that's Harry's only concern."

"I hope you're right. But you can do a lot more for Harry than I can. I'm just a piece of muscle..."

❧❧❧

Wednesday, December 24, 1924:

The fog cutting across the city made Christmas Eve a little bit chilly. Jones and I were just off Central, outside some nameless dive, when a woman's hushed cry floated from an alley nearby, close to a side door to the dump. Her husband was slapping her around because his jingled brain told him she was getting too friendly with a John inside the speak.

Jones stopped the man with his nightstick, a sharp slap across the back. The woman screamed and jerked back, and I led her away to get her statement. Her name was Myrtle Howser and her husband's name was Charles. She said she didn't want her husband hurt because he had a job and she didn't, and she didn't want to have to take care of him.

It was too late. Jones had hit Howser several times hard across the side, at the kidneys. Charley doubled over in pain and Jones pulled him up by the collar, a look of pure delight on his face. He hit the man again with the nightstick, this time straight up between his legs. Howser screamed and collapsed, spewing vomit that just missed Jonesy's patent leather shoes. Jones cursed and straightened Howser, now borderline unconscious. His service revolver clicked and he rammed the barrel into Howser's mouth, smashing several teeth. Howser spit more vomit, mixed with blood and broken ivory.

"Get that on my shoes and I'll knock your jewels clean off," Jones hissed in Howser's sweating face.

Jones pulled his revolver from the man's mouth, spit on Howser again, and hit him again with his stick, this time across the neck. Howser went down silently and lay still. With relief, I saw he was still breathing. Jones was going to hit him again.

I grabbed his arm and pulled him away. Jones turned on me furiously and tried to hit me. Jones was bigger than me, but not by much, and I was in better shape. I held him firmly and yelled at him to calm down.

Finally, he did, but he looked at me with rat-mean eyes that flashed blood red. His nostrils flared. "You're a regular Little Bo Peep. You wanna interfere with me, Bo? Fine. We'll get that settled right enough."

I dragged Jones away from Howser. I looked for Myrtle Howser, but she was nowhere in sight.

We left her husband unconscious on the alley's bricks. I called it in at the corner phone. Said a badly beaten man was still breathing, but we saw no suspects.

"That twist won't say anything." His vicious snarl had no bottom. "She's too scared. She knows I'll kill her."

Next day I asked for a new partner. I did not give a reason and the captain refused my request

Jones raged at me. If I didn't want to be his partner, that was jake with him. But I'd have to take it awhile.

"Let's see what makes you tick," he told me.

The next day I saw him take a payoff. He made sure I saw it.

"Tell anybody, Bo, and you're a dead palooka."

I never saw a man with meaner eyes.

CHAPTER 9

Thursday, September 10, 1931:

I looked in on Cutter, but Tod Markham kept him busy, trying to wrap the thing today so he wouldn't have to worry about his star disappearing again into the world of Lena Landers and her delightful treasures. It was late when I left the stage for my little cubbyhole to go over job-related paperwork and do some thinking. The phone rang an hour later. It was Jimmy Gallen.

"Wire on Carmine wasn't very hard to come by." He almost whispered. "Our Carmine was a very bad boy. Very, very bad. He's—was—a torpedo for Joe Masseria. I'm sure that name rings a loud bell."

It did. Superstitious Italian gangsters regarded Joe "The Boss" as the man who could dodge bullets because he had once miraculously escaped a gangland hit. Masseria had taken on chief rival Salvatore Maranzano to see who would rule the mob in New York City. Maranzano won by a landslide back in April when "The Boss" went face down under a hail of Tommy gun fire he couldn't dodge. Police fingered Charlie Luciano, Meyer Lansky, and Benny Siegel for the hit, but the trail disappeared into the thick haze of mean New York streets.

"Carmine turned to smoke the day Masseria was killed. Police think he might be keeping company with a bunch of tires at the bottom of the East River."

"Carmine from the Lower East?"

"You betcha. Born two weeks before Johnny Cutter and about a block away. They grew up together on those streets. But Johnny was tall and good-looking and he could hoof. Carmine learned to pull a trigger. Carmine's got a rap sheet long as a reel of film."

"So Carmine looks Cutter up out here."

"It would seem. But why?"

"Long-time friends, maybe," I said, but we both knew a darker, sinister reason.

"Maybe." Doubt colored Gallen's voice.

"Or a shakedown if there's something in Johnny's past. And you could probably bank on that. Or maybe they were into something sweet. Something that helped Cutter pay off that million dollar palace floating out in Laurel Bay."

"Don't go there, Neil. Please. I can spin a web to cover those two being childhood friends. But blackmail? Crime partnership? Even Harry'd have trouble fixing that one."

"Let's sleep on it. Figure out our next move."

"Starting to wish we had kept Carmine's ID."

"Bulls will find out sooner or later even if we had. His fingerprints are surely on file and I bet his puss has been plastered in every clubhouse in the country." I had another brainwave. "That bio you wrote on Cutter. Said he had a sister. You make up the sister?"

"Why?"

"Think I ought to talk to her."

The line went dead and I found myself wishing we weren't on the phone. I wanted to look into Gallen's face.

"What I heard, she's mostly jingle-brained," he said at

last. "Don't know if you can get any sense out of her."

"Dig up her address anyway. I'll give it a try."

"Ah, Neil, that's bound to be a waste of time. Besides, she's been out of the pictures so long I don't know what I can dig up."

"Tell me about her."

"She came to Hollywood with Cutter. Their studios gave both of them phony names, so I don't know how many knew they were brother and sister. Fox signed her and she did all right 'til the talkies. She didn't have much of a voice, and booze and drugs had pretty much done her in by then, anyway."

"What name did she act under?"

"Joan Banes."

"You have a photo of her?"

His voice dulled. "She was with Fox and I've got some Fox junk in a file cabinet in the other office. I'll ask Hester to dig it out."

"Get me her address. I'll drop in on her tomorrow if I can."

I heard a sigh I did not like.

"I'll call you right back."

He got back to me in less than an hour. Joan Banes lived in central LA, a couple of blocks off Hollywood Boulevard.

"Thanks. I'll get on that first thing in the morning."

"Wait a minute."

Gallen mingled low, mumbled words with someone in his office. After a few seconds, he was back on the line.

"They just wrapped it up on Stage Two. Johnny retired to his dressing room with a hot little number who was doing a bit in a scene with him."

"Good. I wanna see him a minute."

CHAPTER 10

Johnny Cutter had two surprises for me. He answered my knock on his dressing room door, and he had clothes on. He cracked the door, grimaced a little, and opened it wider.

His dressing room was standard studio fare of long, leather sofa, a couple of wingback chairs, full-length mirror, a dressing table and a big closet. Heavy drapes hid a big window overlooking a flower garden behind the building. A door to the right led to the bathroom. Behind the bar on the left, an open armoire loaded with Johnny's best bootleg booze mocked Harry York and the law. A voice coming out of the floor radio in the corner sang, "Who's that little chatterbox? The one with the pretty auburn locks? Who can it be? It's Little Orphan Annie."

Cutter leaned in to me and tilted his head toward the willowy figure sitting in a chrome and leather chair by the radio, fastening a silver-banded watch around her wrist.

"She likes that show," he said, keeping his voice low.

The voice on the radio went into an Ovaltine commercial.

"Got a minute?"

"Bad timing, fella. Me and the billboard have a dinner

engagement." Cutter ran both hands down his tuxedo jacket. "See?"

"Just need a minute."

"Don't be a flat tire. Can't this wait until morning? I gotta be back at seven. Got a coupla close-ups and some voice-overs. They wanted to do 'em tonight, but I got plans. My contract says I don't have to stay past seven. Twelve hours a day is all I've got to give 'em. I'll do 'em in the morning and then I'll be shut of this damned hole until October." He grinned. "Only gotta do one more picture for Harry this year."

"I want to know about Carmine Broglio."

The canned smile instantly quit Cutter's handsome face. "I don't think I like someone digging into my past."

"You're gonna like it a lot less in the next few days. Cut the static and deal it straight. Jimmy Gallen's gonna try to keep you out of the soup kitchen. I'm thinking that might not be easy. It would sure pay you to help Jimmy."

Cutter pulled me into the room and closed the door. He crossed to the radio and switched it off, right in the middle of little Annie's chatter.

"Johnny," the dark-haired doll squealed. "I was listening to—"

"Go iron your shoelaces." Cutter took the frail's upper arm and jerked her to her feet.

Cutter's date rated high on the eyeball scale—a choice bit of calico, a couple of inches over five feet, wearing a silver evening gown with a bias cut meant to cling tightly and show plenty of curves. Brown doe peepers the size of quarters overlooked her full lips, painted deep red, and absurdly white teeth. Despite her effort at glamour, she was a wholesome-looking bunny, the type you'd put in the background as a salesclerk, or a nurse, or a college student. I didn't peg her as Johnny Cutter's type, but a hot meringue like him easily picked off baby vamps.

"And while you're in there, wipe some of that powder off your face."

Her brown eyes flashed briefly and her lower lip quivered, but she didn't speak. She flounced into the bathroom.

"Stay in there 'til I tell you to come out." Cutter took my arm. "A real flour lover." He guided me to the bar. "I need a drink. You?"

I shook my head no. Cutter popped the cork on a bottle of Cutty Sark and half filled a tumbler. He knocked it down and his nerves seemed to settle.

"You needed that quilt," I told him.

Cutter didn't look at me. "Little edge won't hurt just now."

He poured a stiffer one, replaced the cork. This one he sipped, the closed bathroom door drawing his full attention.

"Carmine," I said. A gentle reminder of why he was drinking with me and not the air-tight fixing her pan in his bathroom.

"Okay. You saw him this morning, but he didn't tell you his name. He wouldn't. In fact, you're lucky you're still breathing."

"That's another conversation. Tell me what he's doing at your place."

"That bastard. He was supposed to drive my bus down here this afternoon. He hasn't shown and I've tried to call him all day. When I heard the knock, I thought you were Carm."

"You two grew up on the East Side," I said, trying to get him started.

"Yeah. How'd you know about Carm?"

"My hairdresser."

"I forgot. You used to be a cop."

"That's right."

"Got busted over a bribe as I remember."

I think a smile flirted at the corners of his mouth. "Nix that or you'll need new teeth." I didn't say it nicely.

"Nice line. Right out of one of Harry's potboilers."

I leaned in on Cutter and locked my eyes on his. We were about the same height, an inch over six feet, but my one-ninety had him by thirty pounds. I was in shape, and I didn't care about my face. "Johnny, this can go one of two ways. I can bust your head and dust out, or I can try to help you."

He held my gaze a few seconds and then remembered the bathroom door. "Okay, old boy. Okay. My apologies." He downed a slug of the scotch and lit a Fatima. He was thinking hard. "Why do I need help?"

"Carmine Broglio's a wanted hood staying at your house. The papers'll have to print extras. Lolly Parsons will have a field day. Harry might blush."

He took a long pull on the gasper. His eyes emptied. "Yeah, me and Carmine grew up together. We ran in the same gang for a while. Just small-time knockovers, y'know. Nothing serious on my part. I mean that. We robbed a couple of places, but I was just the lookout. I got older and the whole thing started to scare me. Carm and some of 'em drifted into harder stuff. Know what I mean? A few of us went the other way. One day I got a job sweeping out a theater. I was watching rehearsals one time and the lead—this guy wasn't much older than me— was kissing this beautiful girl. Kissing her and getting paid for it. That looked way better to me than robbing stores and running down back alleys. So, to make a long story short, here I am."

"What about Carmine?"

"Juvie stuff, at first. Did a short stretch in Sing, Sing. His cellmate was a small-time button man for Joe Masseria's outfit, and that's how Carm got in with that mob. When Carm got out of the pen, we'd see him some around the old neighborhood, bragging about being in with Masseria. Not long after that, I landed a Broadway gig. Harry's people saw me and..."

He shrugged, took a long pull on the Fatima.

"So Carmine came out here just to see you?"

"That big lug might never have known who I was. The name Johnny Cutter meant nothing to him. But he started seeing a sometimes waitress, sometimes pro skirt who worked a clip joint on Forty-Second Street. She dragged him to a movie picture one night, and guess who was up there, his head twenty feet high?"

Cutter downed another slug of scotch. "Carm told me he came right out of his seat when he saw me. Said he told himself right then that one day he'd have to look up his old buddy. I gotta tell you, it was pretty chilling the way he said that."

"Let me guess. He came out here when Joe Masseria went face down in a plate of spaghetti."

"Took him a few months. He said he needed to cover his tracks in case Luciano was looking for him. Carm got pretty high up in Masseria's family. He thought Maranzano might want to take him out, too."

"Don't look good, Johnny, you playing the sap for a trouble boy like Broglio. Hiding a hood in your house is a fast way to get jammed up."

"Don't I know that? If I was Cagney or Raft, I might make hay out of that sort of thing. But I'm the white knight on a white charger. Fans might not forgive my past."

"Anybody else who might come out of your past?"

He pursed his lips. "Naw. Carm's the only one, I think. Listen, most of the others either went straight and wanna forget their pasts, or they went underground. For keeps."

"Okay. Is Carmine just dormy, or does he want something?"

"He just wants to lay low, see if there's any heat. He's talking about Havana. Friend of his runs a casino down there."

"How'd he find you out here?"

"He knew what studio I worked for. Anybody can learn that. Started hanging out by the front gate and one day he saw me. Followed me home. In a bent car."

"When was that?"

Cutter poured more scotch. "Coupla weeks ago."

"I didn't see a car at your place this morning."

"He told me he stole the heap he was driving. Stole several before he found me, trying to stay ahead of the cops. I made him ditch it. Last thing I need is a stolen car in my driveway."

"It's all right to have one of Joe Masseria's trigger men bunking with you?"

"He's not staying with me. He rented a place in Burbank."

"Where in Burbank?"

"How would I know? He wasn't about to tell me."

"What about your butler?"

"I sent that Chink back to Hong Kong to visit his family when Carm showed. Didn't need him to know about Carm."

"Your driver? The maid? Got a cook?"

"Butler cooks when I want. I told the driver time to get lost 'til he hears from me. Same reason. Maid comes in three times a week. Carm said he'd stay out of her way."

"Who else knew Carmine was here?"

"I didn't tell anybody. I didn't want anyone to know. I just wanted him out of my life."

"Not Gallen?"

"Not anybody, I tell you. And you won't spill. Harry'd

can you. Why the sudden sweat over Carm and me?"

"Listen to me. If the bulls come looking for Carmine, you clam. Tell nobody nothing. You hear? Keep your kisser shut to the cops and call Jimmy Gallen. Harry's pull will keep your background hidden and nothing will get into print anywhere. And you won't get smeared all over *Little Orphan Annie*."

"Why should the cops come to me? They don't—"

"I found out and Gallen knows. Carmine's a wanted man. He gets pinched driving a bent car, he might call copper on you. If he does, don't say a damn word to anybody. Call Gallen and clam. He'll get your lawyer or Harry's. Understand?"

He nodded, but he wasn't a good enough actor to hide the fear in his eyes.

"Attaboy. Now take your mother to dinner."

CHAPTER 11

I fired up my boiler. The guard had locked the main gate to the studio, leaving the side gate the only way in and out of the lot. I parked down the block, hiding in the shadows but able to see the side gate. The warm evening had clouded a bit, but the red-and-purple sunset promised no rain.

A Blue Streak dimbox pulled up to the gate shortly after I settled in to wait. Cutter and his evening dessert came out through the pedestrian entrance and slid into the taxi. The cabbie backed out, ran the half block to Sunset, and hung a right.

I pulled out behind them, keeping well back, hiding behind streetcars and other traffic. The cabbie pulled up at the gate to Cutter's place and his two passengers got out. Cutter peeled a bill from a big roll and the cabbie drove away. I had pulled to the side of the road where I had a clear view through the trees. The Blue Streak whizzed by, the cabbie smiling and paying me no mind. Johnny must have tipped him handsomely.

Cutter unlocked the gate and the two of them walked up the drive to his house. A few minutes later, headlights winked through the trees. The throb of a powerful engine grew louder and a Deusenberg rolled right onto Palmero and sped away on the deserted road. I kept well back in my little roadster, the Duesy's distinctive taillights in sight until Cutter began slowing near Laurel City. Soon he encountered traffic and I had no trouble keeping him in sight.

When he turned onto Bay Avenue, I knew where he was going. I slowed and fell way back. I turned onto Angelo, a short street that ended at the docks. Near the bay, I parked the roadster out of sight between low buildings pockmarked by wind-blown salt water, and went the rest of the way on foot. Clouds moved across the moon, but I could see well enough to find the dock I wanted. My dark suit made it unlikely anyone would see me skulking around in the dark.

Cutter parked the Duesenberg at the foot of the dock, and two shadowy figures walked arm-in-arm toward the end of the pier. *Sea Venture* rode at anchor, lights ablaze. I crouched on the slip between two smaller motor boats as a seven-passenger Cadillac V-12 glided to a smooth stop beside Cutter's Duesy. A tall, beefy bruno, who was nothing more than a large shadow in his dark topcoat, got out and crossed in front of the Caddy. He had turned up the collar on his topcoat and pulled his fedora low, but the way he moved made me think I knew him.

The man opened the passenger door and Lena Landers emerged, a little black cloche hat sitting gracefully on her white hair, the tiny brim turned up. Her tight, silver lamé gown ran to her ankles, flaring at the bottom over matching heels. A dark sable stole covered her shoulders. She took a deep drag on a cigarette and flicked it away. The gasper had lit up her face but not her driver's.

The man with her opened the Caddy's back door and five lovely pieces of fluff with curves like a mountain road slid out.

They slithered down the dock, the five beauties talking

and giggling as they studied the white palace floating several hundred yards away.

An electric yacht tender whined its way from *Sea Venture*, sending out a fine spray in the calm water. It tied up at the end of the dock where Gallen and I had pirated the dinghy the day before. One by one, the five frails climbed into the tender, followed by Lena, then Johnny Cutter and his twist. The man who had driven the Caddy got in the tender, and then another man. The boat left the pier, turned easily toward *Sea Venture* and picked up speed. It tied up at the stern, and its passengers went up the Jacob's ladder, being helped by two men aboard the yacht who looked like black ghosts against the white paint.

I wrote down the license number of the Caddy, then found a comfortable seat on one of the small boats closer to the end of the dock, and waited. I turned up my coat collar against the chill of the marine air.

Maybe forty-five minutes droned by, maybe an hour. My brain locked in thought. The whine of the electric tender churning back to the dock brought me back. Lena climbed up the wooden ladder, Cutter right behind her. Another woman came up behind Cutter—slim, wearing a full-length fur and a dark, wide-brimmed hat that completely obscured her face. Three big men followed and the six of them stood at the end of the dock, arguing. They were too far away to hear, but their voices occasionally rose in anger, and I picked out a few words.

"No more...what if somebody finds out...too dangerous...too late...had enough...you can't quit..."

Cutter broke away from the other five and jogged down the dock. One of the men made a move toward him, but the woman I couldn't recognize put a hand on the man's arm. They said something I couldn't hear. Johnny clipped past me and pretty soon his Duesenberg roared to life.

He gunned the brawny engine, the tires squealing when he hit Bay Avenue.

The five who remained talked a while, then Lena and her driver and the other woman started down the dock. I could barely make out their forms in the darkness. They walked past me and the Caddy soon purred away.

The two men at the dock got in the tender and headed north. They tied the tender at the pier and went into a roadhouse on a point of land edging the bay.

Sea Venture's gigantic steam turbines rumbled and the forward anchor chain groaned. The yacht turned its bow toward the open sea and was slowly underway, lit up like W.C. Fields on New Year's Eve.

I drove the Chevy around to the roadhouse and parked it between the only two cars in the lot. A faded sign identified the roadhouse as the Laurel Inn, long and low, shaped like the letter T, the shorter length facing the bay. Salt water and wind had scraped most of the paint off the building, leaving mostly pitted boards.

I went in by the side entrance and found a stool at the long bar. Hundreds of bottles of booze lined up behind the bar, unconcerned about Prohibition. This was Laurel City and the honest cops and booze agents who weren't on the take had long since disappeared into the bay.

I ordered a beer and a ham sandwich. The bartender nodded and said nothing. The ham came between two pieces of stale bread, with a piece of limp lettuce and a sliver of dill pickle. The bartender set down a small yellow bottle that had more mustard crusted around the top than inside. He moved off without saying anything. He fished an Old Gold out of a pack, lit it and nonchalantly leaned against the bar, pretending not to watch me. The two men from the tender were sitting at a corner table, drinking beer and talking quietly, their hands still. One of them faced me, but I had never seen him before. I chewed

on the beer and tried to bite the gristly ham. When the
two men stood to leave about thirty minutes later, I got a
good look at the other man and it froze me. I ducked my
head away so he wouldn't recognize me as they sauntered
by. It was Hiram Strakowsky. I hadn't seen his mean puss
since he was bounced from the force, but I could never
forget that flat face and those hard eyes. Neither man
looked my way as they went out the door. That left only
me, the bartender, and a couple of men shooting billiards
in the far corner of the room. I hooked a finger at the bar-
keep.

"Know a man named Mousey?"

He fixed me with dark eyes. The thin line under his
nose might have been his mouth. "Mister, I don't know
nobody." The lips didn't move. He was better than Edgar
Bergen.

"You'd know Mousey. Long, thin face like a hatchet.
Wispy gray hair that wouldn't be on speaking terms with
a comb. He somehow always has a three-day growth.
Five-feet nothing, hundred pounds tops if you weighted
down his pockets. Could be fifty. Could be eighty."

The eyes didn't change. "Mister, I don't know nobody."

I fished out a sawbuck and spread it on the bar, keeping a hand on it. His eyes got a little bigger and a little
brighter.

Evidently, he knew Alexander Hamilton. His tongue
peeked out between his thin lips, like a tiny worm getting
its first look at daylight.

"No trouble. I just want his best take on Hamlet."

"Who?"

"Hamlet. Mutual friend."

"Like I said, mister. I don't know nobody."

I added another ten-spot to the one on the bar. "Like I
said, no trouble."

He thought that over a few seconds, and then leaned closer to me. "Know a place called Sharkey's?"

He straightened up and walked away. The two sawbucks were gone with him. I dropped four bits on the table to cover the beer and sandwich and slid out the door.

Sharkey's was a dive about a quarter mile to the north in Laurel City, in the basement of the ancient six-story Harbinger Building. Steep steps to the right of the building took you down to Sharkey's, if you were desperate enough to want to go.

Apparently, Mousey was. He and about a dozen other wharf rats scattered their ruined bodies around the gin mill's single room. A couple of them slumped listlessly over the bar. Bare light bulbs lit the place, glaring over furnishings ready for the dump. It stank of cheap booze, bad food, and old vomit. It made the bar in Garbo's *Anna Christie* look like the Waldorf.

Mousey, sitting in the back left corner, seemed right at home. He gave no indication he saw me, but Mousey saw everything.

I bought a bottle of busthead at the bar and took it to the little man. Not even when I set the bottle on the table, did he look at me. I sat opposite and waited. After a little while, his gnarled hands slid from under the table and closed around the bottle, turning it around two or three times. His hands were small but his fingers were long and thin, ending in coal black fingernails.

He looked at me, his narrow gray eyes hooded and barely open. "They make this stuff out of warm piss. When it cools down to room temperature it's ready to drink."

He popped the top and poured some dark liquid into the dirty, paper-thin glass in front of him. "Don't suppose you'd want to join me?"

I turned my right hand just enough so he could see the

number twenty on the corner of the bill. Rotgut had
chilled every lush in the place who wasn't in a coma, but
the hint of a double sawbuck in that place would have
brought out loaded Tommy guns and knives as long as
Swanson's eyebrows. The Jackson retreated into my fist
and Mousey looked at me with dead eyes.

"*Sea Venture*," I whispered.

"That's a hard nut."

"Basic."

"Belongs to Randall Curtiss. He don't like people
talkin' 'bout him."

The name set off warning sirens. Randall Curtiss who
had made a fortune in 1912 in the Burkburnett oilfield
and added to it tenfold with munitions and other ventures
during the war. But that fortune looked like nothing more
than a small grubstake compared to the oil find Curtiss
discovered at Signal Hill more than a decade after Burkburnett.

Now, Curtiss had more money than all of Europe put
together and more political pull than a mile of locomo-
tives. He was a central figure in the Teapot Dome scandal
that disgraced Warren Harding and Albert Fall, but
Curtiss came out of it like a newborn pup. Harding died
and Fall had recently been carted off to prison.

Word was, Curtiss was thinking of running for president.

"Thought the boat belonged to an actor named Johnny
Cutter."

Mousey shrugged, said nothing. He had told me who
owned the yacht and he wasn't about to argue over it. I
could believe him or not. I believed him.

"Where's it go at night?"

"Out. Five, six hours mostly. Always back by daylight."

"How often."

"Once, twice a month. Easy to keep tabs on that big boat."

"What goes on?"

"Ain't got no guess as to that. Ain't gonna try one."

"Went out a little while ago. I saw five good-looking skirts get on board."

"I seen 'em. Seen others before. Ain't never seen any of 'em get off."

"And you got no guess."

"Not even if you were stranglin' a handful of Jacksons."

I stood up and the double sawbuck somehow found its way onto Mousey's lap. He forgot the dirty glass and tilted the bottle to his mouth. I left and neither of us said goodbye. Only the bartender watched me leave.

ℰↁℰↁ

Friday, May 8, 1925:

My late shift was over and I got home a little past midnight. Married nearly a year, we were living in a tidy place over on Hyperion. I had just been assigned a new partner, my repeated requests finally approved. I parked in the driveway beside the house and was coming around the corner toward the front door when he jumped out at me. Jones grinned like a cat in the parakeet cage and swung a nightstick at my head. I ducked and the nightstick knocked my hat off. I stepped in on him, driving a right fist into his chest. He staggered back and swung again, catching me across the back of the shoulder. I went down and rolled and the nightstick slammed into the walk beside me. He kicked at me and I grabbed his leg and twisted. We were both down, scrambling to get to our feet. He tried to take my legs out with his stick and I kicked him in the jaw and drove him backward, but he hung onto the stick.

His rat-mean eyes bored into me and the grin was gone. We were crouched like two tigers ready to charge. Jones straightened and tugged at his suit coat. He found his straw boater on the ground and put it on his head. He touched a meaty hand to the side of his hooked nose and ran his thick tongue over his bottom lip. The grin came back. "Ain't over, Bo. See you around."

I stood panting in the yard as he faded down the street. He had parked his Ford well down the block where I wouldn't see it when I came home. He drove by and flipped me off.

Three days later, two grifters Jones had collared in a robbery beef fingered me for taking bribes. They said they had paid me off to look the other way. The collar was bogus, both men had airtight alibis, but the bribery accusation was there to stay. A cop came forward, one of Jonesy's cronies. He said he saw me taking money. I was temporarily suspended with pay. A few nights later, coming home from dinner with my wife, a car drove by and two gunshots rang out. My wife, five months pregnant, was dead with a bullet in her head. I recognized the shooter. Jones and I had collared him a few months before, but while I was calling it in, Jones let him go. Said the mug got away from him. Said it while he was still stuffing money into his pocket.

My wife's death cut me loose from whatever kept me grounded. The slow downward spiral escalated. I found the shooter, gave him his chance, and left him dead in a back alley downtown. The suspension turned into a long leave with no pay, while the investigation into the charges against me continued, this time with the shooting added.

My brother's health deteriorated and he was off the

force on a disability. Two lost souls wandering in a thick, eternal haze, trying to lean on each other.

I was numb from it all. I was having an out-of-body experience when the decision came down that bounced me from the department. A few cops, Harless included, backed me, but most of them sided with the decision and were happy to see another crooked flatfoot go down for the count.

One morning, I saw Jones sitting in his Ford on the street outside my front door. I came out for him, running down the front walk. He grinned and held up a finger and gunned the Ford. I stood in the front yard, screaming.

CHAPTER 12

Friday, September 11, 1931:

I ate breakfast—bacon, eggs, and biscuits—early the next morning at a hash house just down the street from where I was living. The biscuits were made from something called Bisquick, hailed as a modern kitchen miracle. Two cups of black coffee washed the grub down while I looked over the *Morning Journal*.

A big wind had hit the colony of British Honduras on the northern Caribbean coast of Central America. The hurricane's death toll hit fifteen hundred, best guess. Days would pass before rescuers finished digging through the rubble.

In City Hall, the nonstop election wrangling turned nasty over utilities, especially water. Mayor John Porter pushed for the privately owned Southern California Edison and Los Angeles Gas and Electric. He had a fight on his hands with the Municipal Light and Power Defense League, which backed public utilities. Most of us were just glad we had a pot.

At the bottom of the front page I glommed a far more interesting piece.

Salvatore Maranzano, who had begun calling himself

the boss of all bosses after Joe Masseria's sudden removal, met his own abrupt end in his New York City office. The story said four men posing as policemen had walked into Maranzano's digs on the ninth floor of the Helmsley Building in Manhattan and disarmed his bodyguards. They shot and stabbed Salvatore—who hadn't gotten too soft to put up a strong fight—and got away clean.

The fine hand of Lucky Luciano and Meyer Lansky was all over the thing, setting them up to take over the mob. It was too late for Carmine Broglio. I wondered if he was still resting peacefully at the bottom of a canyon off Mulholland. I thumbed through the paper, but Carmine was blissfully absent.

I glanced briefly at the sports pages. It was going bad for the New York teams. Ruth and Gehrig were having their usual big years, but the Yankees were way back of the Athletics. The Giants were fading behind the Cardinals. Maranzano wasn't going to get to see a New York World Series, anyway. It looked like the San Francisco Seals had the Pacific Coast League title locked up, and the newspaper's college football writer faded USC for the Rose Bowl.

I left the paper on the counter, edged fifty cents for breakfast and a tip under the side of the plate, and walked over to the pay phone. A friend—an air-tight, willowy brunette named Alice Windler—worked at the motor division downtown and I asked if she would run a license number for me. Alice said she would in return for dinner. I said dinner sounded like the berries.

I had two things to do that morning before I hit the studio. I wanted to see Joan Banes—I had the address for Johnny Cutter's sister in my pocket—and I needed to make a stop in West LA. Jimmy Gallen told me Joan Banes would drink whatever hooch came out of a bottle, and I had picked up some decent enough brown plaid from a guy living in the basement of my apartment building. I didn't think Joan Banes would mind I had a bottle and it wasn't even noon, so why not take a chance on stopping by unannounced?

I bought twenty gallons of gas at the corner, handed the pump jockey a deuce, and was on my way to see the one-time heartthrob. Cutter had stuffed his sister into a ratty old building called the Bradford Arms, just off Hollywood Boulevard. Bradford Armpit was a more accurate name. The four-story square building had gone up before running water and electricity and had been haphazardly remodeled somewhere around the turn of the century. I parked beside a light blue Chrysler 70 Roadster that looked way out of place in this neighborhood. The musty smell that wrinkled my face when I walked through the front door must have been a mixture of vinegar and prunes. The builder had cut each floor into four tiny four-room flats, two on each side of the hallway that ran down the center, wall-to-wall. The place didn't have an elevator. I wouldn't have trusted one, anyway. Rickety stairs beckoned the unwary at each end of the hallway.

Joan's flat was on the second floor, at the back. Torn, warped linoleum in faded black-and-white squares each a foot wide covered the hallway. Bare light bulbs hanging from the ceiling would have provided illumination in the dim interior if they had been on. I tried the switch and it laughed at me.

I cursed Johnny Cutter. Movietown's hottest darling had a big, beautiful house in the hills and a fast, expensive yacht on the ocean. His sister had four small, dingy rooms, a drug habit, and peeling wallpaper. Brotherly love, Hollywood style.

I knocked on the door at 2B. After a while, I knocked again and, a little bit later, I knocked louder. I glanced around but no one came to the other three doors to see

who was making the racket. I looked at the closed tran-
som. The milky glass forestalled any attempt to see
through it. After my fourth loud knock, something moved
inside. Something hit the floor and a thin, reedy voice
screeched a loud curse. Footsteps shuffled across the
floor and someone began fooling with the lock. The door
opened with the same creak the Universal sound man had
used for Dracula's coffin.

I looked down into the face of a little old woman
slightly more than five feet tall, reed thin under a light
green, shapeless robe that had once been expensive but
was now threadbare and dotted with heavy stains of various colors, none of which matched anything else. Her
hair straggled out of her head, dark, dirty, and matted.

It couldn't be Joan Banes. Joan Banes was thirty-one,
and the 1925 publicity picture Jimmy Gallen had given
me showed a lovely young lady in her mid-twenties.

"Johnny? Johnny? That you, Johnny?"

Her clouded eyes—once hazel and now blood red—
lurched at my face and locked on the scotch in my left
hand. She shook so badly I thought she was going to collapse.

"No. I am not Johnny. I am a friend of Johnny's."

"Oh, you must be Jimmy then. I'm sorry I didn't recognize you, Jimmy, but I just woke up, you see…"

Her words trailed off as she tried to focus on my face,
but she couldn't manage much more than a blank stare.

I stepped through the door, took her by thin shoulders,
and guided her to the lone chair in the room. The padding
was coming out and the chair was rapidly losing its
shape. A small, chipped table beside the chair held a
small lamp and a rolled up newspaper. Otherwise, the
room was empty. I put the bottle on the table, beside a
filthy glass that might have had something growing in it.
A bunch of autographed movie photos in mostly cracked

frames hung from the peeling wallpaper covering the walls. The photos were a desperate reminder of a failed past. The thin, filthy carpet moved beneath by feet as I went to look at the pictures, photos of everybody who was remotely anybody in movies a decade ago, all signed to Dear Joan. There were no photos of Johnny Cutter. I wondered if anybody hanging on that wall, smiling behind yellowing glass, knew or cared how tenuously Joan Banes held onto life.

I glanced at her. She slumped pitifully in her chair, staring blankly at me. I was pretty certain she didn't know I was there. I started back to her and noticed, on the wall opposite the front door and behind her chair, a photo was missing. The wallpaper was brighter where an eight-by-ten had recently hung. I had an idea and checked behind one of the framed photos. The wallpaper was darker. I checked more photos and the wallpaper was darker behind all of them.

I checked the three doors in the room, all closed. I cracked a door and peered into a bedroom. A bed, dresser, and chest of drawers looked like they could collapse at a whisper. Rumpled, stained sheets covered the unmade bed. A strong floral bouquet stirred in the room, reminded me of roses and jasmine. The small, caked window closed off the sunlight. The closet door in the corner was partially open and I could see a couple of expensive dresses that might have been new a dozen years ago. The two pairs of heels on the floor by the bed hadn't seen polish since the war with Spain.

I closed the door and checked the second door. The tiny kitchen, just big enough for a stove, icebox and sink, had no table. A couple of dirty plates and several filthy glasses perched at the end of the sink. The cupboard on the wall had no door. You didn't need a door if there was nothing on the shelves.

The bathroom beside the kitchen was the same size. Black stains marred the sink and toilet, and the filthy tub might have been the bottom of a dried mud hole. A threadbare washcloth and a sad-looking towel draped over the sink. There was no vanity. A bottle of aspirin sat on the back of the grimy toilet.

I pulled my head out of the bathroom and checked the door in the corner. Inside the tiny closet, a well-worn cloth coat hovered listlessly on a wire hanger.

I started back to her chair and couldn't miss the tip of a syringe peeking out from the newspaper. The corner of the paper was wet and liquid dripped down the outside of the glass. She had opened the scotch. The worn carpet between the table and the chair was wet. I capped the bottle and put it out of her reach.

She was still lost in space. She didn't look at the bottle when I moved it.

"Joan, can you hear me?"

"Johnny? Johnny?" she droned, her voice distant, her eyes nowhere. "Do you still love me, Johnny? You do, don't you?"

"I'm not Johnny. My name is Neil Brand. I'm here to help you."

"Jimmy? Is that you? You still love me, Jimmy?"

She leaned forward, peering at me as if I had just materialized. Her pupils dilated, and her lips began twisting as if she were chewing invisible tobacco. "Who are you? Who?" Her shrill voice rose to a thin screech. "You get out of here. Out of here. Now. Out of here."

She pushed at me and I grabbed her hands. They were cold and sweaty and I couldn't hold them tightly enough to stop her shakes. I pushed up the sleeve of her robe. Needle punctures pockmarked her arm.

I gently pressed her back into the chair and she grew quiet again, the blank stare returning. Jimmy was right. I was not going to get anything worthwhile out of her. The room had no telephone. I took the bottle and left the flat. Bright sunshine glinted on a brand new world. I tossed the bottle into a trash can, got into the Chevy, and stopped at the first drug store I saw, about a block away. Two telephone booths in the corner were both empty. I rang the studio and asked for Jimmy Gallen's office.

"Jimmy, where's Cutter?"

"He was in early for a coupla hours. But I think he's finally wrapped that picture and he's out of here. What's up?"

"I'm at his sister's, Jimmy. You find that bastard and tell him to get down here and take care of her. And do it now. You get an ambulance down to her place and get her some help. They might still be able to keep her alive."

Gallen was sputtering. "Neil—Neil, now wait a minute. Let's don't go off—"

"Jimmy, if I don't see an ambulance down here in thirty minutes, I'm calling Lolly Parsons."

"You do that and Harry will kick you out of town. You'll never work—"

"I don't give a damn. Thirty minutes. What do you think Parsons will make of this? Cutter isn't one of her favorites and neither is Harry. She'll have it all over the radio by tonight."

"Sure, Neil, sure. I didn't know Joan was that bad. I haven't seen her in—"

"Ambulance," I shouted and hung up.

I sat in the vacuum that was the phone booth, trying to calm down, thinking. After a while, I put a nickel in the slot and asked the operator to get the veterans home out near Sawtelle. A honey voice came on the line in thirty seconds.

"Soldiers' home. How may I help you?"

"This is Neil Brand." My voice was back to smooth

and polite. "My brother, Nelson Brand, is a patient. I wanted to know how he's doing today."

"Just a moment, please, Mr. Brand. I will connect you."

After a few moments, another very pleasant voice came on the line. "This is Miss Allenberg. May I help you?"

"I'm inquiring after Nelson Brand, my brother."

"Yes sir. He's resting comfortably today."

"In his room?"

"That is correct. I think we will take him outside this afternoon, however. The weather is nice and I rather think he enjoys being in the sunshine."

"He does, but he gets cold easily."

"Yes, sir. We will be certain to keep him warm and comfortable, I assure you."

"No problem if I come to see him."

"No, sir. That would be very nice."

"I'll be up this afternoon. Thank you."

I started to hang up, but the very pleasant Miss Allenberg spoke up quickly. "Sir, if I may say so. Your brother is very special to us. We are, of course, aware of his war record, and we are most fastidious in his care. Every nurse on this staff treats your brother as if he were also our brother."

"Thank you," I said again and hung up.

I sat slumped over, my reflection in the phone booth glass just as blank as the one on the pan of Cutter's sister. Her ravaged mug burned my brain and spun into Nels. Just now, I couldn't tell them apart. I thought of the .45 back at my apartment. I needed a drink. It was not even eleven and I needed a drink. I knew a scatter where I could get one. I left the drug store, turned into an alley that cut the block in half, and went down a flight of steps. When I was on the force, we had raided Vinnie's dive a couple of times. Always making certain, of course, to telephone first.

This time, I came unannounced, but they let me in any way. I ordered a whiskey straight, made it clear I was not open to bumping gums, and nursed the brown along for nearly thirty minutes. I got lost inside myself.

The unblinking sun was straight up in a practically cloudless sky when I got into the Chevy and drove back to Joan's dump. I didn't see an ambulance, but Jimmy Gallen's Packard was parked by the front door where the Chrysler 70 had been. I went in and heard a siren coming down Hollywood as I went up the stairs.

Jimmy Gallen was banging furiously on Joan's door. He saw me and yelled, "Can't get an answer."

"She's in there."

"Door's locked."

He banged some more and I joined him.

"Where's Cutter?"

"Couldn't find him."

Two men in hospital uniforms, carrying a stretcher, appeared at the top of the stairs. It didn't take much to break in the flimsy door. Joan Banes was still in her chair, still had that blank stare. Her mouth was open, her head was back, and she was not breathing.

"Your mother?" the ambulance driver said, looking at me.

I didn't say anything. Once gorgeous Joan Banes, thirty-one-year-old former motion picture star, was dead of old age.

CHAPTER 13

The soldiers' home dated from the eighties and covered almost seven hundred acres of rolling, treeless land near the village of Sawtelle, just north of Wilshire. One hundred and fifty-seven buildings now ranged around the property, including thirty-three barracks and six hospitals. Four barracks boasted brick walls, and the others were low frame structures with porches running their entire length, all bounded by round shrubs and waist-high palm trees. Winding lanes curved through the property along the front of the barracks, and pines, palm trees and eucalyptus groves lined the roads. Irrigation ditches allowed orchards and vegetable gardens to be scattered over the property. Someone once had the idea of creating a manmade lake on the property, but hard California rains had washed away that plan.

They had recently moved Nels out of one of the frame barracks and into the four-year-old James Wadsworth Hospital that had replaced the Barry Hospital, a meandering structure built in five sections during a nearly twenty-year period. The final section went up in 1909.

Close to forty-six-hundred former soldiers lived at the home. Some had served as far back as the War Between the States.

I found Nels in the garden area behind the hospital. Numerous varieties of bright flowers grew in the large expanse of lawn, the grass interrupted by several flagstone walks, small palms and scattered stone benches. Several soldiers and nurses enjoyed the garden—some soldiers in wheelchairs, others sitting on benches. A few strolled along the immaculate grounds. Nurses or visitors hovered at their sides, although some soldiers were alone. Two small Civil War-era cannons stood guard duty on either side of a tall flagpole in the front corner. A large, new American flag atop the flagpole unfurled itself lazily in the slight breeze.

Nels was asleep in a reclining wheelchair just off the main flagstone walk, a wall of low, round, and very green shrubs behind him. Sunlight on his face accentuated the deep lines of his pale, sagging skin. A light breeze blew in his face, and wispy white clouds hung above us like shreds of torn cotton. Before he went into the hospital, Nels had been my size, but now he couldn't have outweighed the doughboy's gear he used to easily carry on his back.

My pocket watch showed seven minutes past two in the afternoon and a thermometer on the porch nudged just over eighty degrees in the shade, but a heavy blanket hid his ravaged body from neck to feet. The woolen cap on his head covered his ears. A slender and attractive young nurse in her late twenties sat on the bench beside his wheelchair. Nels could not have been aware she was there. When I drew closer, I realized the nurse was reading a book aloud.

She looked up when she saw me and closed the book. She looked at me with large, light green eyes that twinkled in the bright sunlight.

"Oh, you must be Mr. Brand's brother. Miss Allenberg said you were coming."

I nodded and took her extended hand. "I didn't mean to interrupt your reading."

"Oh, that's quite all right." She laughed lightly. "Actually, I was reading to your brother, but he went to sleep." Her genuine smile brightened a bright day. "I think he was bored."

She showed me the book. It was Ruth Suckow's *Children and Other People*. I didn't know anything about it, but it didn't look to be the sort of prose to excite either Nels or me.

"Don't see how anyone could be bored with you around."

She might have blushed, but she most likely had heard a lot of that kind of nifty patter from all the soldiers around her.

"Well, I will leave you brothers alone. I have my duties."

"Sounds like you were waiting for me."

"I thought I would keep your brother company until you arrived. I am Nurse Brownlee. If you need anything at all, please don't hesitate to ask."

I watched her walk along the flagstones, stopping briefly here and there to say a few words to soldiers in wheelchairs and on the benches, and to give them comforting pats.

I sat down and reached out my hand to touch my brother's arm. He stirred a little but did not waken. I sat silently and watched Nels. I watched the soldiers, the nurses, and the visitors. I watched the green grass, the little palms sprouting from the grass, and I watched the round, green shrubs. I watched Old Glory stir in the light breeze, its forty-eight stars and thirteen stripes shimmering in the sun. I didn't wake Nels. I just sat there. This visit was for me as much as it was for Nels.

My mind wandered back to when we were kids, growing up playing baseball and football, frolicking on the white California beaches, and swimming in the clear blue ocean. Whatever we did, we did together, even when we started looking for girls. When I hit five feet and one hundred pounds, so did Nels. It was my idea to join the Army in '17, but Nels was right behind me. When we enlisted, we both stood an inch over six-feet and weighed one-eighty, solid. We went overseas together in 1918, two young men among thousands looking for the adventure of war. We were in the same unit together, and we jumped the Huns in the Argonne side-by-side. We took mustard gas, but I quickly got my mask in place. Nels stopped to help a soldier who was having trouble with his mask. We had been warned not to do that, but Nels never thought of himself first. He took a lungful of the stuff and was soon in a field hospital, then in a hospital far to the rear. They sent Nels home and sent me to hit the Germans again. I kept hitting them as hard as I could right up until Armistice Day. I earned two citations for bravery in action. They called it bravery because they didn't hand out awards for stupidity.

I didn't know how I made it. A lot of the boys Nels and I went over with did not. I knew two things about France. Half of it was ugly, black trenches stretching over ugly, black ground; the other half was tall, white crosses growing out of bright, green grass. Doughboys had a saying for those who found their final resting place beneath those crosses, those who would never go back home across that ocean. They simply said the dead had gone west.

When the war was over, I got back home just in time to be my brother's best man at his wedding to Connie. A few years later, he was my best man. He joined the police force, pleasing our old man, who was by then a desk sergeant downtown. Three years later, I joined. Our bright futures soon got on twisted paths. Mom contracted cancer and died in '23. Connie split when Nels got sick. My wife took a bullet meant for me. I got suspended and kicked off the force.

Nels began losing weight and started coughing up blood. He wouldn't eat because he had trouble swallowing. Each day Nels grew weaker until just getting out of bed was a trial. His voice became hoarse and his breath came in short gasps.

Eventually, we had to put him in the soldiers' home. Finally, a newly arrived staff doctor told Nels he had lung cancer. He wanted to operate, a risky procedure that had been done only a few times. He cut Nels open and saw it was too late. He sewed him up and found him a place in Barracks 18. As in 1918, the year he took the gas.

And now Nels was nothing more than a dried piece of leather with a faint murmur in his chest and maybe a few good thoughts in his deteriorating memory. I knew, sitting there watching him, Nels would never come out of that wheelchair. Sitting beside him, the faint hope I otherwise held out for him was gone. I realized the dim trust I'd clung to was only there in the mornings when I was alone. Alone and staring at the night stand, trying to summon the guts to do the thing Nels wanted. The thought hit me like a cannon blast. I wanted to find his wife and drag her to him, make her look at Nels. But what good would that do? I wanted to kill Johnny Cutter because of his sister. But what good would that do, except make me feel a little better?

I sat beside Nels a long time. The shadows lengthened. Nurse Brownlee passed, stopped briefly, but said nothing, and—just like she had done with the other old soldiers—gave me a sympathetic pat on the back when she walked on. I was crying and she left me to my sorrow. I was crying. Me, the tough doughboy who took on the Huns

without a thought of danger. The one-time LA police officer who was tough enough to walk down mean alleys
on the darkest nights. The sinking sun was taking me
with it, the wind was picking up, and Nels still slept. For
all I knew, he would never wake up. It was too late now
to put the .45 he had begged for in his hand.

At five o'clock, several ex-soldiers appeared wearing
uniforms covering the last seventy years. A few in the
AEF uniforms of the Great War carried musical instru-
ments. They played "Taps" a little off-key while three
relics who had survived the Civil War—one in gray, two
in blue—reverently took down the flag. Two men about
my age—both wearing the uniforms of flyboys—helped
the older men to fold the flag, taking great care it did not
touch the ground. The last strains of "Taps" died out and
the flag bearers disappeared inside, followed by the little
impromptu band. Soldiers who could stand and those
who could not lowered their salutes. Most wiped moist
eyes.

I left. It was getting late. I knew our old man would
stop by after he got off work and I did not want to see
him. Did not want to hear him blame me again for taking
a bribe, for getting kicked off his beloved force. Did not
want to hear him blame me again for taking Nels to war
and giving the son he loved most a death sentence.

And he didn't want me to try to tell him, yet again, I
was framed but couldn't prove it. That if I had not said
let's go to war, Nels would have.

It didn't work. I was halfway down the front steps of
the hospital when the old man climbed out of his black
Model A. I might have found someplace to run, but I
stood out on those white steps like a turkey buzzard on a
poodle. He saw me. He stopped outside the car door and
put his right foot on the running board. He dug a Lucky
Strike from the vest of his plain black three-piece. He lit

his smoke and eyed me the way Mom used to look at moles in her garden.

"Didn't know you ever came out to see Nelson." The chill in his raspy voice crept down my spine.

"I come to see him. Usually don't stay this late."

"I usually get here 'bout this time."

An awkward silence chilled the air between us. He took a long drag on his smoke while studying my face. I think my eyes were red.

"You okay?"

"Ducky."

"Yeah. Lot better than your brother."

What do you say to that? "Nels was asleep out back. Sun's gone now, so I imagine they'll take him inside. You can probably find him in his room."

I started to walk away.

"Neil."

I turned halfway.

"Still Harry York's egg?"

"I still work for York."

My old man shook his head and did not try to hide the hurt and anger in his eyes. He took a deep drag, ground out the gasper with his heel, and headed for the hospital steps. Going to see the son he wanted desperately to live. Leaving behind the son he had disowned. I got into the Chevy and watched Police Sergeant Norsten Brand disappear through the hospital door.

CHAPTER 14

I did not want to go home. I wanted to go on a long bender, but I didn't want to get drunk. I wanted to do something that meant something and would feel good doing it.

I stopped at Clifton's on South Olive for a hamburger with the works. A neon sign over the door flashed *PAY WHAT YOU WISH*. I suspected most customers overpaid because of that sign. A pound of hamburger these days was eleven cents so I left fifty cents for the sandwich and the tip, plus a bottle of Pepsi I took with me. The Pepsi-Cola company had filed for bankruptcy and could use my help.

This year I was hanging my clothes in a coop on Wilshire, just off Grand. I rented two large rooms, along with a kitchen and a bath on the fifth floor, last door on the right as you turned left out of the elevator. I stopped only long enough to change into black trousers, black shirt, and black, crepe sole shoes. I pulled a shoulder holster off a nail in the closet and took my Colt M1911 out of the bottom drawer of the night stand. I filled a seven-shot clip and, this time, I rammed it home. I shrugged into the holster, slipped on a black leather flogger, and dropped four seven-shot magazines into the pockets, two clips in each pocket. A black fisherman's cap completed the ensemble. It was an outfit I had used when I spent two months undercover on the San Pedro wharfs the winter of 1924-25.

I drove fast to Laurel City and parked about fifty yards from the Laurel Inn. The dying sun cast long red streaks over the darkening water. The tethered *Sea Venture's* tender bobbed lightly against the tide at the far end of the dock. When twilight faded out, I crossed to the tender. I started the electric motor and headed to the big white yacht, shadowy in the expanding moonlight. No lights burned aboard the yacht and I saw no one on the deck.

I tied the tender and swiftly climbed the Jacob's ladder. I walked the teak deck and looked into the empty pilothouse. I went into the main salon and switched on some lights. I turned on every light I could find. I didn't care who saw. I wanted someone to come out to see what was going on. I wanted someone to talk to.

I checked out the main salon and the cabins for the captain and his crew. The galley was empty. I looked through the guest cabins, all elegantly done in teak and silver and divided into sitting rooms and bedrooms, and all with private heads. I didn't know what I was looking for. Each cabin was richly furnished and as impersonal as a motel room.

I left the lights burning and went topside. Dark shadows played across the water under the pale moon. I could hear the tide gently lapping against the yacht, along with the faint bump-bump of the tender riding against the steel hull. I stood behind a finger of light spilling from the pilothouse and waited in the deep shadows. I had enough lights on to attract somebody.

Not long after dark, I heard something touch against the electric tender. I pulled the .45 and racked the slide. The bird in the dinghy below was the one who had stopped Gallen and me at the dock a couple of days ago. He hadn't changed clothes. He stepped into the tender and started up the ladder, holding a baseball bat in his right hand. He was chewing on a toothpick. I stepped back and out of sight, went down the stairs toward the salon, and sat in one of the chairs to the right of the doorway. I was out of the man's view until he stepped into the salon. He stopped short when he saw me and lifted the bat so the barrel was resting in the palm of his left hand. He stared at the heavy .45 in my hand. The Colt has a way of drawing your attention when the barrel is looking at you.

"I hope I don't have to tell you not to do anything stupid."

He didn't move. He looked at me like a hitter who had just struck out and didn't want to leave the box. The forgotten toothpick dangled between his lips.

"Put down the bat and kick it away."

Nothing happened.

"Look. This is a Colt .45 and it has some pretty impressive firepower. And trust me on this. I've used it a few times and I know how it works. You just stand there and it makes me jumpy. I get too jumpy and—boom. Know what I mean?"

He took his left hand off the bat and let the barrel rest on the floor. He released his right hand and the bat fell over onto the thick carpet with a soft plunk, the knob almost pointing at me.

I motioned the .45 at one of the chairs.

"Sit down and keep your hands where I can see them. I have a few questions that won't take much of your time."

He lowered his considerable bulk into one of the overstuffed chairs and put his hands on the arms, all the while staring at me. The toothpick snapped between his teeth.

He took out the two pieces and tossed them onto the carpet.

"What's your name?"

"They call me Rigger."

"You remember me, Rigger?"

"Yeah. Seen you a coupla days back, snoopin' 'round."

"As you can see, I'm snooping some more. Where's the captain and the crew?"

"They only come 'round when the boss goes to sea. Otherwise, it's just me."

"And what do you do?"

"I keep a' eye on things for the boss. He don't want no rats gettin' aboard."

"Who's the boss?"

"Johnny Cutter, the picture star."

"You're balled up. Cutter does not own this boat."

"Sure, he does."

"No. Cutter does not own this boat. It belongs to an oilman named Randall Curtiss, who has more walking around money in his pocket than you and I will make in five years."

I could see Rigger was working that bit of information around in his conk. "Well, the man told me Cutter owns it."

"What man?"

"Big guy. Your age, height, a lot heavier. Had a little scar here—" Rigger pointed to his left cheek. "His beak had been batted around pretty good."

"He said he worked for Cutter?"

"Yeah. Said the boss wanted his boat watched. Give me a double sawbuck to keep a' eye out. Said he might be back in two, three days and give me another twenty if he still wanted it watched."

"Told you to keep your lamps trimmed and your trap shut?"

Rigger nodded.

"You don't stay on board. No food in the galley. You're taking meals at the Laurel Inn. Where do you sleep?"

"None of your beeswax."

"Okay. But it ain't on board."

"No, it ain't on board. The man said Mr. Cutter don't want me on board. Just wants me to keep a' eye on his boat case someone comes pokin' 'round."

"What did you do with the booze?"

"What booze?"

"Boat was full of hooch when I was here earlier. You couldn't drink it all. What did you get for it?"

"Say what?"

"How much you sell it for? Get a good price?"

Rigger almost smiled. "Didn't reckon the boss'd care. He always brings plenty when he comes. He expects it to be drunk."

"Ever hear of Prohibition?"

Rigger snorted. "Don't be a sap."

"The man with the scratch say he thought someone might come snooping?"

"Didn't say."

"See anybody but me?"

Rigger nodded. "You and that cake-eater was with you the other day. And another man. Saw him that night the boat went out. He was with them skirts."

"Big gink, wearing a black coat?"

"Yeah. I think he was a bull."

"How's that?"

"I can smell bulls. Saw him another night, too."

"Get a good look?"

"Naw. A real baby grand, though. Had a hooked nose. That's all I can say."

"See anybody with him?"

"Another man 'bout his size. Smelled like a bull, too. And a coupla ripe tomatoes."

"You make them?"

Rigger shook his head. "Naw. One was tall, had white hair like that dame in the pictures. Other was shorter but I never got a look at her face. Always kept it hidden under a big hat. Nice builds on both, though."

"How long you been on the job?"

Rigger shrugged. "Week."

"You see anybody hanging around, how do you get in touch?"

"Mr. Cutter's man give me a phone number. Only called it once, when I seen you two the other day."

"Talk to Cutter?"

"No. Operator said nobody picked up."

"Call again?"

"Yeah. Coupla times that night. Same deal."

"What's the number?"

"Wait a minute."

He dug a folded piece of paper out of his shirt pocket. He read the number. I didn't recognize it.

"Rigger, this boat went out to sea couple of nights ago. Remember? Had a bunch of very pretty, young skirts aboard."

Rigger grinned, showing a few gaps around teeth badly in need of work. "Sure. Bunch of real lookers. They prob'ly swizzled all the booze. That Mr. Cutter sure knows how to have a good time."

"You talk to Cutter?"

"Naw. He never paid me no mind. Don't think he even saw me."

"Man who gave you the scratch with them?"

"Didn't see him."

"Where'd they go?"

"Out to sea."

"Where out to sea?"

"How would I know? I ain't the captain, see? They just went out to sea. Havin' a party."

"And you turned in for the night?"

"Yeah. Mr. Cutter's man paid for a room for me over at the Laurel. I left a few dead soldiers and turned in. Mornin', the *Venture* was riding her anchor, right here. Been untouched since. 'Til you showed."

"Rigger, you are Western Union."

Rigger nodded at the .45 still in my hand. "You got the bulge."

"You seem like a regular fella so I'll tell you what. Your boss won't be too happy with you if you tell him I got on this boat. He'll have some questions for you, and it probably won't work out your way. You don't want to be left holding the bag. Understand?"

Rigger's mind was working again. "You mean you don't want me to squeal to him?"

"I don't care one way or the other. Was me, I wouldn't spill to anybody. You've been helpful. I'm just trying to do you a little favor."

Rigger mulled that over. "You're sayin' you ain't gonna tell Mr. Cutter?"

"Why would I do that? Mr. Cutter is only gonna find out if you tell him, and I can't think of a reason why you'd want to."

Rigger grinned. "I won't tell that goombah nothin'."

"Now you're hitting on all sixes." I picked up the baseball bat and crossed to the stairs. "I'll leave this in the dinghy. See you around." I left him sitting in the salon, trying hard to think. I was halfway back to the Laurel Inn when the lights aboard *Sea Venture* winked out.

CHAPTER 15

Saturday's were regular work days at the York Brothers Studio. Jimmy Gallen was in his office, but he didn't have time to talk. He was taking care of a few details before heading out to Lakeside for a round of golf with a couple of MGM producers and an executive from Paramount.

"You find Cutter?"

"Yeah." He bobbed his head. "He went up to San Francisco. He's at the Mark Hopkins. I called yesterday but he was out. I left a message. Tried again this morning and left another message. My guess, he registered at the Hopkins and now he's shacked up with some dish. Who knows when he'll surface?"

"Funeral arrangements?"

"Not going there. This studio does not wish for anyone to know about Joan's relationship with Johnny Cutter. Joan was a drug-addled has-been who will go out under wraps. *The Journal* this morning had two graphs on her, and no Cutter, and don't expect any of the other papers to be any different."

He looked at me without humor. "And Brand, I don't appreciate being threatened with Louella Parsons. No matter how much that mug Cutter needs a dose of reality.

Besides, how do you think Harry'd like you spilling stuff to Parsons?"

"Don't take it personal. And Cutter needs a sock on the jaw."

"Break his jaw? Harry'll like that."

"I'm beginning not to care very much for Harry." I backed out of Gallen's office. "Good luck with your golf game."

"Thanks. I'll need all the luck I can get against those sharks."

I entered the main building and headed to the top floor to say hi to Betsy. I stopped when I passed the office where two of Harry's best writers, Frank and Meyer Wolheim, hung their hats. The door was open and I saw Meyer's feet propped up on the bottom drawer of his desk.

I stuck my head in the door. The room smelled like a smokestack. A big ashtray full of butts rested atop a carton of Marlboro. Meyer was making notes in red ink on a screenplay. Frank busily tried to pry open a can of sardines.

We chatted a moment and when I turned to leave Frank stopped me.

"Say, Brand, you here yesterday?"

"Didn't know anyone noticed."

"Well, what I mean is did you hear the latest from Harry?"

I perched on the corner of Frank's desk. "Fill me in."

Frank chuckled and waved a hand. "This is a good one, Neil."

"One of Harry's truly sparkling moments," Meyer said. "Frank'll have to spill. I can't get through it for laughing."

"Anyway," Frank said, suppressing a laugh, "me and Meyer are working on a sword and sandal epic for Harry and he's been yelling at us to finish the first treatment so he can read it. Not a good idea when the idea's Harry's. He wants to make a picture about the Crusades. *The Great Crusade*, he's calling it. About some king who wants to take back the Holy Land. Lots of sword fights and nookie. Gonna star Richard Mercer and Evelyn Parker. Harry thinks it'll be a big hit, like *Ben Hur*."

"Listen," Meyer cut in. "If Harry had made *Ben Hur*, he'd rewritten it so that Ben Hur loses the chariot race."

"Never mind that," Frank said. "So me and Meyer take the script up to his office first thing yesterday morning before Harry's even here. When Harry gets in, about the first thing he does is start reading it. Before long, he's screaming his lungs out. Betsy can hear him even through those asylum doors he put in. She can hear things bouncing off the wall, and then he's pounding on the doors. You know he can't open 'em from inside his office because of those damned doorknobs. Betsy opens the door and Harry's yelling, stomping, and cussing, and Betsy has to cover her ears. He tells her to get Meyer and me in his office right now. Tells her to tell us we're fired if we aren't in his office in two minutes.

"So she calls us and we hustle up. We go into Harry's office and he's screaming at us. He tried to throw a telephone at us but the cord didn't reach, and I had to pick it up off the floor and set it on his desk. That got Harry calmed down a little bit. He told us to sit down and he just sat on the other side of that fortress he calls a desk, staring at us, not saying a word. He was breathing hard and his face turns from red to purple—"

"I thought we were going to have to call an ambulance," Meyer said.

"Then he started to talk," Frank said. "Low, barely above a whisper. He was trying real hard not to blow up. He says to us, 'How much do I pay you two bums? Don't answer. I'll tell you. I pay you two bums fifteen hundred dollars a week. That's as much as any writer in this town makes. And for fifteen hundred dollars I get this.' Harry picked up the script, waved it at us, and then threw it on his desk.

"Now, Neil, this thing might not be *King Lear*, but it's a pretty good tale. We worked hard on it and it's a pretty good tale. Got everything in it Harry wanted, with plenty of good lines for his two stars. But we don't say anything. We don't say anything because we know Harry is not through, and Harry does not want to be interrupted.

"Then he says, 'I put you two fifteen hundred dollars a week writers on this because I wanted the best picture that anyone—MGM, Paramount, Fox, those punk Warners—the best picture that could be made. If I had wanted this crap, I would have asked a two-hundred-and-fifty dollar a week writer to do it. But I wanted the best. I turned to the best, I thought. I got crap in return and I am not happy. Do you two bums have any idea how unhappy I am just now?'

"Now, Neil, a question like that deserves a thoughtful answer and neither one of us had a thoughtful answer just offhand. So Meyer asks, 'What's wrong with it, Harry?'

"And Harry says, 'You two bums burn me for fifteen hundred dollars a week—each—because you are supposed to be top of the line writers. The absolute best. You both studied at Columbus—"

"'Columbus,' he said," Meyer cut in. "Not Columbia."

"Yeah, yeah, Meyer. Brand knows how Harry talks. So Harry says, 'You both, I was given to understand, graduated from Columbus. Big Ivy League school, good as this country has. With honors, I understand. You are educated men. Me, I am not, in that way. I learned this business through hard work, with not much formal,' excuse me, Harry said 'former education. I didn't have the easy time of it you two bums had. So I don't have the former education that you two bums supposedly got. But even so—even so—I know, and so does every man, woman, and most little children, that people who lived in the times of the Crusades did not go around saying no, siree, and yes, siree.'

"Now that stopped us cold. We did not write no, siree, and yes, siree in our modest little masterpiece, and we had no idea what in the hell Harry was talking about. So I said, pointing at the treatment, 'Show us, Harry.' Harry opened the thing, scanned down a page, and pointed at a line where a knight says to his king, 'Yes, sire.' And at another place, he says to his king, 'No, sire.'

"I looked at Meyer and Meyer looked at me, and we were both choking on our tongues to keep from cackling like a hen laying an egg. It was all I could do to say, 'We'll take care of that, Harry.' I grabbed the script and we ran through his private door because we couldn't last long enough for Betsy to open the front gates. Harry was cussing us so loud we could hear him all the way down the hall. We were about halfway down the steps when we collapsed, laughing so hard we had to beat each other on the back to keep breathing."

I listened in shock, and then I was laughing. "Everybody knows by now?"

"It got around the lot faster than Aunt Tilly's wig," Meyer said. "I swear, when I finally get out of this place I'm going to find a way to get that scene in a picture if it's the last thing I ever write."

"And this rewrite?"

"We'll leave out the sires in the script and put 'em in when we shoot. Most likely, Harry won't notice when he sees the rushes."

"Good luck on that," I said. "See you later."

"Yes, sireeeeee," the brothers Wolheim said in unison.

The horn was blowing when I finally made it to the cubbyhole that was my office. Karl Behm, the guard at the main entrance, needed me. Behm had been a German soldier in the late war, and the tourists didn't stand a chance of getting by him at the front gate. Karl would look ducky standing at the front gate carrying a long saber and wearing a Pickelhaube. Maybe sew a photograph of Harry York on his left breast in lieu of medals.

"You must come," Karl said in his slight German accent. "A woman here wants in. She is causing quite a rookus."

"What's she want?"

"Her sister. Says she is an extra here and has disappeared. She wants to know what we have done with her."

"Okay. I'm on my way."

"Please hurry. She has a gun."

I hung up the phone and went out the door. I bumped into Theo Stein, another of Harry's top writers, on his way to the commissary. It was Theo who got me on at York studio when Harless called after they bounced me from the force.

When I was still a cop, Theo was writing a war drama for Harry and wanted to talk to some war vets for background. Somehow, he got me. His picture hit big-time and Louella praised him for his realistic screenplay, although I was never sure what she knew about warfare. Theo got a big raise from Harry and I got a good friend who stuck by me when the bribe scandal hit. I looked into a little studio problem for Harry, thanks to Theo. Some of Harry's prop workers were pinching sets from stages and selling the stuff to a mug out near Santa Barbara. An easy thing to break and to keep out of the papers, but it impressed Harry enough that Theo talked him into putting me on to run studio security.

"Wasn't hard," Theo said when I thanked him. "Harry

don't mind a crooked cop." He grinned. "After all, Harry's paid off a lot of 'em."

Now, Theo slapped me on the back and asked if I had a few minutes. "I'm doing a cop story for Harry. Wanted to pick your brains, along with some other cops still on the force. Make it realistic like that war story I wrote."

"Anytime, Theo. Right now I've got something at the front gate I've got to see about. Catch you when I'm finished with that."

I gave Theo a pat on the back and hurried off to the front gate to placate the always stoic Karl, who was never known to crack a smile. Harry dressed his guards in navy chino pants with matching leather belts, white cotton shirts, and black shoes. The York Brothers Studio patch was sewn on both sleeves near the shoulder and each guard wore a name tag on his left breast.

Karl wore his uniform with military precision, clean and neatly pressed. All the more reason I should get him a spiked helmet, except Karl would probably wear it. I hired him on just before Christmas. He looked just the type to hold off an attack of autograph seekers armed with ink pens and publicity photos. For all I knew, we might have been shooting at each other across no man's land during the war, but a dozen years after the shooting ended he was in California needing a job to support his family. Karl spoke English well enough to handle the gate, so I put him there. He showed up on time every day and did his job.

Karl was standing in front of the gate with his legs spread as if he were at attention, his arms clasped behind his back. He was my height and a trifle heavier, especially in the thighs. The California sun turned his light hair almost blond, and his dark blue eyes always showed deep concern no matter what. Now, he fixed his deeply concerned eyes on a slender young twist barely five feet tall, wearing a cheap, shapeless lightweight green dress with yellow trim. She wore no hat and her short brown hair was done up in finger curls that were working loose. Reasonably pretty in a scrubbed-face kind of way, the kind of girl the kid next door would fall in love with, but in this town, her kind of frail was lost in the woodwork. She was arguing with the placid guard blocking her entrance into the studio. I couldn't see a gun.

"What's going on here?" I used my top sergeant's voice.

Karl would understand that tone. He started to answer, but didn't get the chance.

"You in charge?"

The girl across the gate pointed a finger at me. She looked to be about nineteen or twenty, but already getting hard air across her pan.

I held up a friendly hand. "Don't cast a kitten. Calm down and I'll be with you in a snap."

I took Karl by the arm and pulled him toward the guard shack, which had a wraparound window, a sliding door, and a button inside to open and close the gate for cars. It was just big enough inside for a stool, a shelf to hold papers, and a phone.

"You said she had a gun," I reminded Karl. "All I see is a finger."

"I wanted to be sure you came right away," Karl said stoically. "That *dummes weibchen* has been yelling out there for half an hour."

"Karl, that's no way to speak about a young lady. And don't tell me somebody has a gun if nobody has a gun."

"I wanted to be sure you came right away."

Maybe he had a point. The girl in the green dress was little and slight, but her voice was big, and she was yelling louder now, and trying to climb over the gate.

"Stay here," I told Karl and motioned the girl to meet

me at the pedestrian gate off to the side. I pulled the bolt-lock on the inside of the heavy, iron-grated door and let the kitten in. She stopped yelling when the iron door creaked open.

"What's your name?"

"I'm Mary Kamenshek and I'm looking for my sister, Winnie."

I looked at her blankly.

"She's an actress. The name she uses is Winnie Kramer."

"Mary, there are no actresses at York Studio who go by Kramer. Or Kamenshek."

"She works here. She told me."

"Doing what?"

"She was working on a picture called *Doorway to Heaven*. Stars Johnny Cutter and she was really thrilled about getting to work with him."

"Okay." I leaned against the wall. "My guess would be your sister is an extra. That sound about right."

"Well, yes. I guess so. She answered a...what was it...casting call?"

I nodded.

"She said they were giving her ten days' work, maybe two weeks. Thursday, she came for what she said was to be her last day. She called me that evening, said she was going to a wrap party and would be late. I haven't seen her since."

"Did you go to the police?"

"I did. They said she had to be missing for forty-eight hours. And they didn't seem very concerned when I told them where she worked and where she went on Thursday night."

"She tell you where she was going for the party?"

"Something about a big yacht. That's all. I guess she was in a hurry."

"You go back to the cops yesterday?"

"Yeah. They took down her name and information and said they'd look into it. They told me to go home and wait. I did, for a while. Then I came down here, but nobody would let me in. Or even talk to me."

"You have a photo of your sister?"

"Yes. I forgot." She dug around in a little, brown cloth purse and took out an eight-by-ten glossy folded in half. "This is the same photo I gave the police. Winnie had several made, you know, for publicity."

It was the frail I had seen in Johnny Cutter's dressing room, the one who had gone to *Sea Venture* with him. She looked a lot different in the photo her sister handed to me, but it was her all right. "Thursday, you said?"

"She came here to work Thursday. That's two days ago and I haven't seen her or heard from her since."

"Can I keep this photo?"

"Please. Can you help me?"

"I'll ask around. I'll check with the director of that picture she was working on. I'll show her picture around. I'm sure someone will remember her."

"Can't you just check your files? Surely, you—"

"I'll check with casting. They have records on extras, but no one will be in until Monday. They don't work Saturdays. The picture's finished and the director and his crew won't be back 'til Monday. I'll find out what I can. You have a phone?"

She nodded. I told her to write down her name and number on the back of her sister's photo, along with an address. I folded the glossy and put it in my pocket.

"I'll call you Monday night, no matter what. That's a promise."

"But can't we—"

"No. We can't do anything today. I promise to do what I can."

I pushed her toward the door. She was reluctant to go and stood outside the grated door looking forlorn, a lost little bunny. I slammed it shut and shot the bolt.

"Go home."

She looked at me with hopeless brown eyes and I was sure she was going to turn on the faucet. I dusted as fast as I could. I went back into the main building and rustled up Theo Stein, who was easy to find in the office he shared with Margot Rodgers, another writer who came to Harry from the newspaper business.

Margot had been a sob sister for the *New York Herald*, and she penned some pretty successful pictures with the sob sister touch. The three-hankie jobs, the writers liked to call them.

"What's up?" I asked Theo, settling into Margot's chair.

"You remember how Harry got the idea for that war picture I wrote by watching *All Quiet on the Western Front*?"

I nodded. "*The White Crosses*. Good picture, better box."

"Harry could have made *All Quiet*, but he turned down the rights to it because he thought the Baumer character was too weak. He wanted to rewrite it. I told him he couldn't. The book is too popular and he'd be the laughing stock. You know Harry. Hell, he'd rewrite *The Scarlet Letter*, the dope."

"What's that got to do with a cop drama?"

"*All Quiet* was beat out for an award by *The Big House*. I say *All Quiet* was much better, but *Big House* won. Harry's war picture wasn't even nominated. He's been stewing around about *The Big House* ever since he saw it and the other night he was at a dinner at Jack Warner's and Jack showed an Eddie Robinson feature called *Smart Money*. So now, Harry wants a cop story that'll outdo *Smart Money*. He wants me to write it."

"What do you need?"

"First, let me tell you the plot. What I've got so far. The hero's a flatfoot, joined the force after fighting in the Great War. Rises in the ranks 'cause he's smart, honest, and good at his job. He finds out some cops are on the dole and he tries to take them down, only he gets framed by his partner for taking a bribe and gets kicked off the force. He uncovers the real crooked cops and gets a promotion. He does this, of course, with a goofy sidekick and a great looking dame on his arm. Whaddya think?"

"Sounds pretty damn familiar. Except for the goofy sidekick and the swell-looking dame on his arm. And, oh yeah, that part about finding the real crooked cops."

Theo rubbed his chin, a habit when he was thinking. "Thought I'd name the crooked cop Elmer Jones."

"Elmer Jones is pretty close to a real name, Theo."

"Yeah, I know. I know all about him. I already talked to him. You know, picking his brain for my story. Fed him some booze and loosened his tongue. Told him I'd base the hero on him. He ended up telling me a lot more than he wanted to." Theo put his elbows on his desk and leaned forward. "Elmo Jones is the cop who framed you, Neil. The sap basically told me all about it. Not that I could prove anything. Anyway, I just wanted you to know."

"You're a right gee, Theo. But I know all about Jonesy. If he spilled to you, then he knew you'd tell me. And like you, I got no proof. His tracks are well covered."

"I might have something more concrete, Neil. After I talk to a few more cops and flesh out my story. Who knows what might pop into this devious little mind of mine?"

"Flesh it out, Theo. Give me a call when you do.

Maybe I can fill in some details, help you with plot problems. Maybe I can be your Ben Hecht."

"I'd settle for half that good."

"But you stay far away from Elmo Jones. Pipe that?"

Theo nodded. I fished the photo of Winnie Kamenshek out of my hip pocket. "Ever see her?"

"Sure, all over this town. Everywhere you look, you see someone just like her. Why?"

"I think she worked on Markham's *Doorway to Heaven* as an extra."

"Markham might remember her. But she don't look to be his type."

"No?"

"Too wholesome. The schoolteacher type."

"He like his women a little hard edged?"

"Remember couple of months ago he showed up to work with a shiner? Told some cock 'n' bull hokum no one believed. Turns out he picked up some tough-framed dame with a chassis like a brick schoolhouse and she beat the crap out of him."

"Tried to go too far with her?"

Theo laughed. "No. Turns out he couldn't keep up his end of the bargain when it counted and she punched his lights out."

"That's a tough dame, all right."

"Tough, built, and mighty easy on the eyes. I did Markham a favor and smoothed out her hard spots. Bum never did thank me."

"Ungrateful mick. She must've grown fond of you, Theo."

"Say." He grinned. "I didn't get no black eye."

CHAPTER 16

Two eggs and a couple of day-old, one-cent sinkers made a slick breakfast Sunday morning. The stale sinkers were passable dunked in thick, black joe. I thumbed through the *Morning Journal* but there found about a big white yacht, nothing about a body wrapped in blankets in a gulch off Mulholland, nothing about a missing bit player who billed herself as Winnie Kramer.

I showered, shaved, and put on my best tennis whites. I tore a mean swipe in white from head to toe and I thought of Nurse Brownlee, which made me think of Nels. I pushed those notions to the back of my mind as I went out the door and bounded down the steps. I fired up the Chevy and headed west on Sunset toward lower Bel Air, just out of the foothills of the Santa Monica Mountains.

Sunday afternoon parties were a staple of the Hollywood crowd. It was the only day of the week the studios weren't shooting, which meant no lack of partying on big boats or at bigger houses—along with games of tennis, golf, and polo. There were also indoor games. Some of the parties were major blowouts, although most tended to be small and cliquish, and only the highly-anointed bothered to show. Gemma Layne's parties were the former.

She threw them the second Sunday of each month, no invitations needed. If you knew about it, you were welcome. At her parties, top studio bosses and unknown extras could rub elbows with the highest-paid producers and the lowest-paid writers. Which is why, of course, the top people rarely came to Gemma's parties. She had hoped they wouldn't when she set up the idea. Gemma, no face-stretcher, lived as down-to-earth as a picture star could get. On the set, between set-ups, she would rather hang out with the grips and extras, shooting dice, playing cards, and telling raunchy jokes. Gemma's days as the beautiful leading lady were fading, now that she had passed the magic forty-fifth birthday, but she had gracefully glided into the Rock of Ages roles of wife, mother, and mentor without losing a beat. After twenty-eight years on the stage and on the silver screen, Gemma Layne was still one of America's favorite actresses. She was also a favorite of Harry York because her movies continued to rake in lots of dough for him.

Gemma and her husband—one of Hollywood's most respected producers—lived in a modest California ranch-style house just off Sunset Boulevard on Celito Drive, a short, winding road that looped past the Bel-Air Country Club.

The house was hidden by a stucco wall and dense foliage, although it wasn't twenty feet from the road. What gave the place its character was its panoramic views of the Bel-Air back nine, the Los Angeles Basin, and, on clear days, Catalina Island.

The back yard featured a small pool, a tennis court, and an acre or so of nothing but manicured green grass bordered by short round shrubs and brilliant flowers.

I found a hole for my Chevy in the small front yard between a black Mercedes-Benz SS and a light green Bentley 3 Litre. A gray Studebaker Dictator huddled beside them. Not my style, but certainly more in my price range.

The sun was beginning to break through the overcast and the still air was springing some life when I dragged myself out of the Chevy. Some of Gemma's guests, none I knew, strolled aimlessly around the front of her house, maybe trying to escape the boredom. I circled around to the back, like a homing pigeon zeroing in on the laughter and the loud talk.

Larry Farrell—a silver-haired, gracefully aging, fairy character actor at York—was the first to see me. He was putting the finishing touches on a gin and tonic.

"Cheezit, the cops," he yelled loudly as I turned the corner of the house.

A few guests looked up, saw me, and went back to whatever they were doing. Farrell grinned crookedly and honored me with the famous one-eyed squint he had perfected in a couple hundred two-reelers.

"How's it goin', copper?" he asked out of the side of his mouth, still grinning. He set about fixing another gin and tonic in a tall glass.

I clapped the nance on the back and kept going. Two guests I didn't know played tennis and several more engaged in a heavy game of croquet on the sparkling green grass. I recognized two of the players: Loretta Young and her sister, Elizabeth—stage name Sally Blane. Some guests were in the pool, swimming lazily or hanging onto the edges, but most of them sat on Adirondack chairs painted a variety of bright colors at little tables around the pool, talking and laughing. Like me, the men who weren't in the pool wore tennis whites, some in white linen jackets, most with their sleeves rolled up. The women were all dressed in a casual style that tried to say their ensemble was merely thrown together at the last minute, not actually styled, tailored and planned to the last stitch so they bulged in just the right places, and parted in just the right places, and were completely missing in just the right places.

Gemma was sitting at a patio table in the shade near the back door of the house, sipping on a glass of noodle juice. She was wearing a crepe day dress, cream-colored with touches of red that set off her auburn hair. A string of cultured, white South Seas pearls around her neck perfectly matched her pearl earrings. She smiled warmly as I walked up to her.

"Stranger," she said, affecting a perfect deep Texas drawl, "ya'll look plumb naked without a drink in your paw."

"Now, ma'am, I just now got off that there stage and ain't had no chance to make no acquaintances."

"Sir," the round, elderly lady sitting beside Gemma said, "if you'll just get back on that stage, I'd be happy to climb in there with you and make your acquaintance."

I chuckled and looked into the light, twinkling eyes of Alison Skipworth, one of the brightest character actors in Hollywood. Everybody called her Skippy. Her skirt, blouse, and light jacket combination definitely looked thrown-on, and I had no doubt she had grabbed them out of her closet as she was going out the door. An incandescent smile lit up her craggy, sagging face—nobody in Hollywood was more proud of that face than Alison Skipworth because it was making her a fortune. Not that she spent much of it.

She lived in a small apartment in Hollywood and her auto of choice was a Ford Model A.

We spent some time on small talk, until Skippy snapped at me. "Young man, you are wasting your time on two old crones like us. Get yourself a drink and mingle with those lovely young ladies Gemma has invited."

"I always get kicked out of the best places," I said,

pulling the folded photo of Winnie Kramer from my hip pocket. I showed it to Gemma.

"Maybe you remember her. She's worked a little as an extra."

Gemma stared at the photo a while, lightly fingering the pure white marbles around her neck. Skippy craned her neck to look at the photo, pursed her full lips, and quietly shook her head no. Gemma nodded her head.

"Yes, believe I do. Can't swear, but she looks like the girl sitting at a table behind me in a nightclub scene in my last picture."

"When was that?"

"We wrapped about a month ago. So maybe six weeks."

"I'm impressed you remember her."

Gemma laughed. "Saw the picture last night. Harry showed it at his house. That baby vamp was making faces in the scene, and I don't think anybody saw it when we were shooting. I think the little imp was trying to get noticed."

"Seen her since?"

"No, but if I do, I'll give her an acting lesson. Why?"

"Her sister's looking for her. She's turned up missing."

"Oh, that's too bad." Her concern sounded real. "I hope her sister finds her well."

I nodded and tried my Texas drawl again, although I think it came out more like a California twang. "If you ladies will excuse me, I think I'll mosey."

I poured a whiskey and water and took a plate of food. A middle-aged man in a white apron stood behind a table by the bar, trying hard not to ogle the dazzling frails falling all over themselves to stand out. Pushed to it, he sliced the roast beef and the boneless ham and delicately dropped the slices on proffered plates. Each guest could choose from the caviar, goose liver, assorted vegetables, and miscellaneous items gracing the long table. Pies, cakes and a gelatin concoction were available for dessert. Only the men, Alison and Gemma ate. The high-maintenance actresses and the lithe, trim Janes wouldn't be caught dead in public putting anything that wasn't liquid in their mouths. I took some roast beef and ham and a scoop of au-gratin spuds, and found a vacant chair painted vivid blue off to the side of the pool.

When I finished eating, I got a bourbon and water and wandered around, saying hello here and there, showing the photo of Winnie. Nobody bit. I watched a little tennis and a little croquet.

The bright sun pushed the thermometer into the upper seventies. I found a seat in the shade of a tall maple and amused myself for the next half hour watching comely and preening tomatoes spreading themselves around the pool in one-piece suits scooped low in the back so they could get a nut-brown tan they could show off in their backless evening gowns.

"You just plan to look?"

Benny Blackmer, Gemma's husband, stuck out a hand. I was sure he only stopped to say hello because Gemma asked him, but that was all right. Tall and thin with a sallow face, Benny's bald head was ringed by prematurely gray fuzz. A right enough gee, Benny, but he belonged with the talent, not with Harry York's security gink.

We exchanged the usual pleasantries, and Benny pulled up a green Adirondack. He didn't recognize Winnie Kramer.

"Heard you and Jimmy Gallen were present when Joan Banes died."

I looked at him blankly. "Yeah. Sad day. You remember her?"

"I produced one of her first pictures, nine years ago. I

thought she was going to have a big future, but life takes funny bounces, y'know."

"I heard she had a tough go of it."

"I've heard that, too. I just did that one picture with her."

"What do you remember about her?"

"Not much. I can tell you that, even then, she was troubled, although she refused to talk about it. A few months after that picture we made, she was rolling with Jack, Ollie, and Alma. Hooked on junk just like them. Wonderful talents wasted. I wish Joan had been more forthright. I might have been able to help her, but she just pulled everything into herself. Damn shame."

"So you didn't know her very well?"

Benny pursed his lips and shook his head. "Not really. I know her real name was Dorothea Gardner, a good name for an actress but she refused to use it. She said her family would be mortified to know she was in pictures. Herb Brenon, who directed that picture, came up with the name Joan Banes for her. The only thing she ever told me about herself was that she came from Missouri. Some little town I can't remember. A Cape, I think. Girando or something. She told me that when I mentioned I was thinking of doing a costumer about a Mississippi riverboat. Also, Wally Reid was in that picture and he was from St. Louis. She said to please not tell anyone she was from Missouri."

"She say why?"

"Something about her family hating the idea she was in pictures."

I looked at him coldly. He noticed. "What's the matter?"

"I thought she was born in New York City."

"That was publicity piffle. She told everybody she was Upper New York. She let it slip to me that she was just a little girl from Missouri. Seemed very sorry she told me that much."

"Sounds like a movie title. *The Little Girl from Missouri.*"

Benny nodded in thought. "Too bland. No pop. But thanks for the idea."

"Ever do that riverboat picture?"

"Somebody beat me to it."

Benny was gone then, mixing with the right people. I was right behind him. I said my thanks to Gemma, who was mingling herself now, tea in hand. I headed for the Chevy. I turned the corner of the house and bumped into Lena Landers, incandescent in a cream-colored, light silk blouse set off by wide shoulders. There was nothing but Lena beneath the blouse. Her slacks were grayish-brown and elegantly tailored in flowing lines that spread smoothly and tightly around her shapely hips. Her vanilla ice cream hair had lost some of its curl and looked vaguely like cotton candy. Her violet eyes regarded me coolly.

"You bum. Don't talk to me. I'm not ready to forgive you, yet."

"Miss Landers, you're breaking my heart."

"Interrupting me and Johnny. Not a nice thing to do. And I didn't even know you."

"Just a mug doing his job."

"Jimmy Gallen told me all about you. Imagine me, letting some broken down flatfoot bust into my house."

"You can have it fumigated. Send Harry the bill. He won't kick. Seen Johnny lately?"

"That no-good bastard went to Frisco on the sly, but I have an idea who he's with."

"Anyone I'd know?"

"Some dumb Dora at York. A skinny, yellow-haired gold digger with no brains, a pretty face, and peanut butter legs. Just Johnny's type."

"Peanut butter legs?"

"Creamy smooth and easy to spread."

"That why he took up with you?"

Her violet eyes turned a smoldering dark purple and her lovely mouth compressed into a small, tight red line. "You bastard. Just when I was starting to warm up to you."

"I thought you and Johnny broke up a couple of years ago."

"So? There are times when we get together. Y'know, reminisce about old times. Sometimes for two or three days. Maybe next time I'll call you to come over."

"I'm not much good at mulling over old times."

"Who says we'd be mulling?" She looked me up and down. "Why aren't you in pictures? You got the looks. Tall, well-built, all that dark hair. Nice eyes, nice nose. Square chin the camera likes."

"Lena, you're turning my head."

"Maybe some day I'll turn more than your head, you bum."

"Seen Winnie Kramer lately?"

Something flashed in her eyes and was quickly gone. Her mouth set hard for an instant and then she was smiling. The actress in her had taken over. "Winnie who?" She grinned. "Winnie the Pooh?"

There was no reason to press that line.

"Have a nice time," I said and left her.

I backed the Chevy, just missing the fender of a brown-and-black Austin roadster. I looked for Lena Landers, but she was out of sight.

CHAPTER 17

I turned left onto Celito and right onto Sunset. The Chevy sputtered and backfired, sputtered more. I worked the clutch, the gear shift, the gas pedal, and the prayer button. I hit Laurel City and took Bay to the docks. *Sea Venture* was right where it was supposed to be. I walked out to the end of the dock. Rigger came off a motorboat tied to a slip. He was still wearing those same clothes and carrying his baseball bat. His supply of toothpicks had not run out.

"Anybody been snooping around?"

"Just you."

"The man who gave you the sawbuck, he been back?"

"Ain't seen him. If he don't show tomorrow, I'm done 'til he comes back."

"He won't be back." I pulled a ten-spot and a fin from my billfold and held them out for him. "How 'bout the same deal with me. Keep an eye out. Don't try to stop anybody. Just call me if someone comes."

Rigger eyed the scratch. "How'd ya know that man ain't comin' back?"

"He ain't coming, Rigger. That's straight goods."

Rigger looked at me, back at the bills in my hand. He slowly nodded his head and slipped the money into his pocket. I took a piece of paper from my billfold and gave it to him. I had written two phone numbers on it, one to my flat and one to my office.

"See anybody, ring me. Don't do anything else."

"You don't want me to stop 'em?"

"Be best if they don't even see you."

I walked back to the Chevy. A short, fat man in a medium brown suit slid into an outside phone booth by the side door to the Laurel Inn.

He glanced at me when he put his nickel in the slot, glanced at me again, closed the door, and began dialing. He had the blower pressed to his ear when I pulled out in the Chevy.

I was on Bay Avenue and near the Laurel City limits when I heard the siren. A long, black-and-white Ford with Laurel City Police Department lettering on the side doors in black-on-white paint shaped like a cop shield zoomed up, passed me, and slammed on the brakes.

I hit the Chevy's brakes and twisted the wheel. The right front tire jumped the curb as I ground to a halt.

Two beefy twins in blue uniforms took their time unfolding their big frames from the car. Badges glistened in the late afternoon sun and both twins had their right hands on the butts of their service revolvers.

I put my hands on the steering wheel and sat tight.

"I need to see your license," Twin One said.

I handed it to him, along with my employee card for York Brothers Studio. He looked carefully at both and handed them back to me.

"Turn your bucket around and follow me. I'd advise you to be a good boy about it."

"I'm a regular Boy Scout."

"Too bad. If you was a smart mouth, I'd have to straighten your teeth."

Twin One went back to the cruiser. Twin Two opened

the passenger door and wedged himself into the seat. "Don't break any traffic laws."

"I drive like a Sunday school teacher sometimes."

I followed the cruiser into downtown Laurel City. We rolled past the police clubhouse and down to the beach. We turned into the parking lot of the swanky Laurel City Hotel and drove around to the back door. Two broad men in matching dark blue, double breasted suits leaned on banisters, smoking, and watching us. One of the two wore a plain red tie, the other a plain gray tie. They straightened when we drove up and hovered near the driver's door of my Chevy. They were each a half-head taller than me. There was enough material in the two suits they were wearing to cover the Statue of Liberty. I set the roadster's brake and killed the engine. Red Tie opened the door for me.

Twin Two got out and walked to the cruiser without looking back or speaking. He climbed in beside Twin One and the cruiser rolled out. Red Tie motioned me to put my arms out. I followed instructions and Gray Tie patted me down. I was clean.

Red Tie led the way to the door and opened it. I went in with Gray Tie close behind me. We walked down a long, carpeted corridor to the elevator at the end. A nameplate beside the up button told me it was a private car. Gray Tie pushed the button and the grated door opened. Another broad man, this one in a plain black suit and a black tie sprinkled with tiny white polka dots, stood inside. Nobody spoke. I stepped in and Black Tie pushed the button. Only the faint whir of the elevator invaded the silence. The car stopped and the door opened. I stepped out into a big room filled with a bunch of plush leather sofas and chairs. The half-dozen men in the room all wore suits and ties. Only a couple of them bothered to look at me. A short, round man in a tan, double-breasted suit and bright green bowtie hauled himself out of a soft chair behind an oak desk. He looked like the actor Eugene Pallette.

He tapped softly on a door and stuck his head in. "He's here, boss." His bullhorn voice sounded like Pallette's.

I looked at the broad man who had stepped up beside me. He was wearing a navy suit and a red and navy striped tie. "People around here talk your leg off," I complained.

Navy Suit didn't know how to smile. Tan Suit motioned to me and held the door open. I went in and the door closed with a slight click. The room wasn't as big as Harry York's office and not as opulently furnished, but it showed nice taste. The light gray carpet was thick, and two long, overstuffed leather sofas with matching chairs nestled against the walls. Walnut end tables separated each sofa/chair set. Walnut paneling covered the walls, with tasteful paintings hanging here and there. The wall opposite the door was almost completely glass and offered a breathtaking view of Laurel Bay.

In front of the glass, a walnut desk of normal size partly hid the walnut bimbo in abnormal size. He had loosened his dark blue tie at his short, thick neck. Close-cropped salt-and-pepper hair receded across his broad head. Bushy dark eyebrows ran without a break across his face. His nose was slightly bent and his full lips held up a tightly cut mustache. The sleeves of his white dress shirt, rolled to the elbows, exposed massive forearms.

Mack Sanger was always getting his picture in the papers, back-slapping various mayors, senators, and governors. In his younger days, he had been a dock brawler, graduating to enforcer for the seaman's union. Now he was the boss in Laurel City, the man who told his hand-picked mayor and his hand-picked police chief when to chew their cheese and for how long. He had his hand in everything that happened in Laurel City, and outside graft didn't fly unless Mack Sanger got his cut. He was nobody to fool with.

Sanger didn't stand. His dark eyes narrowed at one of the chairs by his desk and he gave a slight nod of his head. I sat down.

"Nice of you to join me, Mr. Brand."

His voice was deep and gravelly, neither friendly nor unfriendly.

"I happened to be in the neighborhood."

"Yes. You've been in the neighborhood several times recently. I thought we might have a friendly chat and talk that point over."

"I seem to have gotten an engraved invitation. Hard to turn down."

Sanger leaned back in his chair and took a deep breath. He dug out a long cigar from an oak humidor and held it up with questioning eyes. I shook my head. He nodded, snipped off the end of the Cuban, and lit it, rolling the end carefully in the flame. He got it going and eyed me like a research scientist studying bacteria through a microscope.

"Mr. Brand," he said easily, "you are a hot sketch. Be a shame to erase you. I'd like to keep this a friendly little gum-beating, as long as you are cooperative. I pray you don't allow it to go the other way. Perhaps you would enjoy a drink. It might help you relax."

"A little brown always makes me friendly."

Sanger smiled a little. He stretched his six-two frame, which was beginning to show a slight paunch, and took a bottle of Glenlivet whiskey and two glasses from the bar to the right of his desk. He poured three fingers in each glass and set the bottle in the middle of his desk.

"Help yourself whenever."

"Cheers."

We sipped and I waited. Sanger took a deep pull on his cigar and blew little smoke rings into the air. They disappeared into the air the same way people Sanger did not like disappeared.

"So you know what I want. You have the floor."

"I'm with York Brothers Studio. I was down here looking over a location for a waterfront picture the studio is planning. Laurel City seems to be a good spot for some authentic footage."

Sanger seemed a little tired. "Mr. Brand, motion picture people do not come to Laurel City to look at anything without first consulting me. Not even Harry York's people."

"This is highly preliminary. Actually, I'm trying to get into the production end and I'm pretty much doing the initial scouting on my own."

"Uh-huh. Stop chewing gum and let me tell you what I know. You run security for York. Taking care of balled-up actors and making sure nobody runs off with the stage lights. You were down here Thursday with Jimmy Gallen, who knows better. You were aboard *Sea Venture*. You came back later and got something to eat at the Laurel Inn. You had a beer and a ham sandwich. You asked about Mousey and then went to see him at Sharkey's, which, by the way, I own, along with the Laurel Inn. And a few other places. You asked Mousey a bunch of questions, primarily about *Sea Venture*. Tell me what your interest is."

Sanger's hard eyes grew harder. I set the glass on the edge of his desk. The six baby grands in the front room danced in my head.

"Gallen and I came down here Thursday because we were trying to find a missing actor who was supposed to be at work that day to wrap a picture. A big timer named

Johnny Cutter. You might have seen some of his mush. Gallen said Cutter owned *Sea Venture*. We thought he might be aboard, probably shacked up. He wasn't. I got word from an extra that Cutter might be on his boat Thursday night, so I came back. A bad line. I knew Mousey from my time as a cop and I went to the Laurel Inn to see him. Mousey knows a lot of what goes on around the bay."

"If you're worried about Mousey, don't be. Mousey's jake. He plays fair and doesn't talk when I tell him not to. He won't come to any harm. But he won't talk to you again."

"I like Mousey."

"Me, too. In fact, I gave him a couple yards because I like him. He wired you on who owns *Sea Venture*, but that's okay. It's an easy thing to find out. Mousey's a fountain of information on some things, but he knows when to clam."

Sanger drained his glass and poured three more fingers. I took another sip.

"So what's your interest in that yacht? You were down there again Saturday night and again tonight. You know Cutter doesn't own that boat. You paid a man named Rigger to keep an eye on it for you and to call you if he saw something."

"Somebody else was paying Rigger to do the same."

A renewed interest lit Sanger's eyes. That was something he didn't know. "Who?"

"His name's Carmine Broglio. Rigger thought he was Cutter's man, but he isn't. Rigger gave me the phone number Carmine left him. I called and got no answer. I'd like to talk to him."

"Why?"

"I think there's a chance some people Curtiss knows are using his yacht without his knowledge."

"Using it how?"

"I think for illegal purposes, though I don't know what."

"Embalmers? You think someone's using a luxury yacht to run illegal booze?"

"It occurred to me someone could take a yacht to the high seas, transfer bootleg aboard and scatter the hooch on any number of smaller boats closer to shore. They could take the booze anywhere. The same could be said for illegal drugs."

I pointed to the bottle of Glenlivet. "Good way to get top shelf booze into the country."

Sanger laughed. "Good thought, but if I were doing that I wouldn't use a boat anchored outside my front door. I'd use a boat that would never touch these shores and had no official connection with me. If I were doing that."

"Never occurred to me you were."

"And you think Randall doesn't know what's going on with his yacht?"

"I think Randall Curtiss is one of the richest men in the universe, and I don't think he's trying to make a few extra bucks in illegal activities. If he's engaged—and I say if—in illegal activities, then he's making a few extra million out of it, and he's far above anything I can do about it, so I don't care. He's not the type to bother with small graft. But if someone is using his boat for something that would get the attention of the bulls, I'd think he'd want to know. I wanted to find some proof before I approached him."

Sanger's eyes turned to slate. "Blackmail?"

"Trying to shake down Randall Curtiss would be a one-way ticket to oblivion. It couldn't be done. The man owns entire governments."

"And you don't think a man like Randall would not know about his yacht?"

"I think, in this case, it's a possibility he doesn't. I think maybe he lends his boat to people he knows, but doesn't know what they're doing with it. He's a very busy man."

"Okay. Here's what'll happen. Rigger will call me and not you. Leave me your number. I'll call if I want. If I don't, I expect you can find somewhere else for your background footage. You don't nose around about me. You don't nose around about Randall Curtiss. Savvy?"

"It's a sharp picture."

"Make sure it doesn't get out of focus. Now give me the phone number for the man who hired Rigger."

I had written the number Rigger had given me on a piece of paper. I handed it to Sanger.

"This looks like a Burbank exchange." He studied it a moment. "Tell you what. I'll find the address goes with this. I'm certain it isn't Laurel City so I'll let you handle it when I do. Discreetly, of course. I'm sure you'll have no problem reporting back to me."

"I'm sure."

"Now, you say hi to Harry for me. He and I do some business from time to time, and I would hate for that business relationship to suffer because some half-brain tried to get smart. I'd like to think anyone who works for Harry would not do anything to damage that relationship. To find out someone did that would make me very un-happy. Do I need to make that any clearer?"

"I'd like to think I'm one of Harry's more loyal em-ployees."

"Darb."

Sanger stood up to walk me to the door. "If Harry wants to do any stock filming in Laurel City, we will bend over backward to help. All he has to do is ask. Tell him that, will you?"

I nodded. "By the way, I think you ought to do something about those ham sandwiches at the Laurel. They're tougher than trying to sit through one of Harry's pictures."

Sanger's eyes turned soft as walnut shells. "I'll speak to the chef."

CHAPTER 18

Mabel Burns headed the research department at York Brothers and was always eager to answer a question. In her mid-fifties, tall, thin and angular, red hair fading to gray, she was a chunk of lead with a pinched face that suggested she was always lost in thought. I hunted her up first thing Monday morning.

"Know a town in Missouri called Girando, or something like it. Maybe starts with Cape something."

She sat at her desk going through a thick, oversized book of intense interest only to her. She put her cigarette in an ashtray, used a long finger to mark her spot in the book, and looked at me over the tops of her wire-rims. A blotch of red lipstick accentuated her plump lips. She made the little hissing sound she always made when thinking. Her dark gray dress had no shape to it, but was perfect for her shapeless body.

"Cape Girardeau is what you are looking for, most likely."

Something like a smile smeared her lips and then her long nose was back in her thick book. I thanked her, but if I had done a tap dance on her lap, she wouldn't have noticed. I had two phone calls to make, the first to Randall Curtiss in Santa Monica. I dropped Harry York's name to see if I could get a few minutes. I bounced like a ping pong ball from secretary to secretary, and I kept repeating Harry's name until at last I got the oilman's private secretary, who called himself Mr. Milner. I told him what I wanted.

"Just a minute, Mr. Brand, I'll see if he has time for you."

Milner was back on the line in two minutes. "Mr. Curtiss has a tee time at noon at Riviera Country Club. He can give you five minutes at exactly 10 a.m., but you must be prompt."

I thanked him and rang off. If Randall Curtiss was willing to fit in a nobody on a moment's notice, it was because he had talked to Mack Sanger or Harry.

The next call was to Cape Girardeau. It was tedious business as phone operators between California and Missouri worked to connect me but, at last, I was talking to someone at the Cape Girardeau newspaper, the *Southeast Missourian*. The lady at the switchboard got me through to a man named Hake. She said he was the managing editor.

"My name is Neil Brand," I told him. "I am with York Brothers Studio in Los Angeles. I am trying to obtain a little information."

"Well, sir. Well, sir. Hollywood. How may I help you?"

"I am doing background information for a picture in pre-production, some of which, by the way, and please keep this under your hat, we are thinking of filming in your fair city."

"Well, well. That would certainly be of interest. The citizens of Cape Girardeau would be most thrilled—"

"Please, please. We are not ready for any publicity yet, you understand. We are only in the planning stages, and anything else would be highly premature. Anyway, in our research we came across a name I would like to get some background on, and naturally thought your newspaper would be the proper place to start."

"Yes, sir, I will be glad to help all I can. What is the name you are interested in? Maybe I will know it."

"Dorothea Gardner. I understand she lived there until the Great War."

"Dotty Gardner? Hot socks. Sure, we know her. Quite notorious, you know. She killed her parents in 1918 and completely disappeared. You have knowledge of her whereabouts?"

I almost dropped the receiver. "Wait a minute. Slow down. Dorothea Gardner. Right?"

"Absolutely. Biggest story of the century in these parts. She killed her parents one night in, I believe June of 1918, and took off in their Ford automobile. Police found the automobile in the river, but no trace of Dotty. She was eighteen at the time. They dragged the river and put out a bulletin, but she was never found. Have you knowledge of her?"

"Just the name. That's why I'm calling. We here in the research department thought the name sounded familiar."

"Way out in California, eh?"

"Way out here. What can you tell me about her brother?"

"Brother? She had no brother. She was an only child."

"You sure about that?"

"Absolutely. Her parents grew up in Cape Girardeau and so did she. The family was very well known."

"You sure she committed such a dastardly deed? Killing her parents."

"No doubt. All the proof in the world. Beat them to death with a fireplace poker. Bloody fingerprints. Bloody dress that she often wore. The amazing thing is that she got away. Every policeman in the state was after her. Is your picture going to be about her?"

"Thanks." I hung up.

I stared out the lone window of my little cubbyhole. After a while, I rang Jimmy Gallen. His secretary said he had not come in this morning. She mentioned something about him being on the beach way out in Malibu shooting publicity stills for a whaling picture. I chewed my lower lip awhile and the horn erupted. It was Alice Windler. She said the Caddy V-12 belonged to Lena Landers. "You know, the actress."

She let that last word hang in the air like a puff of smoke from a cigarette, waiting for me to explain. I did not.

"Sweetheart, I owe you a dinner."

"I'm free tonight."

"Tonight won't work out, but soon."

"I've heard that before."

"It's a promise, but I don't know when."

"Bye."

I hung up the dead line and examined the Studio One wall. I chewed my lower lip until it was time to scoot to Riviera. No way I wanted to be late for Randall Curtiss.

CHAPTER 19

Rotund Oliver Hardy, decked out in smashing blue and yellow plus fours, jauntily tagged along behind a tall, skinny caddy when I drove into Riviera Country Club at a quarter 'til ten.

"What are you boys doing next?" I yelled at the portly half of the famous comedy duo.

He grinned at me. I was hoping for a tie twiddle, but I didn't get it. "Wouldn't know. You'll have to ask Stanley."

He gave me a little wave of his meaty hand and was off to his tee time.

A valet took one scornful look at my Chevy and told me to park in the far corner of the lot. I told him I was from York Brothers Studio and was here to see Randall Curtiss. He gave in a little bit, allowing me to park closer to the clubhouse as long as I was not going to be there long. My heap looked pitiful amongst all the gleaming brass and chrome of the members' ritzy rides, but I was pretty sure the thing wouldn't collapse from the embarrassment.

The doorman ushered me in through a side door and escorted me to a room in the back corner that offered a nice view of the course sprawling through the Santa

Monica Canyon. The Santa Monica Mountains loomed in the distance, bathed in sunshine.

At exactly ten, a slim man about my height, dressed for golf, and wearing no expression at all, opened a door to a small room where Randall sat alone at the only table. He motioned for me to sit opposite. Photos of various golfers filled the walls. I didn't know most of them, but I did recognize Bobby Jones and Walter Hagen.

"You appreciate I am a very busy man trying to enjoy a rare day off from business," Curtiss said, his voice like honey on sugar. "You are here as a courtesy to Harry York. I can give you five minutes."

Tall and lean, Randall Curtiss had strong hands the size of ham hocks, with long and powerful fingers. About sixty, his deeply tanned and lined face spoke of years spent outdoors in all kinds of weather.

His gray eyes bore the look of a man who was not impatient, but who meant to get straight to business. His thick, white hair had been that color a long time, and gray now touched it slightly. His black slacks and white shirt open at the neck would have probably cost me a month's pay. He took a cigarette from a gold case but didn't ask if I wanted one. He lit up, blew a stream of smoke, and regarded me with eyes that held no interest.

"There's a man called Rigger watching your yacht in the bay at Laurel City. A man named Carmine Broglio, who has gangster connections in New York, was paying him. I'm paying Rigger now to keep an eye peeled for Broglio."

Still no interest in the oilman's eyes. "Why?"

"I think the man who wanted your yacht watched is interested in blackmail. I'm interested in catching him."

"Nobody is going to blackmail me."

"Yes, I understand that. I think the man wants to shake down some friends of yours."

"Who?"

"One, Johnny Cutter. Two, Lena Landers. I believe you know them."

"This man has gangster connections in New York?"

"He used to work for Masseria. New York police say he was one of Joe's trigger men. He dangled when Joe was killed, and I think he's looking for another opportunity."

"And you don't know where he is?"

"He's a hard nut to pin down, but eventually he'll pop up."

"How do you know he worked for Masseria?"

"I used to be a cop before I went to work for Harry York. This morning I ran Broglio's name by a homicide lieutenant downtown who used to be my partner. The name rang a bell with him. Seems after the Masseria killing the New York bulls were hot to find Broglio. Sent his mug and paper around the country."

"I would certainly appreciate your finding him and telling me where he is. There might be something in it for you."

"There are some things on this blackmail angle I would like to clear up. Harry York is greatly concerned because it involves one of his stars."

"This involves my yacht?"

"Apparently so, but I'm a little in the dark on how. I'm hoping to find Broglio and ask him. I'm certain you would have no idea."

"I seldom use that yacht, but I keep it for entertainment reasons. I have a lot of clients around the world and the yacht comes in handy at times. I often allow friends to use the yacht for their own entertaining."

"Maybe something happened aboard they want hushed. You know how word gets out. Maybe Broglio found out something. He's on the lam and he'd be looking for another way to make a buck."

"Mr. Brand, your time is up. You find this Broglio and tell me where he is, and I will deal with that. And I will pay you handsomely for that information. In the meantime, you forget about my yacht and who's using it. That is entirely my business. And my business is none of your affair. Good day."

He didn't offer to shake hands. The slim man opened the door and held it for me.

"Mr. Milner will see you out." Curtiss disappeared through the door behind him.

I went out the door I had come in. Milner trotted faithfully beside me. The guy in the parking lot looked relieved as my blue Chevy rolled out of his sight and off the Riviera property.

CHAPTER 20

I went straight to Jimmy Gallen's office when I got back to the studio. He was standing at a table in the corner, going over some one-sheets for a Richard Mercer picture set for preview tonight in a theater in Long Beach. I sat down in a leather chair and stared at Gallen. He held up two posters, one in stark black and white and the other in color.

"Which you like?"

I just stared at him. After a moment, he put the posters on the table and crossed to his desk. He lit an Old Gold and eyed me through the curling smoke. "Neil, it's a busy day. And you have something on your mind."

"First, tell me something. Does a publicity man like you ever tell the truth? Or is everything lies and half-truths?"

He grinned. "The truth is usually not very interesting. The fans like their stories to be exciting. Just like their pictures."

"Right now, I'd be excited to hear any bit of the goods from you. So why don't we start with Joan Banes?"

He exhaled a long stream of smoke and gave me an impatient look. He glanced out his patio doors. A bunch of actors, in period costumes ranging from medieval times to cowboys, wandered here and there. A couple of bit players pranced around in something that looked like spacesuits. Workers moved a Colonial set on a cart pulled by a Fordson Model F. Other actors and assorted studio personnel scooted around the lot beneath a slate sky beginning to cloud over.

"Joan Banes has nothing to do with this studio," Gallen said at last. He forced a smile.

"Johnny Cutter does. You told me Joan Banes was his sister."

A wary frown replaced Gallen's impatient smile. "I think you've been a busy fella."

"Johnny Cutter was born in New York. You said. Lower east side. You said. Joan Banes was his sister. You said. Imagine the funny look on my mug when I found out her real name is Dorothea Gardner and she comes from Missouri and has no brother."

He took a long drag on the Old Gold. "Once a cop?" He quashed the gasper. "I told Harry I could dig up Cutter without help, but he insisted on calling you in 'cause he didn't know what Johnny was into. You were just supposed to help me find Cutter, not go digging around in everybody's past."

"Remember Carmine?"

"Okay, okay. So things just sorta took off on us. And you decided to be a cop again. But, honest to God, Neil, you don't have to go around digging up dirt. This is Hollywood. Dirt's not even skin deep. And it's everywhere."

"If Johnny Cutter's into something deep and nasty, I think you'd want to know."

"I know what I told you."

"Why didn't you tell me the truth then? Especially about Joan Banes."

"I had my reasons. All you need to know is that I'm trying to protect this studio."

"How long have you known Dorothea Gardner killed her mother and father?"

His eyeballs nearly bounced off his desk. His head slowly moved side to side. "So you even dug that up?"

"Wasn't hard. Once I got the scent."

He pulled a bottle of skee and two glasses from the drawer under the table behind his desk. I shook my head.

"Little early, isn't it?"

"No, it's late as hell."

He poured a slug and drank it in one swallow. He added two fingers to the glass and looked at me. "Sure?"

I nodded.

"Okay. What I know is a little sketchy, but here it is straight. Dotty Gardner came to Hollywood just after the war ended. A beautiful, nineteen year old baby with a face like an angel. A natural brunette with the brightest onyx eyes you ever saw. She dyed her hair platinum and got noticed. Somebody at UA spotted her and used her as an extra on a Fairbanks picture. She got a few bits at Fox and then somebody else noticed her and changed her name to Joan Banes. Well, you know why she didn't want to use her real name. She got loaned out to Lasky and got third billing in a Wally Reid picture, right behind Reid and Thiele Garsone, the French actress. Johnny Cutter was in that picture, before he signed with Harry. But there was trouble with Joan right away. She was scared to death and we all thought she was heading for a nervous breakdown. She started drinking heavily and got some morphine from Reid. She met Alma Rubens and started running in that group with Jack Pickford and pretty soon was hooked on coke and horse.

"She gave a good performance in the Reid picture and in her next one at Fox. That was that. Booze and junk took her out in a hurry. One night she was in her cups and started crying. She told me her father owned several businesses back in Missouri, and she started stealing drugs from his pharmacy. He found out and accosted her. She was high at the time and when it was over, she had taken a poker to both her parents. She fled and somehow ended up in Hollywood, scared to death someone would recognize her on the screen.

"That wasn't going to happen. She had a high school picture of herself, said it was the last one taken of her. With her hair color change and picture makeup, there's no way anyone could tell it was the same woman. She'd changed a lot. But she kept changing. Suddenly looked a lot older than her years and by the time she was in her mid-twenties she looked fifty. Her career was gone. Hell, Neil, she could barely remember anything at all. I honest to God don't know how she lived to be thirty."

"Why pass her off as Cutter's brother?"

"Trying to protect her. And him. Cutter was married but he and Joan started fooling around seven, eight years ago. They tried to keep it hushed up, but people saw 'em at the Hopkins in San Francisco. So I put it out that they were brother and sister. Worked up a phony bio that they were born in Upper New York to a well-to-do family. Joan went along with it because that story got her some space from Missouri, but Johnny was upset. He wanted to marry her. I think she was afraid to marry anybody. He got a divorce, but by the time that came through Joan was far enough gone that marriage was out of the question. Johnny got on with his career and Joan disappeared into her drug haze." Gallen finished his drink, heaved a long sigh. "Wish to God I hadn't put that sister thing in Cutter's bio. If I hadn't, you wouldn't be asking questions about her."

"Why tell me where she lived then?"

He waved a manicured hand. "'Cause you were just gonna keep digging. I figured that if you saw her, saw how gone she was, you'd drop the sister angle."

"Who paid for her drugs?"

"Johnny. He wanted to cut her loose but he was scared to death she'd tell someone about herself if he did. If that came out, and if they learned Johnny was covering it up, goodbye career. I don't know if even Harry could keep Cutter out of jail. So Johnny paid for that apartment and bought the junk for her."

"He could have done her better."

"That apartment was good enough for her. She could have been living at San Simeon for all she knew."

"Not what I meant."

"So nobody's blameless."

"Who else knew about her past?"

"Just me and Johnny."

"Thiele Garsone?"

"Theile left Hollywood after only a couple of pictures. Married a count or duke or something and went back to France."

"Did Carmine know? If he did, he would skin Johnny like a dead possum."

"I never heard of Carmine 'til you showed me his body. If Cutter had told me, I could've dealt with Carmine. I got friends on the force who would've loved a collar like Carmine, and I could've fixed it so whatever that mug said about Cutter wouldn't see the light of day. Anyway, back to your question. I don't know how Carmine could find out. Johnny surely wouldn't tell him about Joan Banes. And Thiele's been in Europe for seven, eight years and far out of the reach of a bum like Carmine even if he knew about her."

"Did you kill Carmine?"

His eyes widened in horror. "No. Course not. That's applesauce. I told you. I never laid eyes on him 'til he was stiff."

"Somebody shot Carmine for a reason."

"That reason might not have anything to do with Joan Banes. Carmine was no saint."

"You kill Joan?"

Terrified eyes took over Gallen's suddenly pallid face. His lower jaw trembled. "My God, Neil. No. No, of course not. What do you think I am?"

"I left the door to her flat unlocked. It was locked when I got back."

"I didn't kill her."

"Then who locked the door?"

He poured another drink. His hand shook. "All right. I locked it. I saw she was dead. I knew you'd be coming back. And the ambulance guys. I guess I panicked. I didn't want anybody to know I was in the room so I locked the door and was beating on it when you got there. But, my God, Neil, I didn't kill her. I swear."

"Okay," I said flatly. "Maybe you didn't. Maybe it doesn't matter, anyway. By the way, know anyone who owns a blue Chrysler 70?"

His jaws clenched, but otherwise he was still. "I don't know. Don't think so. Why?"

"Joan Banes has paid for killing her parents. Nobody cares that it was covered up. But somebody killed Carmine, and if we don't find out who, Cutter might get bitten. That bite will reach the studio. If it does, you just think you've heard Harry scream. And there's also the question of what Cutter is doing with Randall Curtiss' yacht?"

"What do you mean? That yacht belongs to Cutter, doesn't it?"

"Randall Curtiss owns it. Know him?"

"I've heard of him." His voice sounded like a condemned man on the gallows, just before the trap door dropped.

"He was letting Cutter use his boat from time to time. My hunch is Carmine got his hooks into Johnny over that yacht, not Joan. I've got a couple leads to follow up concerning Carmine."

"Such as?"

I didn't want to tell Gallen anymore than I already had. I still didn't know everything Cutter was into. "Wire you when I find out more."

"I'd rather you took a long vacation. Listen, I don't like this thing about Randall Curtiss. You know how tight he is with Harry? Couple years ago the government got on Harry and his brother. Something about anti-trust, I think. I don't know any details, 'cept the lot was crawling with feds looking into everything. I heard they were all over the New York office, too. Then Harry had lunch with Curtiss, and the next day the feds were gone. And they haven't been back. If Randall Curtiss told Hoover to fart, Hoover'd smile and say cheese."

"How about Mack Sanger?"

Gallen's eyes blinked rapidly. "Ain't goin' there. But he's tight with Curtiss, too. Look, Neil, I could get Harry to sign off on a couple of weeks' vacation. How about an all-expense paid trip to New York for the opening of Cutter's newest hit? You and any hot dish on the lot. You could represent the studio."

"Me?"

"No one else is going. Harry won't go 'cause he'd have to see his brother. Johnny's contract doesn't call for it, so he won't go. Hilt and Markham have already started their next pictures. Nobody else in that picture will mean anything to New York."

"Sounds like a big opening."

"Just business as usual."

CHAPTER 21

One of Mack Sanger's flunkies called that afternoon. They had dug up the address that went with the phone number Carmine had given Rigger. Two Sanger employees in a dark red Chrysler four-door sedan, the voice said, would pick me up at the studio's main gate at two-thirty sharp. "Mr. Sanger is worried you might get lost on the way," the voice said. "This way, you just sit back and enjoy the ride."

"Like Cagney in *Public Enemy*?"

I heard a click and the line went dead. Maybe the voice hadn't seen that picture.

The sedan was on time. I climbed into the back seat and relaxed against the soft, wheat-colored leather. Trouble boys Gray Tie and Red Tie from the night before were in the front seat, Red Tie behind the wheel. They had changed from blue suits to black worsted with broad white stripes, and both wore plain black ties.

"We'll drive," the man behind the wheel said.

"The quieter you are, the more you'll enjoy the drive," the other man said.

"Either of you boys got a name?" I asked when we hit Burbank. "When you got the same color tie on, I can't tell you apart."

The man not driving turned slightly and said over his shoulder, "Mike."

"Tank," the driver said.

"Tank?"

"Wanna make something of it?"

I did not. I looked out the window and enjoyed the sunshine all the way to the Walton Auto Court off Glenoaks. The hand-painted sign in front offered clean, neat bungalows by the day, the week, or the month. A dozen small, freshly-painted white frame bungalows with red roofs and red shutters lined both sides of a paved drive ending in a circle, a short distance north. Each bungalow had a parking spot. A sign on the bungalow to the left of the entrance told us it was the office. Tank eased the big Chrysler up to the office door.

"We're going in with you," Mike said. "You ask the questions."

"Okay, boys. Follow me and don't stumble."

"Wise head," Tank said.

Mike nodded. "Wise head."

The balding man behind the counter inside the small office must have weighed three hundred pounds, all of it around his waist. He looked like a Disney cartoon character, the kind who'd bounce right back up if he fell down. He lifted his noodle with an effort and his fixed smile slid off his puss like water on a slide when he saw the three of us.

"We're looking for a man who might've rented a bungalow here." I gave him a description of Carmine Broglio. "He would have been laying low."

"That would be private information. I—"

"This is a homicide investigation, buster. Don't mess with us."

The man cleared his throat. "Do you have identification?"

Tank stepped up, opened his coat, and flashed his Laurel City police buzzer. The quick flash didn't give the man behind the counter enough time to see it wasn't a local shield. The fat man only needed a brief flash. He wasn't interested in trouble. One look at Mike and Tank and nobody would be interested in trouble.

"Yes, sir. I remember him. Checked in almost a week ago, but he hasn't been here since Tuesday, I think. May I ask—"

"What name is he registered under?"

The man consulted a ledger. "Mr. James Allen Smith."

"What bungalow?"

"Seven. I remember he requested one in the back."

I snapped my fingers. "Key."

He rummaged around and handed me a big key on a big ring with a little piece of thin white cardboard attached, rimmed in silver foil to keep it from tearing. A large red number seven stood out on the white cardboard. Along the edge of the cardboard above the unit number red letters spelled out Walton Auto Court, with the address and phone number. The phone number Carmine had given Rigger.

"This the only key?"

"We have two keys for each unit. The other key must be with Mr. Smith."

"Phones in each unit?"

"There are."

"How do they work?"

"What? How do—"

"They go through your switchboard?"

"Oh, I see. Yes, all calls."

"Smith make any?"

The fat man consulted another ledger. "Yes, sir. Two. Both to the same number."

"Write down that number."

The fat man picked up a black fountain pen and tore off a sheet from a notepad beside the switchboard. The number he wrote on the pad was Johnny Cutter's.

"I remember he got one call from that number. And one night, Wednesday maybe, somebody called twice looking for him, but he wasn't in. Fact is, Mr. Smith hasn't been here since Tuesday, but he paid up for the rest of this week."

"You got that number?"

"No, sir. There was no answer so I didn't write it down."

"Maid service?"

"Said he didn't need the maid 'til he said so."

"Pretend we aren't here. And never were."

The parking spot at bungalow seven, on the left at the end of the paved drive, was empty. I dug out the key I had taken from Carmine. I pretended to use the key with the cardboard attached, and Mike and Tank didn't notice me use the other key. It slid easily into the lock. The front door opened onto a small room that held a bed, a padded chair and desk, and an electric heating unit. The phone took up most of a small table beside the bed, no notepad beside it. The painted walls had once been white, the thin carpet red. The white curtains over the lone window bore red trim, as did the white bedspread. A piece of white cardboard with a red number seven on it lay on the bedspread where Carmine had thrown it after tearing off the key. I tossed the key I had just gotten from the manager onto the bed, and slipped the key I had taken from Carmine back into my pocket. The bungalow had a small kitchen and a smaller bath, both lit by bare overhead light bulbs. I started with the bath, but there wasn't much to see—a shaving kit, a hairbrush, a toothbrush, and a nearly empty tube of toothpaste. A piece of dried toothpaste perched on the edge of the sink.

Two extra-large double breasted suits—one dark gray, one black—hung from a rod beside the bed. Two white shirts and two plain ties—one blue, one black—nestled beside the suits. A dove-colored size 9 fedora decorated a hook beside the door. I dug out four signed photos from a suitcase on the desk—Johnny Cutter in a tuxedo, Lena Landers in her trademark silver lamé, and two young women who looked like sisters. Someone had scrawled names on the back. One photo identified Joan Banes, short white hair and thin, painted eyebrows. The other name was Thiele Garsone, short black hair and thin, painted eyebrows. I held the photos side-by-side. It was hard to tell who was who.

Mike and Tank leaned by the door, watching me without much interest.

"You boys mind if I call you Gar and Goyle?" I asked, handing Tank the photos.

"Wise head," Mike said.

"Boss said to take you here and watch you, then do our work," Tank said. "He didn't say to mess you up. He didn't say not to, neither."

He stared hard at me until Mike stuck the publicity photos in his hand. He looked, pausing longer on Lena than on the other two, and gave them back to me.

"Not much here," I said.

Mike and Tank didn't say anything. They were just waiting on me, watching my every move with blank eyes.

"Looks like a dead end," I added and crossed to the door.

"Just a minute, pal," Tank said.

He and Mike took thin leather gloves from their coat pockets and pulled them on. They went through the room in unison, like synchronized gears, cleaning it out. They stuffed everything that belonged to Carmine in the suitcase, including the discarded key ring and the other key.

They tossed the bed and left the mattress leaning against the box springs. They pulled out the dresser drawers and went through them like a pair of starving hounds who smelled breadcrumbs. I watched with a grudging fascination. When they were satisfied, they took towels from the bathroom and wiped down everything in every room.

"You boys would make dandy maids."

They ignored me. Tank carried the bulging suitcase to the sedan and threw it on the back seat beside me. Tank stopped outside the office. Mike went in to make a phone call and was back in less than a minute. After a while, a new Chrysler coupe pulled up. A man I recognized from Sanger's office waved his mitt and drove away. The coupe stopped across the street in front of the auto court, and Tank drove past.

"Got eyes on the bungalow?"

Mike let his lips crack slightly.

"Not bad. We got a plant in case Mr. Smith comes back. He sees that room cleaned out he might panic. Leastways, he'll do something that might clue us in."

I didn't say anything. Sanger's plant would grow roots waiting for Carmine.

"Mr. Sanger said to watch you and we've done that." Mike twisted in the seat to look at me. "He didn't say nothin' 'bout anything else. We'll tell the boss you took four photos and we seen 'em. If he wants them, you fork 'em over."

"Any questions?" Tank asked.

"Yeah. You fellas ever go surfing?"

"Wise head," Tank said.

Mike nodded. "Wise head."

CHAPTER 22

I wanted to see Jimmy Gallen but he had dusted. No one at the studio knew where he had gone, only that he disappeared faster than a politician in a room full of preachers. I got a meatloaf sandwich at the nearly deserted commissary and was about to leave when a director named Gordon Lewis joined me.

"Grabbing a bite while they do a camera set-up," he said.

I knew Lewis was directing a potboiler over on Stage Five, featuring the bouncy Beryl Lillie as a woman framed for murder. Beryl had just finished third lead in *Doorway to Heaven*.

"How's it going?"

"On time and on budget." Lewis smiled. "Which is a good thing at all times, and even more so today."

"Why today?"

He looked at me over a forkful of spinach and chicken. "You haven't heard?"

I shook my head. "I'm about the last to hear anything around here."

Lewis put down his fork and looked around. We were pretty much alone. He leaned forward and spoke in a stage whisper. "Jerry Hilt got canned this morning."

"Hilt? He's Harry's top producer."

Lewis nodded. "Jerry's a lucky man. Now he can go to that job at Paramount."

The rumors had been circulating for several weeks that Hilt had lined up a production job at Paramount and was going there the second his contract with Harry ran out. The office pool pretty much split evenly between Hilt lasting his contract and Harry firing him first.

"What happened?"

Lewis grinned. "Well, Hilt was at a story conference this morning with Harry and some others. They got around to a picture preview set for tonight. Harry got on a kick about what made good pictures and went on and on about it. Finally, he told the others that he could feel a good picture in the seat of his pants."

"His pants?"

"Yeah. He said if he sits still during a picture, it's a good one. If he starts wiggling in his seat, it's a bad picture. He says that's how he knows beforehand if an audience will like a picture or not.

"So, Hilt says, 'Think of it, fellas. The whole world wired to Harry York's ass.' Well, Harry exploded and fired Hilt on the spot. Jerry packed some things and was laughing when he went out the front gate."

I rubbed my chin. "Gordon, the only dull stuff around this place are Harry's pictures."

"Ain't it the truth. Ain't it the truth." He grinned at me. "Except my pictures, of course."

Lewis was still talking to himself when I left the commissary. I called Gallen from my office. He was still missing in action. I left a message for him to call me, not expecting he would.

I busied myself with some neglected work and left a little after five. I hadn't been home ten minutes when the phone rang. It was one of Randall Curtiss' flunkies.

"Mr. Brand, Mr. Curtiss wonders if it would be a great inconvenience for you to be his guest on his yacht, *Sea Venture*, this evening about dusk. He is most desirous that you be able to attend a meeting."

"Tell Mr. Curtiss I would be most delighted," I said in my most formal manner.

"I shall inform Mr. Curtiss. Please come as you are." The voice got a little edge to it. "And bring the photos."

I showered and put on my tan gabardine. I took along my Colt and stuffed it under the Chevy's front seat. I stopped at Barney's out on Route 66 for a quick bite, then drove on out to Laurel City.

The area between the docks and the Laurel Inn looked like a new car lot. The cars were expensive jobs, except for my Chevy and a Laurel City police cruiser. I pulled the Chevy up at the end of the dock in a spot beside the black and white. The twins sat on the running board and watched me without interest. The calm bay doused the sinking sun and a stiff wind kicked up. Off to the left a couple hundred yards, between some wharf buildings, I saw the front end of a Caddy V-12 that had been backed almost out of sight.

The twins frisked me then nodded toward the end of the dock. The deck of *Sea Venture* looked like an ant farm. Several men in white were running around on it, and one wore a sea captain's uniform. Halfway down the dock, Randall Curtiss and Mack Sanger huddled together, backed by a bunch of Sanger's boys I had seen up at his place Sunday night. I guessed the others in the group belonged to Curtiss.

Mike and Tank watched me walk up. The others were talking quietly among themselves. Tank held up a hand the size of a pillow. I waited until Sanger motioned for me.

"Brand, you got those photos?"

I gave him the signed pictures of Lena Landers, Joan Banes, and Thiele Garsone, along with the unsigned photo of Winnie Kramer. Sanger and Curtiss looked them over, but recognized only Lena. A blind man would notice her. The photos made the rounds to the rest of the group, then back to me.

"Who are those two?" Sanger asked. "Banes and Garsone?"

"Joan Banes died a couple days ago. I'm told Thiele Garsone went home to France five, six years ago."

"I saw something in the paper 'bout that Banes dame dying, boss," Mike said. "Just a coupla graphs. Cops said it was a Dutch act."

"That pretty much means no one cared," I said. "Suicide, case closed."

Sanger nodded. Curtiss hovered in the background like a hawk eyeing a mouse, saying nothing.

"The other one?"

"Just an extra. Her sister gave me that photo. She's been missing about a week, and her sister's looking for her."

Sanger handed me a woman's wrist watch and cameo. "Know anything about these?"

I nodded and pointed to the picture of Winnie Kramer. The watch and cameo in the photo were identical to the watch and cameo Sanger had just given me. He studied the photo and took the jewelry from me. He handed both pieces of jewelry to Tank.

"I don't want those to turn up anywhere," Sanger said.

Tank nodded.

"You know anything about her?" Curtiss tapped Winnie's face with a powerful finger. A crease marred her chin where the glossy had been folded. "We found that watch and cameo's she's wearing in this picture in a guest cabin on my boat, tied to the bed springs."

"She did some extra work on one of Harry's pictures a few days ago. She's on the books for having worked three days on that picture. Before that, she had one day on a Gemma Layne picture. That's all anybody at York knows about her. I sent the name around to the other studios, but nothing came up."

Sanger and Curtiss exchanged glances. Curtiss put an arm around my shoulder and we walked down the dock twenty yards, Sanger close behind.

"Harry speaks highly of you, Mr. Brand. Answer this honestly. I don't care what the answer is, but I want it straight. When you were on the police force, did you take a bribe?"

"I got framed for taking a bribe because I wouldn't take one. Got kicked off when I couldn't prove who did it."

"And you know?"

"Elmo Jones. Like I said, no proof."

Sanger snorted. "Elmo's the dirtiest bull in the state. I thought he was smart enough to not step foot in my city. I don't like to step off the reservation, but I might have to look up Sergeant Jones."

"What's your best guess what's going on with my yacht?" Curtiss slid his arm off my shoulder.

"Best guess is somebody's using your boat to take young women out to sea. They lure them on board with promises of a big party and pump 'em full of booze or drugs or both. Take these girls out to the high seas, put them on another boat—a freighter maybe—and they're never seen again. They're taking extras and bit players with no studio contracts. Hundreds of those Janes come to Hollywood every year and ninety-nine of every hundred get their hopes crushed and go back home.

"Nobody here misses them and if they don't go back home, probably nobody there comes looking for them.

Unless you've got a baby sister like Winnie Kramer has."

Sanger and Curtiss looked at me with sour faces.

"And," I added, "I expect whoever's running that ring is bringing *Sea Venture* back loaded with cocaine or heroin."

"That's why you wanted my boat watched?"

"That's it. Frankly, I'm surprised you weren't watching it."

Sanger's sour face turned mean. Curtiss didn't change expressions.

"I don't check up on Mr. Curtiss," Sanger grunted. "His boat's his business. It comes and goes without me."

"And I didn't know it was coming and going," Curtiss said. "I made a mistake in trusting a friend."

"Why was that other man, Broglio, watching it?" Sanger wanted to know.

"I find him, I'll ask."

"No," Sanger said. "You find him, I'll ask. I get answers. What about Cutter? He must be in on it. He's got the use of *Sea Venture*."

"I can't figure Cutter's angle, unless he's being blackmailed. Right now, he's laying low out of town. He might not be back until October. His next picture is set to start October fourth. I'm skating on thin ice here. After all, Cutter is one of Harry York's top properties, and I work for Harry York."

"You leave York to us. We'll reach a deal with Harry."

"Mr. Curtiss, what do you plan to do with *Sea Venture*?"

"She's going to sea tonight." Curtiss had no intention of telling me more.

"Brand," Sanger said, "you're out of this for now. Go back to your studio and mind the store. We'll take care of this little problem."

"How?"

"Like I said. Go back to your job. We'll do ours."

"I'd like to ask a favor."

"Possibly not a good idea," Sanger said.

Curtiss touched Sanger's arm. "What kind of favor?"

"Give me a few days. Sure, you put the arm on Johnny Cutter, he'll spill so fast he'll spit all over you. But I think this thing goes deeper than Cutter, and I think I can get to it and keep it quiet. All Harry wants is his boy safe and no noise."

"No dice. Whoever's behind this is gonna run when *Sea Venture* disappears," Sanger said. "We want him before he takes a powder. I'm gonna cut off his dong and stuff it in his mouth. Nobody comes on my turf like that."

"You know where Cutter is?"

"We'll find him. Don't matter where he's trying to hide. We're taking it from here and you're on your way. Don't ask for any favors and don't ask any questions."

Sanger walked away. Curtiss shook my hand. "Mr. Brand, I thank you for your efforts. Tell Harry we'll protect him. He's got nothing to worry about."

Curtiss went back to his people and I went back to the Chevy. I threw the photos on the front seat then sat on the hood and watched Curtiss and three of his people get in the tender and cross to *Sea Venture*. The big white boat was soon under way, steaming toward the little piece of sun sticking out of the water far to the west. Sanger and his men came down the dock, along with the rest of Curtiss' people. They got into their cars and drove away, leaving Mike, Tank, and me. Mike got into the Chrysler sedan. Tank paused at the driver's door.

"Boss says you can sit there 'til morning if you want. But come sunup you best dangle. Won't be nothin' good in Laurel City for you."

Tank got into the Chrysler and, in a few seconds, all I

could see of it was the taillights growing dimmer. It was dark now. The only light filtered through the dirty windows of the Laurel Inn, three hundred yards to the right and across the smaller boats tied to their slips. Far off to the left, a couple of lights near the wharf gave off just enough glow to see the Caddy V-12 still there, still mostly hidden.

I got the .45 from under the Chevy's seat and tucked it into my belt. Its two and a half pounds didn't feel good, but provided a certain comfort. I started toward the Caddy, keeping as far left along the wharf as I could, and in the darker shadows. I went slowly and quietly, stopping often to listen. It was too dark to see anything. It took me a half-hour to reach the V-12. I struck a match to look at the plates and quickly put out the flame. It was the same Caddy that had brought Lena Landers and the five fluffs to *Sea Venture* on Thursday night. I looked through the window, but the big car was empty. There was no registration on the steering column. I walked around it and found a place in the shadows to hide.

The long night turned chilly in the early morning, but it gave me lots of time to think. An hour or so before daylight, I gave it up and started back to the Chevy. I stayed near the water going back, still moving slowly and quietly. Crates had been stacked on this side, about two feet from the water. I walked between them and the bay's edge. From my pocket, I took out Carmine's bungalow key and threw it as far out into the water as I could. I felt a sudden movement behind me. I yanked on the Colt's grip and tried to turn, but something hit me just above and behind the right ear. The dark form of a hulking man flashed at my side and then I hit the water head first.

I never heard the splash and it was too black to see anything. I had a vague feeling I was an anchor plunging to the bottom…

e/ɔe/ɔ

Tuesday, October 12, 1926:

Frank Harless called, wanted to know how I was doing. I was living on what little I had saved while on the force, and on the few pickup jobs I could find. Frank threw some work my way when he could, mostly small security gigs. He said he had another one for me, would last maybe a week. Fine, I said, and then the conversation somehow got around to Elmo Jones.

"He'll slip up somewhere, Neil. Goons like that always do. He's on the list for lieutenant, but he's a few years away."

"Lieutenant Harless. Lieutenant Jones. There's both ends of the spectrum."

"I'm doing everything I can to prevent that."

I took the job, babysitting a warehouse at night while they installed a new alarm system. Two nights after I took the job, a bomb went off in a corner of the building, blowing out a hole about the size of a truck. They fired me unceremoniously and it was nearly three years before Harless offered me another gig.

The day after the bomb went off Jones called me at home.

"Tick...tick...tick. Wonder what's next? I'll be in touch. I'm not close to through with you, Bo. Tick...tick...tick."

CHAPTER 23

Tuesday, September 15, 1931:

A pink whale dressed like Betty Boop but with extra-large Mickey Mouse ears stared at me with a curious, lopsided grin. A neon sign on the whale's side flashed two words—Harry York—in large scarlet letters. A purple tongue curled around my face and massaged my head just behind the right ear. The lopsided grin disappeared and the whale morphed into a mermaid who looked exactly like Lena Landers. Daggers shot out of her eyes and turned into reels of film, slowly unfurling as bright blue water carried them toward a big white yacht. I looked again and Johnny Cutter's empty eyes raked me. Then water splashed in my face and I was looking into the rat-mean face of a crooked copper named Elmo Jones. I tried to spit at him. He turned into a giant octopus, poking at me with eight tentacles, with huge meat hooks at the end of each tentacle.

I coughed and spit out water. My thick tongue tasted like rubber, and my head felt like an overripe watermelon that had been dropped on cement. I wondered what that red stuff was. It oozed out of my noodle, grew wings and feet, and began dancing like a barefooted Fred Astaire on hot coals. I heard a voice from somewhere far away, and it wasn't Betty Boop. The meat hooks and the tentacles disappeared and turned into large, rough hands attached to a gink wearing a red and black plaid shirt and faded dungarees. His spinning head looked like a shining base-ball. The man was soaked from the waist down but he wasn't as wet as me. I was at the bottom of a bottomless sea, my feet tied to an anchor.

Cobwebs spun in my head, but they shredded and grew fainter. I closed my eyes and slowly reopened them. The bright baseball over my head turned into a full moon, and the bruno shaking me came into focus in the dim light. He had a log in his mouth. No, wait. It was a tooth-pick. Was he crying, or was that just water on his puss?

"You okay?"

I don't know where the voice came from. I don't know how I managed to answer. "Huh? Okay?"

"How you feel?" The voice was a little closer.

"Peachy."

The toothpick waggled through a light chuckle, but stayed put. Calliope music blared between my ears. The man chewing the toothpick seemed to enjoy this, like a bored man who just happened upon a car wreck.

"Peachy or peachy keen?"

"Peachy."

"You got whacked purty good. Take it easy."

The whale and the Mickey Mouse ears had disap-peared, but not the lopsided grin. Rigger sat back on the dock, leaned against a tall crate, and eyed me like he'd just landed a lousy mudsucker and was trying to decide whether to throw me back in or use me for bait.

He had three faces and they were all dancing around. I tried to focus on one of them. I didn't have much luck. I'd have to try later.

My tongue felt thick as gumbo paste. "What happened?"

"Somebody sapped you on the conk. I couldn't see much, just shadows. Big, beefy guy. That bull I told you about, I think. The baby grand with the hooked nose. But I seen you hit the water. The mug hit you took off, got in a fancy boiler, and tore out."

"The gink you saw the other night with the women?"

"Same."

I tried to sit and my head nearly exploded. I put my fingers behind my right ear and found a hard-boiled egg. It had a crack in it and red lights flashed when I gingerly touched it. I put my head back against the hard wood of the dock and watched the moon dance around. It was doing the Charleston.

"You pull me out?"

"Yep."

"Wasn't part of our deal."

"Nope."

I remembered Curtiss, Sanger, and the big white boat disappearing into the sinking sun. I remembered a Caddy V-12 hidden between two buildings. I remembered something hitting me on the head. I remembered a redhead I knew back in high school. I had almost got her out of her clothes one day, but her mom came home. I sighed and tried to focus on Rigger.

"That man, he drive off in a big Caddy parked up between those buildings to the east?"

"Might've been a Caddy."

"Lot of people here last night. Don't recall seein' you."

"Stayed out of sight. Seen you, all right. You was talkin' to Mr. Sanger and a tall fella that even Mr. Sanger seemed to bow to."

"Boat's gone, and your job of watchin' it with it."

"Seems like."

The moon stopped dancing and Rigger's face cleared a little in the growing light of dawn. He eyed me with no emotion. I dug out a soaked fin and two singles. I held them out to him.

"No more boat. Guess this is the last of it."

He ignored the money. He handed the Colt to me and held on to my fedora, which looked like a drowned musk-rat.

"Keep your dough. Take your gat. I found it on the dock against a crate." He turned the fedora around in his hand, trying to return it to a reasonable shape. "Good thing you was wearin' this. I could use a new hat."

"My blessings. Can you help me up?"

"Sure you can stand? That was a hard crack you took."

"Standing's been a specialty of mine for a long time now."

Rigger snapped the fedora over his head. It seemed to fit him all right, but maybe it would shrink when it dried out. Rigger took me under both arms and helped me stagger to my feet. I wobbled like a grazed ten-pin on a warped lane, but I managed to stay upright. I looked around and tried to focus. The effort of standing up started my eyes spinning again.

"Got a car here somewhere."

"Yeah, I know. A Chevy."

He hooked a heavy arm under my left shoulder and led me back down the dock. It took about ten hours to get to my Chevy. I got out a blanket from the back of the road-ster and Rigger threw it over the cloth seat for me. He saw the photos, Lena on top.

"That's the dame I seen down here." Rigger picked up the photos and ran a finger over Lena's glossy face. "Yeah, that's her for sure."

He looked at the other three photos.

"Don't know her," he said, shuffling Winnie Kramer's photo to the back. He looked at the other two. "These the same woman?"

"No. Make one of them?"

"Looks like the same woman. Purty sure I seen one of 'em down here one night."

"When?"

Rigger shrugged. "One night. Two, three nights back."

"Sure?"

Rigger tossed the photos on the blanket. "I ain't sure of nothin'." He slammed the door.

I threw my wet suit coat in the back and got in behind the wheel.

"You okay to drive?"

A vagrant on a chain gang pounded the rock that was my head, but I was focused. I pressed the starter. The engine sputtered and coughed. It sounded like my head felt, but it caught and rattled its usual rattle.

"Sure. Thanks, Rigger." I ground the gears into reverse. "You telling Sanger about this?"

"You bet."

"All of it?"

"All of it."

"You take care of yourself. See you around."

He watched me until I had passed Angelo Street then turned and disappeared behind a crate. I had trouble driving in a straight line and I ground the gears to mush, but I got home just after sunrise without being pulled over for being a menace to mankind.

I took off my wet clothes and managed to take a shower without drowning. I took a handful of aspirin, put on clean pajamas, fired up the coffee pot, and called the studio to tell whoever answered I wouldn't be in this morning. I poured a cup of joe, put it on the table beside the bed, and stretched out on the mattress. I passed out the second my throbbing noggin hit the pillow. It was dark when I came to.

A fire bell was ringing. It was incessant. It jangled my ears as if it were in the same room with me. I saw no fire, smelled no smoke, felt no heat. The throbbing in my head had calmed down, but my apartment walls were waving. Maybe it was an earthquake. Maybe I was just one of the lucky few whose walls waved. I closed my eyes tightly, rubbed them with hands that felt detached, like two pieces of hard rubber at the end of short hoses. I opened my eyes. The walls quit waving, but the fire bell kept ringing. I looked at the ceiling but couldn't see it. The faint glow from the street light below crept through the window and let me know I wasn't blind.

I turned my head toward the table and felt for the lamp. My hand hit the full coffee cup and tipped it over. The fire bell wouldn't stop. I managed to click on the light and saw the broken cup on the floor, black coffee circling around it, staining the carpet. The fire bell kept ringing.

Not a fire bell, you idiot, a detached voice told me. *It's the telephone.*

I sat up on the edge of the bed, but knew better than to try to stand. The clock's hands showed a little past ten. I had been out for nearly fifteen hours. I fumbled for the blower and finally got it to my ear. I didn't say hello. I didn't have to.

"How's your melon, Bo? Sore?"

"Whyn't ya come over and let me show you?"

A chilling chuckle at the other end of the line helped dry my waterlogged brain. I could see red, rat-mean eyes shining in the dark.

"Just a warnin', Bo. Stay out of my affairs or the next time you won't get such an easy tap. Just a friendly warning."

"You're a sick man. I got a cure."

The chuckle turned into a harsh laugh.

"*Tick...tick...tick.*"

A loud click and I was holding a dead phone. I just held it, sitting there on the edge of the bed, in the glare of the lone lamp. I sat there a long time. I wondered where I had left the Colt.

I needed to hold it. Cuddle it. Get the feel of it again.

I had a feeling I might want to use it.

CHAPTER 24

I sopped up the wet coffee, drank two glasses of tap water, and swallowed a handful of aspirin. I went back to sleep and didn't wake until dawn. Sunlight filtered through the window and a marching army would have choked on the dust dancing around in the shafts of light. I took another shot of aspirin, showered again, and shaved. I used a hand mirror to check behind my ear. The small, ugly lump throbbed in a montage of reds, blacks, blues, purples, and polka dots. The bleeding had stopped, and what more could I ask for?

I scrambled three eggs, ate almost all of them with a piece of buttered toast, and drank two cups of thick, black coffee without spilling either cup. I didn't turn on the radio. I didn't pick up the morning newspaper. The disagreeable world wobbled by and I didn't care. I let the time drag, trying to remember every detail about the past night. Maybe I forgot some of it, but the key points throbbed in my battered head.

Finally, I called the studio and asked for Gallen. He wasn't in and wasn't expected. I got back to Gertie at the switchboard. I begged off another day, not that anyone down there would care. The only way Harry would know I wasn't on the job was if he yelled for me.

Two minutes after I hung up, the phone rang. "Morgue. You stab 'em, we slab 'em."

"Heard that line in a picture once. I think it was one of mine. Can't imagine it got any laughs then, either."

It was a woman's voice, low, throaty, and sexy enough to curl my hair.

"I got a lot of cheap patter," I muttered.

"I assume you are Neil Brand."

"Smart doll."

"Do you always talk like that?"

"Only when I'm thinking. Is there a dragon or something you need slayed?"

"This is Lena."

I guess she thought she didn't need a last name. She was right.

"Graveside services for Joan Banes are at eleven-thirty out in Glendale. You going?"

"Planned to," I said. "Wanna see who shows."

"Good. Me, too. But don't expect Johnny. He won't do funerals."

"Not even his sister?"

"You know she isn't his sister. Throw on some glad rags and I'll pick you up. We can talk on the way."

"About what?"

"I'll surprise you."

"I like surprises sometimes."

"See you in an hour."

I propped myself by the Gramercy's front door and tried not to fall down when Lena pulled up in a sleek, black Cadillac Town Brougham with a tan top. I didn't make the Mexican driver when he climbed out of the open air cockpit and held the door for me. He wore a wide black hat, kept his head down, and avoided my eyes. I slipped in beside Lena, radiant in a high-belted black mourning dress with a wide-brimmed black hat and matching veil turned up over the front of the hat. The hat completely hid her vanilla ice cream hair and shaded her violet eyes. Long black gloves rested on her lap, a row of seven pearl buttons gleaming on each glove. Black was Lena's color. I couldn't think of a color that wouldn't be hers.

The Town Brougham pulled smoothly and silently into traffic. The sliding window behind the driver was closed and curtained, as were the side and rear windows. She had switched off the speaker tube to the cockpit, cutting us off from the spinning world.

"Spiffy," she said, looking me over from head to toe. "Regular Joe Brooks."

"This is swell." I ran a hand over the soft calfskin leather of the Brougham's rich interior. I admired the solid silver decorating the doors and the overhead light. A silver latch fastened the flap to a cherry wood bar underneath the sliding window behind the driver. The rich carpeting and the elegant leather upholstery surrounding us were tan, to match the outside top. I tried not to admire Lena, but it wasn't easy. Just looking at her made my head feel better. "You handing out tickets for a ride on the merry-go-round later?"

"Cheap patter. Is that what you said?"

"Who gave you my phone number? I'm not in the book."

"Jimmy Gallen, of course. And your address."

"Where is Jimmy?"

"Nice day for a funeral."

"Hell of a thing to go to a funeral in," I said, indicating the Brougham.

"Gives us privacy. To talk."

"About what? You? Joan Banes? Johnny Cutter? Coney Island? Maybe saps to the side of the head?"

"Yes, I see that." A touch of real sympathy might have

stained her voice somewhere in that banana cream purr. "I bet that hurts."

"Only when I think."

"I guess you bumped into a door."

"Doors are getting to be a little complicated for me these days."

"Well, other than that, you look very nice this morning. I wasn't sure you cleaned up so splendidly."

"It was the least I could do."

"Spiffy. I like it."

"Didn't do it for you."

"Joan? She wouldn't care."

"You must have known her better than I thought. I don't picture you running around to graveside services."

"I knew her. I only worked on one picture with her, when I was under contract to Fox but, after that, we were sort of in the same crowd. You know, Jack and Olive, Johnny, Alma, Joan, me, a few others. We had a good time. We liked to drink, screw, and raise hell. We were fast and footloose, young and reckless. It caught up to some of us way too soon."

"Joan, for one?"

"Yes. For one. We thought—all of us—that she was going places in this business. I mean right to the top. We all told her that. But she was so sad, down deep. So sad. She drank far too much, we all did. You know, Prohibition had just come in and what better way to stick it to those do-gooders than to guzzle all the illegal booze we could find and flaunt doing it."

"Why was she so sad? Her career was just taking off."

Lena fingered the gloves on her lap, stared silently at the cherry wood. "Who knows?" she said after a moment. Maybe Gallen hadn't wired her on what I knew. Maybe she was just being coy. "She wouldn't talk about it. Not to anybody. But her depression overwhelmed her. She just kept sinking. It was a short walk from hooch to dope for her."

"Didn't her friends try to help her?"

"We tried. She didn't want help. I really think that deep down she wanted to die. I think she really thought she didn't have the right to live. Strange, I know, but that's what I sensed. She got on a downward spiral and couldn't be helped. She'd only made a couple of pictures, and nobody really knew her. Some of us tried to get her to open up, but it was a no go. She'd hang around the seedier places in town where nobody had any idea she was in pictures. In those places she was just another down-and-out chippy looking for a good time and an easy way out."

"Her so-called friends could've looked after her better. No matter what, she didn't deserve to die the way she did. Look at the way she was living."

"I didn't know anything about that. Johnny told me he was taking care of her, was paying for a place for her to stay. I thought she was in a sanitarium. Johnny told me she was. When I asked about seeing her, he told me Joan's mind was gone and she couldn't recognize anyone. So why bother? I closed the door on Joan, I'm sorry to say."

"So why today?"

"I feel like a real heel about it. Really, I do. I should have done more. I should have pressed Johnny, but he and I were in and out. We could go months without seeing each other, and we weren't that close. Just pals who'd get together every once in a while for a good time."

"You knew nothing about Joan's past, then?"

"No." She toyed with the pearls on her gloves. "We didn't talk about our pasts. I knew nothing about Joan. I know very little about Johnny, just that he came from a bad part of New York several months after Joan got here.

I hardly knew Alma or Olive. Jack? Well, everybody knows Mary's little brother. And none of them know about me. We were merrily going to hell."

"Wrap yourself in enough satin sheets you might not get scratched."

"Didn't work. I got deep scratches, you just can't see them. Didn't work for any of us. We were just in the present, not thinking about the future. Turns out, most of us didn't have one. Alma, Olive, Joan, Wally. Seen Jack lately? I doubt he'll live another year the way he's going. We were all of us too interested in playing the roulette of life."

"Frances Marion said that about them."

"The one true genius in this town. She knew us well. All too well."

"There might be a few other geniuses."

She laughed lightly, a beautiful sound like tiny wind chimes tinkling in a light breeze.

"You know what Herm Mankiewicz told Ben Hecht? 'Millions to be grabbed out here and the only competition is idiots.' Mank must have met Harry York when he got off the train."

A dark green Indian motorcycle sped past us. My old man owned one just before the war. Nels and I took it out of the garage one day when the old man was at work and took turns riding it. I was the one who wrecked it. Something else Los Angeles Police Sergeant Norsten Brand would never forgive me for.

"Anyone ever come nosing around about Joan?" I asked. "Cops maybe. Private dicks."

"Oooohhh, private dicks."

"Straighten up. You're on your way to a funeral."

"Oh, so you're the morality police, too. All right, then. No. No cops, private dicks, or anyone else tried to pry into her life, as far as I know. The publicity guys ground

out the usual hooey about her, but the fan magazines never got around to her. Before the mill could get going, she
was gone from pictures."

"Her real name was Gardner. You know that?"

Lena shook her veiled head. "Not really. I knew Joan
Banes wasn't her real name, but nobody in this town goes
by their real name. I don't. Johnny doesn't. Tell me, is
Neil Brand your real name?"

"No. It's Clara Bow."

"Ha. Ha. Ha. You ought to be a screenwriter. That
lame line might be funnier than anything I've had in my
last two pictures."

"Saw your last one."

"Really. Have your hat in your lap? I'm told most men
do when they watch me up there on that big silver
screen."

"Naw. I was too busy yawning."

"You can be a real bastard without even trying."

"Know anyone who owns a blue Chrysler 70?"

We were in Glendale now and about to turn into the
cemetery. She pulled down the hat's veil and ignored my
question. "Maybe I can entice you to an evening on the
town some time. Perhaps I can keep you from yawning."

"Have your people call my people."

The Caddy eased up beside the burial site. A white
tent covered the small plot beside the winding road, the
cheap metal casket suspended by thick straps over a deep
hole. Two workers in overalls leaned against an elm tree
several yards away, shovels in hand. They were bored
until they saw Lena. They got a look at her and came off
the tree as if they were on springs. The driver opened the
door for us, then handed Lena a small white bouquet,
which she held at waist level. The small, silver-tinted
gravestone was in place, with engraved lettering painted
white.

Joan Banes, 1900-1931
A star dimmed long before her time.

I was wondering who thought that up when a black, older-model Plymouth pulled up and the minister slid from behind the wheel. His black suit matched mine. He looked questioningly at Lena and then at me.

"I believe we are all here, pastor," Lena said. The overt sultriness of her motion picture voice was missing.

The preacher nodded, took his place at the head of the casket, and opened a little black book that wasn't the Bible. He read a few words and seemed to have nothing to say that wasn't written down. For all I knew, he was a studio bit player.

He asked if anyone had anything to say. Lena and I shook our heads no. He nodded and asked us to bow in prayer. It took twenty seconds, but I guess God was already well versed in the short and tragic life of Joan Banes. He probably even knew about Dorothea Gardner.

When the preacher was done, Lena put the flowers on the casket, shook the preacher's hand, and a rolled-up piece of green passed hands. I wondered what the going rate was for a boozed-up, drug-addled ex-actress nobody cared about. Lena turned and went back to the long Caddy. I tagged along like a lost puppy. The swarthy driver held the door for us.

The Caddy pulled out. Lena took off her hat and veil and shook out her curled white hair. Her scene was over. She had played her part well and I hoped I had kept up my end. She opened the curtains and leaned back against the plush seat to let the bright sunshine play across her flawless face. After a minute, she opened the liquor cabinet and dug out a bottle of plaid. She looked at me with expectant eyes.

"Drink? It's top scotch. Cutty Sark."

Just like Johnny Cutter. I shook my head. Lena didn't bother about a glass. She held the bottle to her mouth and worked down a long pull.

"I wish I hadn't come." She stared at the bottle, maybe looking for a way to crawl inside.

"Why did you?"

"I thought somebody ought to. Somebody besides you."

CHAPTER 24

Lena was asleep—or maybe those gentle snores were just acting—when her driver pulled up at my place. He didn't get out and open the door for me. I slipped out and closed the heavy door without bothering Lena. The Town Brougham purred away and disappeared around the corner. I filed the license plate number into my memory bank. It was mid-afternoon. My head hurt. I felt like I had just gone ten rounds with Jack Dempsey with my hands tied behind my back. I wanted to go to bed and stay there until Christmas. Instead, I got in the Chevy and headed to the studio.

When I got back to my office a message from Jimmy Gallen was pinned on my desk. It was Merly's handwriting, a scrawl I had seen many times. Gallen had left a telephone number I recognized as Johnny Cutter's home phone. Gallen could wait. I called Alice.

"Afternoon, sweetheart." I tried to sound cheery through the banging in my head.

"It would be very nice if this call was an invitation to dinner."

"How about Saturday night?"

"Expect to take me somewhere very elegant and very expensive."

"Deal. How about running another plate for me?"

"I should have known." Her voice turned icy. "That's what this is about, not a dinner date?"

"Sweetheart, we are definitely on for Saturday night."

"Definitely?"

"Cross my heart."

"You don't have to hope to die, but if you don't show up, I might have to kill you. I have a very nice get-up, and I feel like showing off."

"Can't wait to see it."

"You won't beef. What's the number?"

I gave her the number of the Cadillac Town Brougham.

"I will bring you that license number Saturday night. I will give it to you after you have paid me in full."

"That sounds a little distrustful, sweetheart."

"You bet your ass it's distrustful. And don't call me sweetheart until after I've eaten. I'll expect you at eight Saturday evening."

"With bells on."

"No need for bells. Just some dough. Somewhere very elegant and very expensive. Remember that."

I dialed Cutter's number. Gallen answered on the first ring.

"Neil—" It didn't take Sherlock Holmes to hear the panic in his strident whisper. "I need you here right now. Do not tell anyone. Get a wiggle on."

He rang off.

Two minutes later, my Chevy roared past a Sunset traffic cop. I did a Gallen through the traffic lights and a geyser of boiling water spewed from the roadster's radiator when I raced through the front gate to Cutter's place. Gallen's car was parked in front of the garage. I pulled up beside the Packard and looked in the garage window. Cutter's Duesenberg and his Caddy were inside. Gallen waved frantically from the front door. The natty Irishman might have been trying out for the role of the condemned man in a Harry York potboiler.

"What is it?"

"Come in here. Come. I'll show you."

Gallen ran me through the foyer and down a short hallway to the master bedroom. It was the kind of room you'd expect Douglas Fairbanks to live in. The furniture was big and dark with broadly carved wood. Manly paintings, all outdoorsy, covered the walls over wallpaper of ships on an ocean. The faint aroma of roses and jasmine hung in the room. I had glommed that smell before, but it was way out of place here.

The carved headboard and complementary footboard of the big, solid bed spoke of old California. The bedspread had slipped to the floor and the rumpled white silk sheets showed the effects of some serious frolicking during the night. A heavy maroon duvet with narrow white stripes covered a lump in the middle of the bed. I looked at Gallen, who shook so hard he could have made buttermilk. He inclined his head toward the lump and said nothing.

I pulled the covering back. Johnny Cutter stared at the mirror on the ceiling, but the light had gone out of his wide open eyes. I held the duvet up to see more of Harry's suddenly late movie star. Cutter was naked. My headache went away.

"You cover him?"

Gallen nodded. "I couldn't stand those eyes staring at me."

"Why didn't you close them?"

"What? Touch him? Good God, Neil."

"Where'd you get the cover?"

"From the hallway closet."

I tossed the duvet at him. "Get rid of it."

Gallen nodded.

"Toss the place?"

"Just this room." He indicated a brown valise on a big chest by the door. "Everything I could find I didn't want the police to see is in there. Letters. Photos. Other things nobody needs to see. I want you to go through the house with me. Make sure I didn't miss anything."

I nodded. "In a minute."

I pulled the sheet down to Cutter's waist. His cold, pasty white skin showed red-purple discoloration here and there. I pushed lightly on a discolored spot on his lower left side and the skin blanched. Rigor mortis had set in along the jaw and neck, and had started down his torso. He had been dead eight hours at the most.

I checked his arms first and paused over the small needle puncture at the inside of his right elbow. I looked closely at both arms, but saw only the one mark. Gallen gaped at me, wondering how anyone could touch a dead man, I guess.

"He wasn't snowed?"

"God, Neil, no. Johnny couldn't possibly stick a needle in himself. Far as I know, he never touched the junk. Any of it. Booze and skirts did it for him."

I showed Gallen the puncture wound. "He was right-handed. There are no other marks on his body that I can see offhand. I'd say somebody shot him up with something."

"An accident?"

"Maybe."

Gallen stepped back and stared at me. "Are you saying murder?"

"Coroner will know pretty quick. But here's guessing you haven't made that call, yet."

"Not 'til I'm certain the house is properly taken care of."

"How much have you done?"

"The master bedroom, so far. I need to go over it again, just to be absolute. I called a couple of my boys and they should be here soon. There's three guest rooms, four baths, the main living room, a library, the kitchen, the garden room, the storage room off the kitchen, and the garage. I want them spotless before the cops are called in."

"What about Harry?"

"I'll tell Harry before I call the cops. That won't be pleasant. He'll insist on coming up, I imagine, and when he gets here it'll all be in his hands. If he doesn't get here before the bulls do, we'll both be selling apples on a street corner."

"How'd you know Cutter was here? Thought he was in Frisco."

"Called me last night about ten. Just got back into town. Wanted me to come see him first thing this morning."

"Why?"

Gallen shrugged. "Didn't say, but, frankly, he sounded nervous, scared."

Car doors slammed outside, and Gallen ran to the front window. "Here they are now." He rushed to the front door.

Tay Fishback and Cecil Griffith came in and immediately went into a huddle with their boss. Drained and pinched faces greeted me when the conference broke up. They took furtive glances at the master bedroom, but didn't go anywhere near the door. They completely ignored me. Gallen went back into the master bedroom and began going through drawers. Tay and Cecil took two of the guest rooms and I took the third. I tossed it completely and went through a couple of other rooms, but there was nothing you'd mind the town gossip seeing. The three publicity ginks came up with a few hinky items that went into the brown valise. After an hour, they were satisfied.

"Make sure there's no booze in the house," Gallen told his two assistants. They both nodded. "There's a well-stocked bar in the living room and another in the master bedroom."

Gallen stood at the phone in the main room and looked around. "Okay," he said softly and picked up the horn. He asked for York Studio and told the girl at the switchboard who he was. She immediately connected him to Betsy Hammerlin in Harry's outer office.

"I need to talk to Harry." He listened a couple of seconds then broke in. "I don't care who he's with, Betsy. This is urgent. Get him now."

A second passed. "That's right, Betsy. It's my ass and Brand's and maybe yours. Get him now...Good."

I headed outside, through the kitchen, where Fishback and Griffith were going through the cabinets. Two bottles of O'Keefe beer on the counter were both empty. Tay tossed the dead soldiers into a cardboard box as I walked outside. A small hut behind the pool stored gardening and pool equipment. I looked inside the hut, then the garage.

A commotion at the back door brought me outside. Gallen's two assistants dragged Cutter's body, now clad in white swimming trunks, out the door. They heaved the body into the pool. Gallen watched Cutter gently bob face down in the water while the other two went back inside. After a couple of minutes, Tay came out carrying a big cardboard box full of bottles. Cecil, brown valise in hand, followed a few seconds later, headed for their Plymouth. They went back inside, came out with two more cardboard boxes full of bottles.

They conferred briefly with Gallen, got into the Plymouth, and tooled down the drive. I had no idea where that valise would end up. I had an idea about the bottles.

I nodded at Cutter's stiff body. "Your idea or Harry's?"

"Never mind. Harry's on his way. He wants us to stick around and do nothing until he gets here."

"Bulls won't buy accidental drowning."

Gallen grinned bitterly. "They'll buy whatever Harry pays for."

CHAPTER 26

Harry York stared at Cutter a long time, silently, the way a plumber would study an overflowing toilet. I got my orders and Harry and Gallen took off. I called the buttons and then parked my Chevy on the street so I could get away when I wanted. I carried a light blue Adirondack chair to the jacaranda and sat in the shade, waiting and thinking while my melon tried to melt. Eight Bells and his boys showed up and the DA and Gallen weren't far behind. Neither were the newspaper boys. I slipped away behind them, leaving Gallen to do his thing.

I went home. I kicked off my shoes and got lost in my easy chair by the window. I didn't turn on the radio. My head hurt. It hurt a lot, and I figured to soothe the pain with a bottle of decent brown I had picked up at a speak a couple of months ago. I sat in the chair until it got dark. I sat there until it was almost midnight, sipping the whiskey, and thinking. I did a lot of each and finally went to bed. I wasn't feeling any pain by then. The pain would return in the morning.

Harry York's studio lot throbbed with chin music over Johnny Cutter's death when I got there early Thursday morning. Harry tried to make it business as usual, but not much about the place looked normal. Everywhere I went, small- to medium-sized groups huddled in subdued conversation while the day's work faded beyond thought. I waved off a bunch who wanted to talk to me, giving them the simple excuse that Harry York demanded my presence. They gave me knowing nods and left me alone. I called Betsy first thing after I got to my office.

"Harry yelling for me yet?"

"Not right now," she said softly.

"Who's there?"

"Call you back with your appointment time," she said, loudly this time.

Betsy hung up. I sat at my desk and stared at the fascinating Stage Two wall. The horn sounded. I got it before the second ring.

"What a morning. Sorry, but couldn't talk before. The district attorney was here, waiting to see Harry."

"He kept the DA waiting?"

"Only a few seconds. He had to finish a phone call from his brother in New York. Wow, Neil, it must be five o'clock back there."

"I figured Harry'd be yelling for me."

"Give him time. His plate's full this morning. What a sad thing about Johnny. The studio's in a turmoil. Wait...gotta go."

The line went dead again. I didn't want to run around the lot. I'd have to beat gums with people I didn't even want to see. I remembered Mary Kamenshek. I'd promised to call her Monday night, but things had gotten a little out of hand since then. I called the number written on the back of her sister's photo.

"Hello." The little girl voice was weak, full of suppressed emotion. It had been more than a week since her sister had gone missing.

"Mary, this is Neil Brand at York Brothers Studios."

"You promised to call me Monday."

"Things have been pretty busy. Do you have a radio?"

"I heard a little while ago about Johnny Cutter. How horrible."

Maybe she wanted me to say something. I did not. I could hear her shallow breathing, and I anticipated her question. "Is my sister involved?"

"No. Have you talked to the police again?"

"Yesterday. I thought they were going to arrest me for making such a fuss. I do not expect the police are going to be very helpful. Can you tell me anything at all about my sister?"

"I have checked thoroughly, Mary. She did indeed work here last Thursday, but I can't find anyone who saw her leave."

I hated to feed her a line, but I wasn't ready to tell her what I really thought. *Let's wait a bit and make sure*, I told myself. *Piker*, came the reply.

"Thank you for checking, Mr. Brand."

If there was any air left in her balloon, I just heard it go out.

CHAPTER 27

Betsy Hammerlin called about eleven. She sounded all in. "He's screaming at me because you aren't in his office." She hung up.

I hot-footed it to his asylum and cooled my heels for a half hour while he was on the blower again with his brother in New York. Betsy finally got the call to send me in. I got my marching orders—find out why Cutter was killed and make sure Harry's people were protected—and left Harry staring at his ceiling, thinking about Lazarus and mulling over a name change to Cutter's last picture.

I bummed some aspirin off Betsy and we jawed a few minutes in her office. She was all over me about seeing a studio doctor for my head when the Wolheim brothers and Theo Stein bustled in. They didn't look happy.

"Hear you boys are in the undertaking business now."

"Unbelievable."

"Only Harry."

"Wish it was his funeral we were writing."

"Nobody'd come to it."

"You kidding? Harry'd be the biggest funeral ever," I said. "Give the people what they want and they'll turn out for it."

Betsy tossed me a frustrated glance. "He's waiting," she said, crossing to the door.

Theo looked at the imposing doors. "That isn't the doorway to heaven."

The three of them disappeared into Harry's inner sanctum. Betsy looked curiously at me. "I get a little worried about you. There are things going on around here I certainly don't understand."

"Me either. And you're better off that way."

"Keep my mouth shut. Do my job."

"Exactly. Gallen in to see Harry this morning?"

"First thing. And for almost an hour."

"Who else?"

"A man from the district attorney's office right after Jimmy. Then you. Harry's had a busy morning and I don't think any of it has to do with making pictures."

"His lawyer?"

"Having lunch with him later. In his private dining room."

"Harry's brother is coming."

Betsy smiled brightly. "More fun."

A telephone on her desk jangled. I winked and headed for the door while she said hello. Another blower on her desk started hollering. Betsy was having a good day, too.

I had been turning a thought over in my mind since the night before and, when I got to my office, I called Hutto Hay, who did security for Fox.

"Hey, what about Johnny Cutter?" Hutto asked when I got him on the line.

"Busy over here."

"I bet. You calling for advice?"

"Hutt, a decade ago Fox made a picture starring Wally Reid, Joan Banes, Alma Rubens and Theile Garsone. Remember it?"

"Don't hardly remember last week."

"Can you find it? I'd like to screen it if possible."

"I'll check, get back to you. Got a title?"

"Just the cast. Made in '23, I think. Herb Brenon might have directed it."

"I'll see what I can do."

⌗

Friday, January 17, 1930:

The stock market crash at the close of October signaled the end to the rollicking thunder that had been the Roaring Twenties. The roar turned into a wail of hard times as despair slowly dissolved into chaos. I landed a security gig in Long Beach, but the plummeting economy forced the firm to shut down when the New Year dawned. Work proved hard to come by. I didn't know it at the time, but I was two weeks from landing a job with York Brothers Studio.

This night, I was in a gin mill in central LA, drowning my woes in a bottle of rotgut that passed for whiskey. The doctor at the soldiers' home told me that day there was no hope for Nels. Too late for surgery and death was just a matter of time. He was a strong man and doctors said he might last a year, two at the outside. My old man had stopped talking to me. He blamed me for Nels getting gassed in the war and, in his mind, the gassing and the cancer went hand in hand. My getting kicked off the force was a blow to him, and he would never forgive me for letting it happen.

The only son who had made him proud lay dying. The son who had disillusioned him continued sinking into the bottle.

I downed the last slug in the glass in front of me and there he was—Detective Sergeant Elmo Lawrence Jones.

He was permanently off the lieutenant's list now. He got suspended for two weeks while the department looked into a complaint filed against him by a man in traction with a cracked conk and several broken bones. A couple of other ginks came forward and pointed at Jones, and his career path suddenly took a downward spiral.

Harless had invited me to his house New Year's Day to listen to the Rose Bowl game with him. It was seventy-four degrees. We ate a couple of steaks with trimmings and sipped from a pre-Prohibition bottle of smooth bourbon Frank's commander had brought back from Kentucky and given to him for Christmas. While Racehorse Russ Saunders and the rest of his USC Trojans were kicking the stuffing out of the Pittsburgh Panthers, Harless told me Jonesy's personnel file was taking a number of hard hits and a promotion was no longer in the cards. Jones still had his value to the department, but the ceiling was falling in on him, much like the previously undefeated Pitt players were collapsing in Pasadena.

Now, this night, Jones leaned against the wall beside the front door of the speak, his rat-mean eyes fixed on me with deadly intent from under the turned-down brim of a battered fedora that badly needed cleaning. Other than his eyes, his washed-out pan was a blank mask with a dark slash that formed a mouth. We stared at each other a few seconds, then his right arm slowly lifted and his forefinger pointed directly at me. He mimed pulling a trigger and his lips formed words I didn't need to hear. "Tick...tick...tick."

Jones was gone out the door and I sat there like a ventriloquist's dummy, waiting for Edgar Bergen to stick his hand up my back. I studied the door Jones went through and figured he'd be waiting for me out there in the alley, hidden in the shadows with his throw-down in his hand. I was unarmed and a little bent, but I wanted to get my mitts on him. I went into the men's room, but didn't hit the light switch. The corner street lamp let a tiny bit of light through the awning window that opened onto the alley. I felt around the window and found the crank. The window groaned loudly when I twisted the crank. When the window fully opened, I grabbed a small, round trash can beside the sink and threw it into the alley. Three staccato gunshots rang out, battering the metal can.

A nasty laugh followed the three shots.

"Nice, Bo," I heard Jones say. "Afraid of your own shadow? You should be. From now on we play for keeps."

I heard footsteps fade down the alley.

Just over a week later, Frank Harless called and said York Brothers Studio needed someone with police experience to quietly dig into some thefts on the lot. Harless recommended me to a screenwriter named Theo Stein. Harless told me to put on my best suit, go down to the sprawling studio the next day, and look up a fellow named Harry York.

CHAPTER 28

Thursday, September 17, 1931:

The Aliso Club was an upscale drum just off Sixth Street, along the Red Car line and a quick hop from the viaduct. It took up most of the basement of the old Snyder Building, pretty much unchanged from its pre-Prohibition days. The red-letter neon sign no longer blinked, but a bright light flooded the outside of the heavy gray door at the bottom of the steps along an alley. The owner put a new lock on the door in 1920, added a small square peephole, and hung a lamp over it. Now you had to knock to gain admittance. A hidden rear entrance connected to the basement of a luggage store fronting Sixth Street.

Before Prohibition, the Aliso had been an off-duty hangout for Los Angeles policemen. When that joke became law, the Aliso remained an off-duty hangout. I spent more time than I needed to in the joint when I was on the force, first with Frank Harless as my partner and then, briefly, with Elmo Jones. I enjoyed my time there with Frank.

I had switched autos with a second-unit director named Hughie Dunnum, and I backed his Nash into a short, dead-end alley off Alison, a half block from the Aliso's entrance, out of the light, the top up. The black breezer was tucked in, so I had a view of the steps going down to the club. The front of Dunnum's bucket might have been visible if someone looked hard enough. Jones knew I drove a Chevy. I figured he wouldn't be looking for a black Nash.

I had called the central division a half hour ago from a drugstore phone a half block away, and was told Detective Sergeant Elmo Jones had left for the day. I called the Aliso and asked for him, using the name Frank Harless. The hack who answered the phone said Jonesy was there, slightly bent and getting more so. I hung up. Jones drunk or sober did not matter.

I drove to the club, parked the Nash, and waited. My right hand idly fingered a leather-covered sap on the seat beside me. It was a long time before Jonesy came out and, when he did, he had a slight stagger about him. He leaned against the wall and fired up a gasper. The match threw eerie shadows over his rat-mean pan. Jones looked around and dragged on the cigarette. He might have seen the Nash—his eyes lingered in my direction a couple of seconds—but a Red Car came along. He threw down the gasper and jumped aboard.

I gave the streetcar a few seconds then followed, far back but close enough to see anyone get off when it stopped. The streetcar went east on Sixth. Jones got off at Lorena and walked south, not bothering to look around. Halfway down the block, the Ridgeway Apartments loomed along an alley that ran off Lorena. I guessed Jones was staying at the Ridgeway, but it didn't really matter as long as he walked that far.

I rolled the Nash past Jones, with my hat pulled low to the left to hide my face. Two flivvers took up space in front of the Ridgeway. I eased up behind the second boiler, just past the alley. Jones gave the Nash a cursory glance and started to walk by. I jerked the door open and jumped out. Jones started to turn my way but I rammed my left shoulder into his side and drove him into the alley. He cried out and reached for his service revolver, but I hit him hard on his right forearm with the sap. He yelped in pain. I tapped him lightly above his left ear just enough to stun him, then took a handful of his coat collar and dragged him, struggling, into the darkness of the alley.

I kicked him hard in the side to keep him down, found his revolver in a belt holster, and threw it to the far reaches of the alley. It clattered against something that sounded like wood and bounced a couple of times on the alley bricks.

He tried to push me away and I gave him another little tap, same place. I found his throw-down piece, the Smith & Wesson snub-nose he had fired in my office, in the pocket of his flogger and tossed it. I drove a gloved fist into the side of his thick neck. It felt good. He yelped again and struggled for breath.

"You're a little out of shape, Jonesy."

"Brand." His voice squawked from the pain in his throat. "You bas—"

I hit him again, harder. That one felt even better. "Let me talk this time, Jonesy. You did most of it the last time."

Jones tried to roll to his feet. "I'll kill—"

I hit him on the knee with the sap. I heard a loud crack. He screamed and I hit him again. Another gloved fist, this one to the jaw.

"I'm the law—" he gasped.

I hit him again with the sap, hard, about four inches below the knee. Another crack, louder than the first. He screamed again. I looked down the alley, but didn't see anyone. If anyone heard his yelps, they probably wouldn't have come anyway.

"Don't know how many men I saw you do this to when I had the lousy luck of being tagged with you. Enough that I learned how to do it, didn't I?"

Jones didn't say anything. He was breathing hard, grimacing against the pain. I gave him a couple of playful little slaps to the jaw.

"Thing is, Jonesy, you meant to chill me at the wharf, and don't deny it. I guess you're slowing down in your old age. When I hit the water, you heard a man yell out and you ran. Didn't get the chance to finish me."

"Why'd I want to kill—"

I hit him hard with another fist to the side of his neck. He yelped and retched. Pain laced his weedy voice, and his thick chest shuddered with short, sharp gasps. I waved the sap in front of his rat-mean eyes.

"You framed me for a bribe and got rid of me because I knew how dirty you were. Dirty, yes, but I didn't know how depraved. I know it was you behind that racket with the girls. You as much as told me so when you came at me. Way I figure it, you got some paper on a Missouri girl named Dorothea Gardner about a decade ago, and somehow connected her to a girl in the pictures calling herself Joan Banes."

Jones rolled his bleeding head toward me, a cold and desperate look clouding his eyes.

"She was wanted for knocking off her parents and you wired that. Simple blackmail for a year, maybe two. Then her career flagged out and she quickly ran out of dough, so you came up with another scheme. A real pip. One that involved a big yacht and a bunch of doe-eyed dolls with pretty faces and no one to look out for them. Sweet deal, you rat bastard."

"So you know—so what? You're dead."

"Best look out for yourself, Jonesy. I'm not your big worry. You bumped off Carmine Broglio because he found out about your caper with those girls and wanted a cut."

Jonesy awkwardly pushed himself into a sitting position. Blood smeared his pan, hideously twisted because of the pain in his leg. I might have cracked a bone below his knee.

"Yeah, that New York goon thought he was tough. Thought he could cut right in on me. Needed a good lesson." Jonesy forced a grin, but I could see it hurt. I wanted to knock his teeth out, but I was through hitting him. "Carmine's body ain't been found, Bo. You know he's dead, means you moved it, or you know who did. That's 'gainst the law, bucko."

"Might have to give myself up, Jonesy." I bent down to look him in the eyes. "Why kill Johnny Cutter? He getting hinky? Maybe about to queer your deal?"

"Make up more stories."

"No need to. Like I said. You got plenty to worry about—"

"Can't prove nothin'."

"Not even gonna try. But just now Randall Curtiss knows what his boat was being used for, and Mack Sanger knows who was running a white slavery ring right under his nose. Those two boys are a much bigger worry than me or the law."

His face froze in a mask of fear, although he tried quickly to cover it. The broderick I had just dealt him smacked easy as a Sunday social compared to what he had in store when Sanger's trouble boys got around to him. He could have been the governor of the state, those boys wouldn't care.

"You were seen, Jonesy. Last Thursday night you were down there with Lena and Cutter and a bunch of swell-looking young kittens. Carmine had a man watching that boat. You didn't see him. He saw you. Described me to you, but I was down there, too."

Jones tried to move, but it was too much trouble, and he gave it up. I stood and put my left foot on his right mitt. I put a little weight on it, enough to make him groan.

"When Curtiss and Sanger found out it was a dirty LA bull doing that to them, why you should have seen the look on their pans. I think you'll get to see it, anyway. I just don't think you can run fast enough to not see it."

Liquid glass replaced the rat-mean eyes. Jonesy was tough when he had the upper hand, but he wasn't so tough sprawled in a dark alley, his future leaking away with his blood.

"Tick…tick…tick…" I said.

I left Detective Sergeant Elmo Jones sprawled in the alley with a mashed-up face, a bad leg, and a bleak future. He was trying to figure out where to run, I guessed.

I walked to the Nash, fired it up, and looked in the mirror. The face staring back at me was drawn, old, and tired, but my head didn't hurt anymore. I pulled out and went down Lorena. I drove past a dark red, Chrysler four-door sedan with two baby grands sitting in the front seat, like they were waiting for the milkman. They saw me but showed no recognition.

They had come for Jones sooner than I had figured. I was glad I had gotten there ahead of them, if only by a few minutes.

I hung a right at the corner and headed home.

CHAPTER 29

Frank Harless dropped in on me early the next morning.

I was in my office. The window had been fixed, but the hole in the Stage One wall was still there. I turned on the radio and heard the last strands of "I'll be Glad When You're Dead, You Rascal You." A farewell song for Johnny Cutter? An announcer broke in with an update on the death of the York Brothers motion picture star. I wondered if Harry paid these guys to put York Brothers in front of Johnny Cutter's name whenever they mentioned him. The guy on the radio didn't tell me anything I didn't already know.

The phone rang. It was Karl at the front gate. He said a button named Harless flashed his buzzer and walked onto the lot. He was coming to see me.

I didn't get up when Frank walked in. Taller than me by a couple inches, Frank's broad shoulders accentuated a slender frame. Wavy, dark brown hair cut to a deep widow's peak centered over wide-set, dark brown eyes and a straight nose over a slightly rounded chin. His arms were long and well-muscled and his hands were big. A couple of months ago, he had turned forty-six. He looked at least a decade younger.

Harless glanced around my cubbyhole like a bear looking for a place to hibernate. "See your station hasn't changed."

"One of these days I might get around to redecorating."

"Wouldn't take much."

Harless threw his gray fedora on top of a filing cabinet. He thrust his hands into the pockets of his charcoal three-piece and regarded me with the same look I had often seen when he began interrogating suspects. His friendly, fatherly look drew you in and then spit you out.

"Speaking of redecorating, Sergeant Jones had a little work done on him late last night or early this morning."

"Says you."

"Found him in an alley this morning beside his apartment house. Somebody tattooed him pretty good."

"He ought to have expected that at some point."

Harless nodded. "Don't suppose you'd know anything about that?"

"Who's asking? Frank Harless or Detective Harless?"

Harless nodded again. "We'll get to that. Straight out, you kill Jonesy?"

"I had an idea someday I might get around to it, Frank. But first I wanted to prove he framed me."

"We all know he carved your frame. We just don't have the goods. Jones was as dirty as a cop could get, and I thought some day I'd catch him. I can't say I'm sorry he came to such a sudden end. But after all, he was police. Cop getting killed is bad for all cops, and everybody on the force wants to do something about it. The department is going to look hard into his death. Especially seeing how he died."

"How's that?"

"A pro worked him over, then sliced off his whacker, and stuffed it in his kisser."

"I didn't kill him."

"I know you wouldn't do that to him. I can't speak for what others in the department might think, though. Understand?"

"I had a giddy moment for a second. Now you're being a wet blanket."

"God knows what Jonesy was into, and who he might have been in it with, but somebody was sure as hell miffed with him. Thought you might know who it was."

"I could toss out a hunch or two. You know what Harry says about verbal contracts?"

Harless twisted his head at an odd angle and squinted at me. "No. What?"

"Verbal contracts aren't worth the paper they're written on. Same with hunches."

"Humor me. Just for old times."

"Not even."

"All right, I'll make a hunch. Mack Sanger. That work on Jones was the kind of thing his boys are good at. And the way they tossed his place. Cleaned it out crisp. You'd think a choir boy lived there."

"Mack Sanger."

"That's my hunch. I'm not sure even the LAPD would take a run at Sanger."

"You'll need a good place to start."

"Got one. You."

I stared at him and tried to look as blank as an actor without a script.

"Okay, you won't squeal. Boys downtown will find it a lot easier to take a run at you than at Sanger. You'll have to watch your backside a while."

I grinned. "Too bad Jones never made lieutenant."

"Too many higher-ups on the force didn't like him. They believed the stories about him and thought he'd be of more use where he was than as a lieutenant."

"You mean beating ginks to pulp on the streets."

"Tell me about Cutter."

"I don't know who killed him, either."

Harless laughed. It wasn't humorous. "He drowned, didn't you hear? Leastways, that will be the official ruling. DA's up in Harry York's office right now, closing out that deal."

"How much you think it'll cost Harry?"

Harless shrugged. "Don't know. Between this and the Minter thing, the DA will be able to pay off that cabin up at Arrowhead. And York will have to add something for the county. The sheriff's tweaked we stepped on his toes, and the county DA is mad as hell."

"It's a wonder they aren't up in Harry's office with your guy. By the way, you come here with him?"

He shook his head. "Saw the gimp arrive. Limped right in the main door and right up to Harry's office. When he gets back downtown, he'll make it official. Death by drowning."

"Are they going to do an autopsy, anyway?"

He shrugged again. "Ask Harry."

My turn to shrug. "Harry might want to know what really killed Cutter. He's going to want to know a lot of things about Cutter. He's going to have to cover it up to protect the box office. Cutter's new film opens in New York tomorrow. Harry's had people working around the clock to get it ready. Hired a Lockheed Orion to fly it to New York. They'll still be cutting that picture when the plane lands. The studio always expected to make a lot of money off it. If Cutter's death plays right, the box might even be bigger than their dreams. But it'll all dry up if the public finds out he's not exactly an angel. He and Jonesy."

"Jones kill Cutter? They into something together?"

"Cutter drowned, Frank. Remember? Nobody from the

King of England down to the City Hall janitor is going to look into it any further than that."

"You are trying hard to tell me something without telling me anything."

"What I'm trying to tell you is there isn't a thing you or me or anybody else can do about any of it."

CHAPTER 30

The high sheriff of Laurel City called a few minutes after Harless left.

"Okay, Brand, you're back in play. Mike and Tank say that was a swell piece of work you did last night."

"Just business."

"I'm sure. But our associate doesn't have any worries, not any more. Got time to visit?"

"Nothing but time."

"Send a car?"

"I'll drive."

The line went dead.

I had parked Dunnum's Nash beside my Chevy and it was gone. I drove straight to Laurel City. Two blocks from Sanger's office, I drove past the twins, both leaning against the hood of their black and white. Both gave me thumbs up. I was coming up in the world.

Tank and Mike were having a smoke by the back door of the hotel. They had on their dark blue pinstripes. Tank had a red tie, Mike a gray tie. But there was something different about them. They were smiling.

"Hello, Brand," Tank said.

"Nice piece of work last night," Mike said.

"Glad you boys approve."

"Copacetic," Mike said.

"You made it easy for us to do our work," Tank said.

"I'm a regular Boy Scout."

"We just wanted you to know we appreciate it," Tank said.

"Didn't know you fellas would be on it so soon. Had a score I wanted to settle before you boys went to work."

"We know," Mike said. "Why we let you. We was sitting there waiting on that bum to show. Saw you and decided to let you make a play. You could even come along with us one time if you wanted."

"Pleased to have you," Tank added.

"Boys, that is really an honor. I have to say you did a nice job, too. What I hear."

"Our specialty. 'Cept for that last part. We didn't want to do that, but the boss was clear. He really wanted that goon to get his message, loud and clear, if only for a brief moment."

"A painful moment," Mike added.

"Boss give us a bonus," Tank said.

"We had to flip to see who did the finish." A little smile curled Mike's thin lips. "I won."

I wasn't sure that meant who did what, and I did not want to ask.

"That flatfoot sure was into the some nasty stuff," Tank said. "Almost made me blush seeing that garbage he had."

"Cop I know said Jonesy's place was tossed."

"Frank Harless," Mike said.

"You know him?"

"We get around."

"Harless is looking into that copper's sudden demise," Tank said. "He's gonna find the goods that'll hang that killing on a San Pedro wharf rat who's about to turn up in a garbage can missing a few parts. The DA'll close the case and that'll be that."

"Those goods come from Jonesy's place?"

"Tossing the flatfoot's joint was part of the job," Mike said.

"Just like at that place over in Burbank."

"We gotta be thorough, see," Tank said. "Make sure nothing's left around to gum up the works later. Unless we want it to be there."

"Still watching that place in Burbank?"

Mike nodded. "Yeah, but it looks like that bimbo done one of two things. He took air or he took dead."

"But we got eyeballs on it, just in case," Tank said.

I could have told them not to bother, but I didn't want to answer any questions about Carmine Broglio just now.

"That bum Jones had just over twenty thousand dollars stashed away," Mike said. "In a cheap, cracker box inside a big chest. Like who wouldn't think of looking for a safe there? You'd think even a dumb cop wouldn't be that dumb. Leavin' that stash, a bunch of gats, passports with his mug but different handles, dirty pictures of people you'd know, other stuff."

"Pictures of famous people, like motion picture stars?"

Mike nodded. "People you'd know."

"Stills?"

"Piles of stills," Tank said. "Lots of film reels in tin cans. Closet full of it. Stuff that won't get shown down at the Bijou. Know what I mean?"

"Also found keys to safe deposit boxes at a bunch of banks. Too bad none of 'em are on our turf." Mike looked sadly at me. "Means we can't get into 'em."

"Whaddaya s'pose we'd find in 'em?" Tank asked.

"Cash," I said. "Lots of it."

"It'll stay there 'til the banks open 'em," Tank said. "Honest banker'll call the bulls."

"What did you do with all that stuff in his place?"

"Burned what would burn, 'cept the cash. Got rid of the rest."

"Where?"

"In a safe place," Mike said.

"Ain't ever gonna be found," Tank said. "Take it to the bank."

"That kind of stuff would be worth a lot of money. If you had that bent."

Tank shrugged. "Boss said burn what would burn, get rid of the rest."

"That's what we done," Mike said.

"What kind of guns?"

Tank put his head back and looked skyward. His brain was peeling rubber. "There was a silver .32 with a short barrel and a pearl handle, a .45 Colt with a walnut handle, two .38 Specials with walnut on one and ivory on the other, a Webley top-break, a twelve-gauge pump, and a couple of choppers."

Mike smiled at Tank, then me. "Good, ain't he?"

I nodded. "Play a mean game of tag with those babies."

"Not anymore," Mike said.

"You boys know what the boss wants with me?"

They didn't know.

"You heeled?" Mike asked.

I shook my head and started to open my coat. Tank stopped me.

"Go on up."

Tank and Mike were still smiling. I was really coming up in the world.

The same big man filled the elevator, but he gave me a nod this time as we rode up. The Eugene Pallette looka-like said hello to me and opened the door to Sanger's office. A bottle of Glenlivet and two tumblers sat invitingly on the corner of his desk. Sanger got up, shook my hand, and poured two fingers into each glass. We sat down and sipped the amber fluid.

"Ever hear of the Zwi Migdal?"

"White slavers. From Argentina. Having a tough time of it just now. In fact, I thought they were dissolved."

Sanger took a sip, eyed me.

"Pretty much. A bunch of kikes, but not a lot of support from the Jews at large. They trafficked in women from the shetls in Eastern Europe, but they took a big hit a year ago. Argentine convicted more than a hundred of them."

"You do quick work."

"Oh, I've known about them for a long time. They got started in Warsaw, calling themselves the Jewish Mutual Aid Society. Helluva name for that outfit, huh? Short story, they moved operations to Buenas Aires about sixty years ago. Worked out for 'em 'til a little while back when they tried to cut in on a tough whorehouse dame goes by Rachel Lieberman, a ballsy broad who didn't take to a bunch of dirty kikes trying to cut in on her turf. She turned to the city's top cop, guy named Elsogray. Pimps ran the city and Elsogray went after them with a vengeance. Imagine, a cop who couldn't be bribed. So the whore goes to this guy and they shut the pimps down, working in secret. The Zwi Migdal traded in women while building synagogues and wrapping themselves in old, God-fearing traditions. They turned it into a business worth millions, using corrupt cops and politicians, violence, rape, and anything they needed to make the thing work."

"Thought those convictions put 'em out of business."

"Mostly, but there's a few hardliners left."

"I'm going to guess they approached you."

"Few years ago. I wouldn't have anything to do with

214

Ray Dyson

it. Disgusting. Told them there'd be trouble if they came at me again."

"So they found out about Elmo Jones somehow and came at him. Jonesy wouldn't see anything disgusting about it. He'd just see dollar signs."

"He would. But he wasn't in it alone."

"Who else?"

"One of the reasons you're back in play, Brand. We're sure Cutter was in it. Maybe others with pull. We think you're the one to quietly look into it. Seein' as how you're Harry's man and already wired."

"We?"

Sanger nodded, didn't say anything. I guessed he was including Randall Curtiss.

"We have the funds and the contacts," he continued. "We know that some young women—we don't know how many and we certainly have no names—were being lured onto Randall's yacht—without his knowledge, be clear on that. For that matter, without mine—and taken to sea. Randall asked me if he could keep his yacht in the bay here. I didn't see any reason to watch it, since it was his boat, and neither did he. He just gave some friends the loan of it. You know, Hollywood types on the sly. 'Til you come around, we didn't know what was going on. Makes us feel a little sheepish. And pissed. A lot pissed. Anyway, a ship with Argentine registration met up with them at sea. Right now American and Argentine authorities are working on that. Maybe they'll get some of those girls back. I hope so."

"I'm getting a new perspective on you."

"Don't. My business interests are far ranging." Sanger jammed a brawny thumb against his thick chest. "And I don't take kindly to competition. But there are some things that turn my stomach. White slavery, taking young

American girls against their wishes to a life like that—makes me sick."

I sipped and looked at him.

"Prostitution, drugs. That ain't me. I got a lotta stuff goin'. Sure, I've got some gambling joints. I run a little booze. I got my own places I gotta stock, and I have some private clients. I don't force my booze on anyone, and everybody plays by the rules."

"Your rules."

"My rules, but everybody understands them."

"Prohibition won't last much longer."

Sanger shrugged. "I made a lot of money before. I'll make a lot after. Most of my enterprises are strictly legit. I run the politics in this town so I can keep out the riff-raff. The undesirable element." He smiled. "I'm the only game in this town."

"So I'm told. You want me to find out who was in it with Jones then?"

Sanger nodded. "We know about Cutter and Lena, but you've given us to believe they were being blackmailed by Jones. I need to know if there was anyone else."

He dug into his pocket and handed me a slip of paper. The initials SV were printed in ink at the top, and below were eight names. I didn't know any of them.

"Jonesy had that on him. I'm guessing the SV is *Sea Venture*. We'll find who those names belong to. One of my boys made one. Says he worked at the San Pedro wharves. You don't worry about those names. I'll find out. You do what I asked."

"Then what?"

"You bow out. I take it from there."

"Don't know if I can help you."

"Why is that?"

"Might be a conflict of interest with Harry. The man I work for."

"You think the people in this deal might work for Harry? Other than Cutter."

"No. I'm saying some of it could come back and bite Harry. I'm supposed to protect him from goblins."

"I don't want Harry getting hurt, either. Shame about Cutter, but I think Harry will survive that. Harry doesn't much sound like it when he talks, but he's smart and wily, and he knows his onions."

"Harry wants me to find out why Cutter was killed. He doesn't particularly care who did it because he doesn't intend to do anything about it. If he can't control the publicity, he might not be able to control the finish."

"Wants to know why so he can cover his ass?"

"This other thing, I don't know about. Maybe after I find out why Cutter was killed."

"Okay. First things first. They might be connected."

"Thought has crossed my mind."

"Fair enough. I'll tell my friend. We think we can count on you to do what's right."

By that, I knew Sanger didn't mean what was legal or fair or the Boy Scout thing to do. He meant what was right for him, Harry—and their friend.

"It's going to take a while," I said. "The next few days are going to be busy. I'll have to step easy. I'd appreciate it if I wasn't pushed."

"No problem. You got time. Things might go slow on my end, too."

CHAPTER 31

Merly, his wire-thin frame wrapped around my desk chair, frowned at me, held up the empty Canadian, and shook his head.

"Sorry about that, Merly."

He slid out of the chair. "Okay. Got a message for you from Hutto Hay over at Fox. Said he found a copy of the picture you asked about. You want a private screening, he can fix it."

"You could have written that down. Didn't have to hang around." I tapped the warm bottle. "Seein' as I'm so inhospitable."

Merly shrugged. "Nothin' else to do, anyway. See ya."

I had the phone in my hand before Merly got through the door. Hutto said this afternoon was convenient.

Hay fixed it for me to see the picture in the smallest projection room on the Fox lot, where I would have relative privacy. He handed me a piece of paper on which he had listed the pertinent information about the picture: The studio, the director, the producer, writers, photographer, cast, and running time. I scanned it and saw the names I was looking for.

Wise Wives, produced by Benny Blackmer and directed by Herb Brenon, who had a richly-deserved reputation for being wildly temperamental, had been written by former actress Louise Weber, who was now only a writer. *Wise Wives* ran a lackluster seventy-eight minutes.

The slim plot starred Weber as a wife who tried too hard to please her husband and almost lost him to the married other woman, played by Alma Rubens. The weak, restless husband rejected Rubens in the last reel and returned to his own wife. Rubens saw the light and went back to her husband. End of story.

Wally Reid had the lead role as the first husband, and Johnny Cutter the minor role of the second husband. I saw Joan Banes on the screen in the first reel and my mind instantly flashed back to the white-haired girl who had tried to climb the wall when the Homan Dennes party turned bad—the bearcat Elmo Jones had grilled that night back in '24. Joan and Thiele Garsone had small roles in *Wise Wives* as sisters, with their hair dyed bright white and identically styled. They looked so much alike they could have been sisters in real life. A dark-haired Lena Landers was almost unrecognizable in a brief bit as Weber's best friend.

The picture had done well at the box office, but tragedy struck like an irritated cobra soon after its release. Wally Reid died of a morphine overdose, trying to get over an injury. Alma Rubens and Joan Banes quickly sank deep into a booze and drug haze that eventually claimed their lives. Now, Johnny Cutter was also dead too young.

Thiele Garsone, who had married well and moved to France, escaped the jinx that seemed to surround *Wise Wives*.

I thanked Hutto and let him walk me to my car even though he was full of questions I didn't want to answer. We passed director Raoul Walsh, sitting in the warm sunshine on the steps at the back of a sound stage, smoking a

Lucky and reading the *Daily Racing Form.* A long time
ago, I had worked as a stunt rider on a horse-racing picture Walsh had done called *Should a Husband Forgive?* I
had seen him a few times since then, just enough so he
remembered me.

I hailed him and he waved back. I went over. "Working hard, I see."

"Eggs in coffee. Hope to wrap this turkey 'fore the
week's out."

"What's it called?"

"*Yellow Ticket.* Old play reborn."

Walsh regarded me with his one good eye. He had lost
his right lamp a couple of years back when a jackrabbit
crashed through the windshield of his car late one night
while he was driving across the desert. That ended his
acting career, but he kept directing. He took a drag on his
cigarette and nodded to Hutto, who had put a foot on the
bottom step beside Walsh.

"Hutt showing you how to do the job?"

"I need all the help I can get."

"Sorry about Johnny Cutter. I bet Harry York's jump-
ing like a bean. Always been glad I never worked for
Harry."

"Cutter started with Fox, you know."

"I remember Cutter hanging around, trying to get
started, but I never worked with him."

"Do you remember Joan Banes?"

"Not really. Somebody mentioned her the other day.
Died, they said. Booze and drugs. The downfall of many
of us."

"Ever work with Lena Landers?"

Walsh grinned impishly. "Not on a picture."

"How about Theile Garsone? She was once with Fox."

"Remember her." A twinkle lit his left headlight.
"Sweet young thing. Thought she might have a career,

but she dropped out of sight. Must've been six, seven years back."

"Heard she went back to France. Married a count or something."

"Back to France?" Walsh laughed. "Well, she was from Paris. Paris, Texas."

He rubbed the side of his nose with his left forefinger. "French poodle with a phony accent. I think her real name was Thomasina something-or-other."

"Thomasina?"

"Everybody called her Tommy. When you change your name from Thomasina to Thiele, people grin and remember it. Even in this town."

"You lived in Texas once, as I recall."

Walsh nodded. "Did some 'cowboying' down there for a spell, long time ago. That got me in the business, riding a horse on a treadmill in a theater."

"Everybody gets started somehow."

Walsh shook his head. "The Good Lord works his wonders."

The door behind Walsh opened and a grip stuck his head out of the darkness of the sound stage. His eyes squinted against the bright sunshine. "Ready when you are, Mr. Walsh."

Walsh stood, folded the *Daily Racing Form*, and put out his smoke. "Back to the grind."

CHAPTER 32

Johnny Cutter's funeral arrangements plodded on. Harry and his three writers huddled most of Thursday afternoon and again Friday morning, and then Harry began to inundate them with memos. Rearrange this, change that, fix it. We all thought Harry was grooming Cutter for his greatest performance. Maybe they'd both win an Academy Award.

Harry decided the funeral service would be at his studio. He could completely control every nuance—arrange the flowers, fix the set to his ideal, and work it out to every tiny detail. He had decided this was going to be the most elaborate funeral in Hollywood history. No one would be able to look back and say Harry York was a piker.

The services would be on the new Stage Ten, not only the studio's biggest sound stage but the largest in Hollywood.

The writers worked on a script for Cutter's send-off and Harry gave them Wilton Wilmette, his best director of musicals, to help them iron out the details. Canaries went into rehearsal—Harry insisted on women singers only, no men—and set designers got in everybody's way. Harry had ordered his set department to put together mas-

sive flower arrangements and sent down orders that he
had to personally approve every petal in every bouquet.
Fortunately, Wilmette convinced Harry a choreographed
dance for the funeral would be a trifle too tasteless, even
for this charade.

Harry asked Hughie Dunnum if he could gather a
hundred horses, line them up on both sides of the funeral
procession, and have them bow their heads low to the
ground when the hearse passed. Harry thought that would
make a wonderful front page picture, especially with a
big York Brothers banner stretched over the roadway facing the camera. Hughie allowed as how he didn't have
time to train the horses to do that and, anyway, nobody
could be sure the horses wouldn't raise their tails and re-
lieve themselves at the wrong time. What kind of a picture would that make?

Harry worked it around in his head and decided to dis-
pense with the horses. "That bastard Cutter bombed in the
only western I ever put him in, anyway," Harry grumped.
He then told Dunnum not to bother him with any more
lousy ideas.

Gallen and his publicity gang set to work, priming the
press, and greasing Louella and the radio heads. A rumor
surfaced that Johnny Cutter had died trying to rescue a
puppy that had fallen into his swimming pool. Or maybe
it was a baby. Gallen hadn't decided. He was merely test-
ing the waters, so to speak.

Harry decided on Tuesday for the services. It took
time to arrange such a production. Louis York was going
to the hastened *Doorway to Heaven* premiere tonight in
New York. A good box office would make for a happier
funeral. Louis would take the *Twentieth Century* out of
New York immediately after the premiere. The brothers
had to figure out what to do with the properties they had
been preparing for their late star. They had a lot of money

invested in Johnny Cutter and, privately, they were cursing him soundly for having the ingratitude to leave them in such a financial jam.

Everyone but the general public would be invited to the services, but the burial in Hollywood Memorial Park was to be a private affair. Only the studio moguls and the cream of the motion picture crop would be invited to the graveside services.

Late Friday morning, Betsy summoned me to Harry's office. His physician, Dr. Melville Carpathia, sat in the middle chair in front of the barge. The chief medical examiner for Laurel City hadn't grown but a couple of inches over five feet, and his unremarkable faced pinched like it hurt. He could go unnoticed in an empty room. Harry held the Cutter autopsy in his hands. No one else was ever going to see it. I wasn't asked to sit down. This wasn't going to take long.

"Tell him." Harry nodded to the doctor. "Just the pacific highlights."

"Mr. Cutter died of an injection of high levels of cocaine and heroin. There was also a high level of alcohol in his system, and a large dose of a particularly toxic venom from a species of snake known as *Bothrops Jararcussu*. That species is commonly found in South America."

"Argentina?"

"Argentina, Brazil, Bolivia, Paraguay."

"What was the alcohol level?"

"Almost zero point two when I tested him. That would definitely have caused loss of consciousness for a considerable period of time."

"I believe that's all you need." Harry grunted like a hog with colic. "Good work, doctor."

Harry nodded at me. The man could give you the bum's rush without getting out of his richly padded seat.

Betsy stood beside the open door when I got to it.

I turned back to Harry. "Yes, sireeee," I said and walked out.

I thought Betsy was going to collapse. She closed the door as quickly as she could, but Harry's face snarled at the autopsy, paying me no attention. Betsy gave me a wan smile. Her tired eyes looked out of a strained face.

"You holding up?"

She smiled tightly and nodded. A few strands of out-of-place hair straggled over her forehead. Betsy's hair was never out of place. "Long days."

"Tomorrow's Saturday."

"Oh, I'll have to work tomorrow. Sunday, too. The entire studio is on edge. Nobody wants to have anything to do with Harry just now, because nobody truly knows what to do or what to say."

"Harry looks like he's on dope."

"He's wearing himself out, which makes him even more irritable than usual. Eggshells have replaced the carpeting around here."

"When does his brother arrive?"

"Monday night or Tuesday morning. Depends on what train he catches. Premiere's tonight and somebody in New York is going to call in the numbers to Harry. Hope they get a connection. Hope its good news for Harry."

"He change the name of the picture?"

"No. Left it alone. He brought it up in a meeting, but the publicity people went wild. Not enough time to fix all the advertising."

"Like a zoo around here."

Betsy nodded. "And the zookeeper's crazy."

"Least the pay's good."

"What do you think keeps me going?"

CHAPTER 33

Saturday morning awoke warm and hazy. I sat by the kitchen window, sipping coffee and watching the sun burn off the haze. The voice on the radio was all about Johnny Cutter's impending funeral. It shaped up to be the biggest event in Hollywood's brief history. Services were set for two Tuesday afternoon. Authorities prepared for several thousand spectators to line the procession route from the studio to Hollywood Memorial Park.

I called Betsy and asked about Friday's premiere.

"It was a panic. They packed the theater for five consecutive showings. Harry's been dancing this morning."

"You sound pretty happy yourself."

"It's a big relief, I can tell you that."

"Louis on his way?"

"He is. Took the *Twentieth Century* overnight from New York. I heard this morning he's expected here early Tuesday on the *Chief*."

It was twenty hours from New York to Chicago by train, and sixty-three hours from Chicago to Los Angeles on the *Chief*.

"Cutting it close."

"It'll work out. Trust me. Harry and Louis have both planned it."

"Even God wouldn't mess with their planning."

"Harry's newsreel unit is already at the station arranging their set-ups. Harry will meet his brother with every important member of the studio bowing and scraping and the cameras grinding. And there will be a live radio feed."

"You and I won't be there."

Betsy laughed lightly. "I don't know about you, but Harry's got me plenty busy up through the funeral."

"Yeah. Me, too. Harry wants me in first thing Monday to go over my security plans for his big production. A lot of people will be glad when Tuesday's over."

"Better make that Wednesday. Louis is not scheduled to return until Thursday morning. That means he'll be in the studio all day Wednesday."

"Be a good day to be sick. Maybe we can go to the beach?"

"You have no idea how much I'd like that, but I'll have to wet nurse the Brothers York all day Wednesday. I only hope I can skip the going away party that night. Then Thursday I'll have to oversee the commiseration party. I don't expect to be off before Sunday, and I plan to spend that day in bed."

"Alone?"

"Asleep."

A loud commotion crackled across the line.

"What's that?"

"Harry just kicked his writers out of his office, and he's yelling like a banshee for me."

She hung up and I went back to studying the sky through my kitchen window. The haze had lifted and jays and swallows danced through the branches of a maple tree. Theo Stein had given me a copy of Jack Pershing's memoirs. I sat in a chair by the window and held the book on my lap a while, but I wasn't ready to wrap my mind around the Great War. Thirteen years later, the real thing was too vivid.

I tried William Faulkner's *Sanctuary*, found I couldn't concentrate. I took a long walk. A good way to think. I showered and shaved about six and got dudded up in my best suit, a navy pinstripe with matching vest, plain white shirt, and maroon tie with navy pinstripes angling across it. I stopped on the way to Alice's and bought a large, fresh bouquet. A prune pit, maybe, but I felt old-fashioned this Saturday night.

Promptly at eight, I knocked on the front door of Alice Windler's small, white bungalow on Cabrillo, off Palms. She accepted the flowers and put them in a tall vase while I watched her with appreciation.

Alice was an eyeful in a red crepe faille dress with a ribbed, dull surface and matching red lacing on the bodice, her small, firm breasts showing no cleavage. Alice was tall. In her black suede shoes—with Louis heels and leather trim, strapped around the ankles and cut like opera pumps—she was only an inch or two shorter than me. The dress had wrist length sleeves, with more lacing just below the elbows. Get-ups like that were meant for a long, slender chassis like hers. Her festoon necklace—colored in reds, greens, and blues—fitted high around the base of her creamy throat because of her high neckline.

The flowers arranged, she stood in front of a small mirror by a fireplace and put her hat in place. The smart, shallow-crowned, black hat with a little black bow on the front crown fit snugly over her waved, light brown hair cut to barely cover her neck. The hat, wired around the edges, jauntily stayed where she tilted it.

Her black suede, slip-on gloves each had a row of six glistening, black buttons lined up to face each other if she pressed her palms together. She picked up a small, black calfskin clutch purse, higher than it was wide. She snapped the silver latch and was ready to go. I looked her over. Wide at the shoulders, narrow at the skirt hem, slim at the waist. She was the perfect picture right out of the fall fashion magazines. Alice flashed her lovely white teeth. She was much prettier than I had remembered— and I remembered her as being a good-looking broad.

She was twenty-five, with smooth, unblemished skin and large sparkling brown eyes. Her pert nose accentuated full red lips not drowning under the weight of too much lipstick. Her slightly rosy high cheeks added to the waterproof face. A night of dinner and dancing with Alice Windler stacked up to be a lovely evening.

Reservations were for nine at the swanky Laurel Beach House, north of Laurel City on a high bluff overlooking the Pacific. The long, low-shaped, stone and wood building featured a large bar on the north side, several dozen round dining tables in the center of the main room, and rows of curtained booths along the south and east sides. Open booths on the west wall were set against large bay windows offering stunning views of the ocean. A big band played modern favorites and the large dance floor allowed the struggles and the smudgers to discount the floorflushers and the heelers. A guarded staircase west of the bar led to the private basement casino, which offered a full line of games of chance. And all on the up-and-up, it was rumored.

The place belonged to Mack Sanger.

The yellow-orange sun cooled itself in the ocean when I pulled into the north lot. We dawdled an easy quarter-hour on a stone patio that ran the length of the west side of the beach house, watching the sun go out and feeling the gentle sea breeze on our faces.

The Laurel Beach had several specialties in liquor and

food. Mack didn't bother hiding the booze or making any bones about it. Nobody was going to raid his joint. His steaks were thick and juicy and his seafood freshly caught.

The maître d' led us to an intimate booth on the west side, far enough from the dance floor and the band so the music wouldn't overwhelm our conversation. The sun, sinking into the ocean's rim, offered a spectacular view. Alice ordered a dry, Royal Manhattan cocktail, and sipped it slowly and daintily. I had a whiskey and water, which I didn't sip particularly slowly and not daintily at all.

We both decided on porterhouse steaks—hers rare, mine medium—smothered in sautéed mushrooms, with baked potatoes swimming in butter, along with the house salad. The steaks and everything else were perfect. Alice was darb, too.

We ate and ordered another round of drinks for dessert. Mack Sanger appeared, wearing a white dinner jacket over a lacy, white shirt and a black bow tie slightly askew. He shook my hand and smiled at Alice.

"You don't brighten up the joint much," he said to me, "but your charming companion certainly does."

I introduced them. Alice didn't seem to know who Sanger was, definitely a point in her favor. He told her he owned the place, but didn't tell her anything else.

"No handcuffs?" He grinned at her. "This drugstore cowboy turns out to be a flat tire, give me a whistle."

After some chit-chat with Alice—me mostly listening, only occasionally joining in—he asked me about the Cutter send-off. He planned to be there. He was, of course, invited to the private graveside services. So, he said, was Randall Curtiss.

"Sounds like Harry's turning the thing into the grandest circus this side of Moscow," Sanger mused.

"Nobody's turning out to say goodbye to Johnny Cutter. They just aim to glom Harry's sockdollager."

Sanger nodded. "He's pulling out the stops, all right."

"Most entertaining funeral in history."

Sanger bowed slightly to Alice. "You and Father Time have a good evening."

Alice showed gameness taking to the dance floor with me. The band went into "Heartaches" and followed with "Sweet and Lovely." The piano player touched off "When I Take My Sugar to Tea," and we came back to the table, leaving the floor to the hoppers. Alice went to the powder room and I opened the folded check tucked under my plate.

"Save your kale. On me and happy to do it." The scrawled handwriting had to be Sanger's. "But you can leave a big tip. By the way, that's an air-tight woman. You could do worse than get her insured."

We had a third drink each, but Alice begged off a fourth. I had to drive and did the same. We danced through a couple more numbers and left. When we got in the Chevy, Alice handed me a piece of paper.

"That's the number you wanted," she said, smiling sweetly. "Now you can dump me if you want."

"Not what I had in mind," I said.

Alice kept smiling.

CHAPTER 34

I slid the Chevy into a shady spot in front of the soldiers' home in Sawtelle, early Sunday afternoon, and finally got around to looking at the dope Alice had given me the night before. She had printed a phone number and an address in Beverly Hills, along with a name—Thomasina Edith Garston, owner of the Cadillac Town Brougham I had ridden in to Joan's graveside services. I let out a long breath and stared at the blue, nearly cloudless early afternoon sky.

Another beautiful day, but a storm nobody else could hear rumbled in the distance.

Nels was sitting in the sun in nearly the same place as the last time I saw him, watching a military band set up for an afternoon concert. Nurse Brownlee sat beside him, but she wasn't reading to him. His knit cap covered his ears, and a wool sweater stuck out underneath the blanket around his wasted body. I kissed Nels on the forehead. He gave me a weak squeeze with his right hand and smiled. Nurse Brownlee started to rise and excuse herself.

"Please, stay. Listen to the concert with us."

She smiled and nodded. "That would be very nice. There are some extra chairs on the corner of the veranda. I'll get one."

"Allow me."

I sat the chair to Nelson's left just as the band's twelve pieces started sawing. They played a mixture of modern tunes, Souza marches, and old favorites. They played well and alternated up-tempo and slow works, finishing with a popular gospel tune, "Take My Hand, Precious Lord." When the band finished, Nurse Brownlee excused herself. She had duties to see to.

I told Nels about Jones. I told him every detail and left out nothing. When I was done, he had a wry smile on his sunken face and a fire suddenly in his eyes that had long been absent.

"Darb," he said weakly. I had to put my ear to his mouth to hear him. "I think the force can do without that goon." He gave me another weak squeeze. "I know we can."

He let go of my hand and made a motion with his right index finger, simulating a man pulling the trigger of a gun. I shook my head.

"I can't do it," I said softly.

"Doing me a favor—" His voice was so weak I could barely hear him.

I felt tears welling. "I can't do it, Nels."

"I know. Don't worry—it's not so bad. I'll soon go west, anyway."

We beat our gums a while, me doing most of the talking, and little of it was meaningful. The only meaning was two brothers sitting together in the fading afternoon light, trying desperately to hang on to the few healthy parts left of each other.

Nels fell asleep about four-thirty and I sat there quietly another thirty minutes. The old soldiers would come out soon to take down the flag. I spotted my old man on the veranda, staring at us, wearing a black suit, the coat opened to show red suspenders. He watched us several minutes and I held my breath he might come to us, but he turned and went inside. I found him on the outside steps leading up to the front door, dragging on a Lucky Strike.

"You kill him?"

Circles of smoke hung in the air and drifted away.

"No, Dad."

Cold, glassy eyes looked me over. "Lotta cops think you did."

"I beat him. I beat him hard, but he was alive when I left that alley."

"What the hell have you turned into? You're not the son I brought up."

The sun hung low now, sending long shadows across the parking lot and up the steps where we sat. There hadn't been much of a breeze all day, but now the air had as much life to it as a moldy stump.

"You know who killed him?"

"I can't prove anything. And even if I could, the man who killed Jones is pretty much out of anybody's reach."

"What kind of people are you dealing with?"

I had no easy way to wire him about Harry York, Mack Sanger, and Randall Curtiss. Tough, rich bastards who got what they wanted or made somebody pay for what they didn't get. What could I tell the old man about three people as shallow as Johnny Cutter, Joan Banes, and Lena Landers, who did what they did without thought of anyone else? "The kind who don't think like most people," I said at last.

A long silence hovered while the old man dragged on the Lucky. "Well, keep your neck tucked in."

That sounded a little bit like fatherly concern. We looked at each other, but there was nothing in his eyes.

I changed the subject. "Nels was asleep when I left him. A military band played and he stayed awake for it. Enjoyed it."

"Yeah, I saw them leave."

I raised my eyebrows. "How long you been here? I just saw you."

He almost smiled. "You been off the force too long. Good cop would have seen me. I watched the two of you for fifteen, twenty minutes. I was standing back on the veranda, near the door. You should have seen me."

I shook my head. "You didn't have to hide."

"Not hiding." He scowled at me. "Didn't want to interrupt, that's all."

"Don't know why you'd think that. What could be more natural than a father and two sons—"

"Don't know that I got more than one son." He stood and ground out his cigarette. "Time I went to see him."

I didn't watch as he went up the steps and through the door. I had a feeling he stood up there a while, watching me before he went inside. Staring at my back while I stared at nothing. Maybe he didn't. It was just a feeling.

I sat there a long time, watching shadows disappear as twilight settled down on the land like a soft, dark sheet. I had something I had to do even if I didn't want to. Trouble was I really didn't know what I wanted to do.

I got in the Chevy and drove toward Beverly Hills.

CHAPTER 35

I stopped at a drug store near Beverly and Sunset. I found a phone booth in the back corner and gave the operator the number Alice Windler had given me. A man answered. His voice sounded vaguely familiar.

"Sorry, wrong number." I hung up.

Somebody was home.

I soon found Camas Drive, a short unpaved road that circled east. I drove past the address I was looking for, not being able to see much of the house from the street. There was no wall and the drive was open, lined by a row of maple trees obscuring the house. It was the only house on Camus Drive. I parked down the road out of sight, took the .45 out of the glove box, and slipped it into the pocket of a lightweight flogger I kept rolled up in the back of the Chevy. I put on the coat and turned up the collar. I pulled my fedora low and walked back toward the house. The slight cut of moon gave off only a faint shine.

I went up the driveway and saw several lights glowing softly in the windows of the California style, white stucco ranch with a red tile roof the color of dried blood. A two-car garage attached itself to the east side of the house and a wide parking area beside the garage would easily hold five autos. I looked in the window cut into the east side of the garage and saw a light blue Chrysler 70 Roadster and the black-and-tan Cadillac Town Brougham I had ridden in to the cemetery with Lena Landers.

I walked around to the small back lawn, stood on the small empty patio, and looked through the window by the door. I could see a tiny foyer and a piece of the kitchen. I tried the door, but the knob wouldn't turn.

I walked around the house toward the west, looking through the windows into the lighted rooms. Most of the blinds were drawn but I could see into the window on the front left corner. Shadowy forms of a man and a woman filtered through the curtains. The man—tall, beefy, and broad-shouldered—had his back to me, his face hidden. The front window gave me a better view. The black-haired knockout, her hair cut in a Louise Brooks bob, wore a loose-fitting, yellow silk blouse with padded shoulders and tailored navy slacks pleated in the front.

The tall man stood by the fireplace, wearing a striped sports jacket and dark trousers. The woman paced slowly as they talked, her hands working overtime.

The tall goon stepped forward and grabbed the woman by the shoulders, holding her firmly but apparently causing no physical pain. He was doing some hard talking. I got a good look at his flat face then, and a cold hand slapped me across the jaw. The goon was Hiram Strakowsky, one-time partner of Elmo Jones before his talent for graft got him tossed from the force.

I stepped to the front door and pounded the brass knocker against the polished oak. I stopped after four hard licks, waited three seconds, and pounded again three times. I was about to hit the knocker once more when I heard a scraping noise and saw the knob turn slowly. My right hand closed around the handle of the Colt in my pocket, lifting it up. The door opened a crack and I saw

Hiram's scowling face. I put my weight to the door and pushed hard with my shoulder. Strakowsky staggered backward. I slammed a forearm across his chest. He tumbled to the hardwood floor, losing his grip on the Smith & Wesson .45 semi-automatic in his hand. The gat bounced toward the fireplace.

The woman screamed and reached for the .45. I swung my automatic toward her, but she had no eyes for me. Her beautiful face froze in a harsh mask, her large, dark eyes spitting hatred. She pointed the gun at Hiram and pulled the trigger twice. The .45 barked loudly in the confined room. The explosions opened the hurt in my head. Strakowsky jerked on the floor. One of the slugs missed him, but the other found his chest, a little left of center.

"You bastard," the woman yelled. Her black eyes smoldered.

She squeezed the trigger a third time and I heard the bullet slam into Strakowsky's limp body. I jumped toward her, slashing the edge of my hand against her gun arm. The roscoe fell with a heavy thud against the flagstone hearth. She grabbed her arm and shrieked in pain, or maybe it was simply a cry of overwhelming hatred. She tried to pick up the .45. I caught the fragrance of roses and jasmine as I leaned in against her.

"Leave it be, sister."

She blinked at me and took an involuntary step backward. She started screaming, like a voice in a Universal horror picture. I slapped her hard. She buried her face in her hands and racking sobs shook her entire frame. I looked at Strakowsky. The second bullet had struck just below his ear. Ghastly dark fluid spread out across the sea green rug beneath his head.

I grabbed the doll and pulled her into the next room. A smaller room, with a short sofa and three matching, over-stuffed chairs in Queen Anne design, just like in Harry's office, but the leather was beige. A couple of unlit floor lamps filled opposite corners. A large desk sat near a window, the lamp on it lit. A small crystal bottle marked *Joy de Jean Patou* glinted in the light. A golden silk thread wrapped the neck and when I lifted the cap the rose and jasmine perfume overpowered me.

The woman started screaming again. I slapped her once more, harder, and dumped her on the sofa. She stopped trying to split my ears and looked at me, breathing hard. Her wild, hate-filled eyes reminded me of Elmo Jones.

"Stay put." I pulled the Colt from my coat pocket and waved it in a tight little circle, hoping the sight of the gun would freeze her.

She reacted as if she hadn't heard me. I don't think she even knew I was in the room. She stared blankly, all the while cursing the dead man in the front room. I had seen her face before. The same face that seduced the camera in the 1925 publicity still Jimmy Gallen had given me. The same face I had seen on the screen in *Wise Wives*. The same face I had seen Jones putting the screws to at the Dennes party seven years ago, not far from where we were now.

"You ought to use a different perfume, Joan."

Her eyes hardened even more as she looked at me for the first time. I think I heard a small hiss escape her lips. I told her again to stay put, but I was sure she didn't hear me.

I went into the other room and knelt beside Strakowsky. His shoulder holster was empty but I found a snub-nose strapped to his ankle. Using my pocket mop, I unstrapped his throw-down piece and put it in his right hand, stuffing his forefinger through the trigger guard. I pointed it at the fireplace and pulled his finger. A slug slammed into the mantel. I moved the gun slightly left and sent another bullet into the back of the chair. I let the gun slip from his hand. It fell on his belt and slid to the floor. I unfastened his shoulder holster and threw it beside the front door, along with the ankle strap. I was guessing neither of those guns was registered, certainly not to Hiram.

I went into the other room. Joan Banes was still on the little sofa, calmly smoking a Parliament. I sat on the edge of a chair, watching her, keeping the Colt where she could see it.

After a while, I said softly, "Talk to me, Joan."

"What do you want?"

Her voice was thin and faraway.

"Maybe I want to pick up where Elmo Jones left off."

Her black eyes hooded before showing some life. I don't know what she was thinking, but she was doing plenty of it. If she had been in shock, she was out of it in a hurry. It occurred to me she had just been acting.

"I don't know what you're talking about. If this is a robbery—"

"It isn't. You know who I am and you know why I'm here. Maybe you don't know how I found you, but you know why I'm here."

"Please enlighten me."

"You're a pretty good actress, Joan, and a pretty good shot. But I know why you got out of the picture business."

"Do tell."

I slowly ticked off names, carefully watching her expression

"Dorothea Gardner. Joan Banes. Johnny Cutter. Thiele Garsone. Lena Landers. Elmo Jones. Jimmy Gallen. Carmine Broglio."

Her expression didn't change when I spoke each name.

"Winnie Kramer." A slight flash lit her eyes. That name didn't register with her. "I'll bring you up to date on her later," I said.

"You might as well kill me now because I will call the police and I can give them a perfect description of you. I will tell them you broke in and killed Hiram."

"Buttons, dear Joan, are the last people on earth you want to see just now. Among other things, they take fingerprints."

I held up a hand, fingers spread. I tapped the barrel of the Colt against my forefinger.

"Let's start with your real name. Dorothea Gardner. You killed your parents in 1918. With a fireplace poker, a Cape Girardeau fella told me. Left a lot of evidence behind. Bloody fingerprints. A bloody dress. Pretty sloppy, but you were in a hurry. Took the family car, ran it into a river, and somehow made your way here. How am I doing?"

"Your fantasy, Abercrombie. My name is Thomasina Garston."

"You changed your looks. White dye job, cut shorter. Some cosmetic changes done with makeup. Got hooked up as an extra. Changed your name to Joan Banes."

"You'd make a good scenario writer. But prune pits are out of style."

Her voice was stronger now and her dull eyes searched my face.

"You were at a party not far from here in July 1924 when a drunken second-rate actor named Henderson Pettigrew found out the hard way he couldn't fly. The buttons came and you tried to climb over the garden wall in the moonlight. Nice scene if the lighting's right. Bull named Elmo Jones stopped you and grilled you. I was there. Once upon a time Jonesy was my partner. After Hiram."

Her eyes began to show interest in me.

"Some paper came out from the Missouri cops after you lammed. LAPD gets a lot of paper and most of it gets posted and forgotten. But Jonesy read that paper and made you. You were nervous beyond reason the night Pettigrew died. You were plenty scared but not because of Jonesy's act. You being so bent made him hinky. He glommed the paper at headquarters and put your pan to it, but he wasn't about to collar you for anything. He saw a meal ticket. He saw a budding picture queen with murder behind her and mazuma around her, and Jonesy knew how to write himself into that scene."

Her eyes closed and her head rolled back. Her breath came in short, sharp gasps.

"You might have had a career in the pictures. Had a good part in a few of them, one called *Wise Wives*, but you were hanging on a shaky limb. Jonesy had found you despite the change in your looks and your name. If a dumb flatfoot like him could blunder into you, then someone with brains might do the same. You had to get out of the picture business. And Jones respected that. You were still valuable to him, but not in jail."

She took a long breath and her lovely head bobbed a little.

"When your money dried up, Jones blackmailed you into a prostitution ring that soon turned to white slavery."

She swung her head at me. "Tell that static to Sweeney."

"There's a man down at the Laurel City docks saw you with Lena and Jones. Carmine Broglio hired him to watch *Sea Venture*. He knows all about what was going on, and he made you."

"You can't prove any of that."

"Okay. Let's me and you and the bulls go down there and see him."

I don't know which opened wider, her eyes or her mouth. She had suddenly gone from resigned to frightened.

"That whole nasty business finally caught up to Jones. I'm sure you've seen the newspapers. I guess you thought you were out of it with him bumped off. I think you figured you could get around Hiram."

"I had nothing to do with any of it."

"You can tell that to the man who had Jones killed over this mess. All I have to do is give him your name and tell him where to find you. You were working that ring out of his backyard down in Laurel City and he takes that sort of thing very personally."

"How much do you want?"

"Good question. But answer a few more of mine first. What I do next depends greatly on your answers. Don't think you can lie to me. Lies will only get you a hard send-off. Maybe even worse than what happened to Jones."

There was no fight left in her. "What do you want to know?"

"Tell me about Johnny Cutter. Tell me about Thiele Garsone. And Lena Landers. Start with Cutter."

"I met Johnny a few months after I came to Hollywood. We both started as extras. We started getting noticed and got better work. We fell in love on the set of *Wise Wives*. I told him about my past. I knew I could trust him. We were goofy for each other."

"I think you told him because a bull had his horns in you and you thought you could talk Cutter into killing Jones. If he got Jones off your back, you could deal with Johnny. Problem was Jonesy buffaloed Cutter. Jones didn't worry about mugs like that. Jones dragged Johnny into his scheme to sell young women to slavers because Johnny had a lot of contacts. He was a famous picture star, and handsome, and frails flocked to him. And he had secrets in his past. Maybe Jones wired those secrets. Maybe Cutter was just afraid he'd find out."

"Because Johnny knew about me, Jones said it was the same as if Cutter had helped me kill my—my—"

"Skip the theatrics. Cutter knew about you, sure, but Jones scared him and he went along. Cutter was all celluloid. What about Lena?"

"Johnny fell for her and told her about me one night when he was zozzled. He told her about Jones. Johnny was desperate for a way out and begged Lena to help. But Lena knowing about me was all Jones needed to rope her in, same as Johnny. We were all scared to death of that man. We knew he had killed people while hiding behind his badge. We had to do what he wanted, or he would have ruined us all."

"Thiele?"

"Her, too. She was part of the circle."

"Tied to the same bag as the rest of you and slung over Jonesy's shoulder."

"Only Thiele fought back. She tried to get Jones and he—he—he shot her full of dope and hid her out and kept shooting her up. He liked to have killed her with the junk."

"And seeing what happened to her kept the rest of you in line."

"It scared us plenty. All we could do was what he wanted. He would have killed any one of us at any time if we defied him."

"And anything you did would have landed Missouri on your head. And washed up Lena and Cutter."

She squirmed on the sofa. "Yes. Yes."

"Carmine Broglio?"

"Johnny knew him when they were kids. He was a hoodlum in New York and came out here after some shooting back in March. A gangster or something. He and Johnny were from the same neighborhood and somehow he found out Johnny worked at York. He found Johnny and somehow found out about us. He wanted a lot of money to keep quiet."

"Carmine wanted in. He tried to bleed Jones and Jones killed him."

"Yes."

"How much does Jimmy Gallen know?"

"Everything about me. Johnny told him when he signed with York. He knew Gallen would protect him."

"The girls?"

"Jimmy didn't know about that. He always thought there was something else going on, but he didn't know what. After Jones had a talk with him one night, Jimmy didn't want to know anything else about us."

"You killed Cutter because he couldn't take it anymore. He was holding himself together with booze and about to crack."

"No. No. I didn't kill Johnny. It was Jones."

"Convince me."

"Johnny took off to San Francisco when Carmine disappeared. He was scared. I think Jones was, too. The body of that gangster should have been found in Johnny's house and, when it wasn't, Jones got worried. He had a man watching Cutter. The man tailed Johnny to Frisco and when he told Jones, Jones made Johnny come home. Johnny called me that night, wanted me to come over, said he just couldn't take it anymore. Only that man out there—"

She nodded her head toward the living room, where the late Hiram Strakowsky was planning his next scam.

"—he was here. He listened in on the other line and called Jones. Jones made me go to Johnny's. He stayed outside when we got there. Johnny was already fried and he was still drinking. I tried to calm him down and he tried to make love to me, but he was too drunk. I lay with him in the bed until he passed out. Then Jones came in. He took a hypo out of his pocket and gave it to Johnny. Said Johnny wouldn't talk to anyone, anymore."

"That was a mixture of dope and snake poison. Jones got the poison from the Argentines he was in business with, right?" She nodded. "It was a simple thing for you or Jones to shoot that junk into Cutter while he was passed out," I continued. "He would have died pretty quickly from that mix."

"'The lucky slob won't feel anything.' I remember Jones saying that."

I flashed on two empty O'Keefe bottles in Cutter's kitchen. I pictured Jones sitting there, drinking his beer, and waiting.

"Who was the plant watching Cutter. Recognize him?"

"I don't know his name. Orry something. He was one of the sailors who went out with us on the yacht. One of the crew."

"That leaves Thiele. And that's partly my fault. I insisted on going to see her because I thought she was you. Gallen told me you were Cutter's sister and I fell for it. But you had changed places with Thiele. You looked enough alike to pull it off, especially since Jones had her hooked on junk and booze and she looked twice as old as she was and her mind was jingled. You people should have killed her sooner than you did."

"How did we know you would dig the whole thing up? Jones wanted to kill her right away when I told him Jimmy said you were digging around, but we begged him not to. I don't know why, but he gave in as long as we kept Thiele under wraps. Several years ago, Jones helped me change places with Thiele so that she became Joan Banes and I became Thomasina Garston."

"Living a quiet life in your little Beverly Hills dream home. Off the scratch you made selling baby vamps like Winnie Kramer."

"Who's she."

"A kid you sent to that boat. An extra at York."

"I'm sorry for her."

"That'll square things. When you found out I wanted to talk with Joan Banes, you knew you had to do something. Kill Thiele and get her buried as yourself. Shut off a lot of questions. You were in her rooms the morning I was there."

"Yes. I was hiding in the bedroom closet."

"You shot her up that morning, expecting the dope to kill her. But she was still alive when I got there. When I left to call an ambulance, you finished her off. How?"

"I smothered her with a pillow. I thought that with all that dope in her system that's all anybody would look at."

"Yeah, nobody was wasting any time over a kicked hophead. Gallen know?"

"Not until he showed up. My car was outside. He saw it."

"Blue Chrysler roadster?"

She nodded. "Jimmy came in just as I was—just as I was—It was too late to save her. He told me to scram because you were coming. I got out as fast as I could. He told me later he locked the door and was beating on it when you came."

I stared over her shoulder, not seeing anything. I was drinking in a speak while Joan Banes was draining the life out of Thiele Garsone.

"I left the door unlocked. When I saw Gallen beating on it, I thought he popped her." She didn't respond. "A picture was missing from the wall?" said. "What was it?"

"Me, Thiele, and Johnny. We didn't want you to see it."

"That would have got me thinking, okay. What about those other pictures on the wall, signed to Joan?"

"Mine. I took them over that morning and hung them on the wall. Just something else to make you think she was Joan."

"Trouble is you people thought I was a pushover for any line Gallen fed me. You hadn't counted on me digging into your background. It didn't occur to any of you that I might dig out a copy of *Wise Wives* and screen it. That I might run the plates on that Town Brougham you let Lena take to the funeral. That was a big mistake."

"Johnny's idea. He thought you might do that because he was beginning to understand what you were doing. He thought it would force a showdown with Jones. He thought you could take out Jones and you'd be easier to take care of."

"Cutter was an actor. Brains were not his long suit."

"We were trying to find a way out. We were twisting in the air. Going from one mad scheme to the next."

"You people should have hired a good screenwriter. Jones use you to kill Carmine? He didn't do it himself."

"No. No. I swear I had nothing to do with that." She looked up at me briefly, the light of defiance in her eyes. "I didn't know anything about it until Johnny told me. I can even prove where I was that morning."

"Okay. I'm going to call the cops. Keep your mouth shut and they might not find out who you really are. Get a good lawyer and clam up. Don't tell the buttons anything, and especially don't lie to them." I took her chin in my hand and lifted her face so I could look in her eyes. "Hiram is a clean case of self-defense. Don't spill about him. Ask for a lawyer and clam. If they dig and wire you, the Missouri boys will crawl all over you and the California boys won't have a better reason to keep you. The only way the boys here will find out you killed Thiele is if you tell them. If you don't want your neck stretched, keep your mouth shut and let your lawyer do the talking. Cutter and Thiele and anything else won't matter. Nobody can prove anything."

"I don't have much money. Jones never gave me much more than what I needed to live on. Kept me in this house to impress those young girls I invited over. Gave me the Brougham for the same reason."

"Jones gave you that car?" She nodded. "He put it in your name so it couldn't be traced to him."

"Yes, I know. You can have what I've got if you just let me go. You can get rid of Hiram's body and keep me out of this. I'll make it worth your while."

"Forget it. You'll need all the dough you've got for a good mouthpiece."

I called the Beverly Hills police station. A sergeant answered the phone. I told him there had been a shooting, apparently in self-defense, and told him to bring a body bag. I walked down to the Chevy. I put Hiram's shoulder rig and ankle strap in the back, drove my boiler to the house, and parked in front of the garage.

A half-dozen uniformed cops showed up and locked down the scene, stashing the woman in a separate room from me. They asked no questions. Two of them stayed with the skirt, two with me. The other two made sure Hiram didn't run off.

Two plainclothes detectives arrived several minutes later. Those boys asked the questions. A uniformed cop showed the detectives the bullet holes in the mantel and in the chair. They checked the gun beside Hiram and called it a clue.

"Looks like he shot twice. Missed both times. Took one in the chest and one in the head."

They bagged both guns.

I showed the two detectives my York Brothers identification card and they got polite. I told them I didn't know anything about the shooting, I was just making a social call. They sized up the twist in the other room and gave me a knowing leer.

They questioned the woman. The only thing she said was, "I want a lawyer." She kept repeating it the way a novice actress firmly follows the instructions of a seasoned film director.

Finally, the lab boys showed. They fingerprinted Hiram and put him in a body bag. They printed me, apologizing for disturbing a member of the motion-picture community. They took their fingerprint kit into the other room. I heard Joan scream defiantly, but they printed her anyway. The detectives told her she needed to leave the house, but could go where she wanted as long as they knew where. They told her to be available for more questioning.

She said her lawyer would call them.

They told me to go home, but to stay available.

I didn't argue. Pre-production on Johnny Cutter's big send-off was almost over and the *Real McCoy* was about to start.

CHAPTER 36

The AAEF victory parade in New York was a barn dance compared to the York Brothers lot when I pulled in at six the next morning. I went directly to Jimmy Gallen's office. I knew he'd be there early. Harry York was putting the finishing touches on his preparations for Johnny Cutter's Technicolor funeral, and everyone who worked there was on notice.

Gallen said hello. I didn't. I ignored him and watched the bustle around the lot through the spotless sliding door. A little past six, and the place was on fire.

"Beverly Hills buttons pinched Joan Banes last night at Thiele Garsone's place," I said.

"Yes," he answered cautiously, turning to stare out the door with me. His plain, dark blue suit had no frills, no mop in the breast pocket, no stickpin. He looked as if he had aged ten years in the past week.

"She would have called you. She killed Hiram Strakowsky just before the bulls showed."

"She talking?"

"I told her not to. She kept asking for a lawyer last night. Said she'd call one this morning. Maybe you want to check with her."

"I might."

"I don't know what those Beverly boys will do. They've only been in business about four years and they work overtime to protect their own. They printed Joan. If they dig, they'll find out about her past. In which case, Missouri will be all over her."

"I'm a little behind you."

"She keeps her mouth shut, the less chance anyone here will dig into her past. You'd be better off if they didn't."

"Yes, I see."

"She killed Cutter. She and Jones. Proof will be hard to come by, but you might want to cover that angle anyway. That kind of publicity could turn nasty."

"You haven't told Harry?"

"Harry doesn't care who killed his star. He wants to make sure no dirt gets shoveled on his little kingdom."

"There won't be."

"You know Joan killed Thiele."

"Anything she did that does not personally affect Harry is of no consequence."

"No bad press?"

"No bad press."

"No pangs of conscience?"

"Not in this business. You check your conscience at the door when you take this job. You do what needs to be done."

"Broom and a rug."

"Broom and a rug. Oughta be my slogan."

I headed for the door.

"We do what needs to be done to protect this studio, Neil," Gallen said to my back. "Nothing else matters. We'll work around it."

I walked out and bumped into Merly. Harry was looking for me. I should meet him at the front door to the main building.

"All right if I just bow? Skip the hand-kissing."

Merly grinned and scurried off.

Harry stood impatiently at the door, growling orders to one of Betsy's assistants—a short, plump bug-eyed Betty named Hilda. Harry wanted us to walk with him from the front gate to Stage Ten. He wanted to rope off a circuitous route from the gate to the stage so the sheer size of his lot would impress the visiting moguls and near moguls. It would reinforce his stature as one of the industry's major studios. He ordered most of his thousand-plus employees to be outside when the procession entered before the services, then to move to the after-services route so they could stand in a long line and bow their heads when the hearse bearing Johnny Cutter passed from the lot. A few of the pictures in production were on tight schedules so Harry would allow them to keep working. He ordered every "no admittance" light on every stage to be lit, regardless of whether shooting was in progress.

Everything needed to be in its proper place. Harry had no color productions on the schedule, but he rented every color camera the Technicolor people could spare and placed them just outside various stages, with workers ready to start carrying them inside as the procession passed. He ordered his best equipment put where it could easily be seen, and equipment showing wear and tear hidden. Everything would be painted, whitewashed, cleaned, and wrapped in satin Christmas ribbons.

We walked. Harry talked. I listened. Hilda made copious notes. It took nearly three hours but we finally got back to the main building. Harry told Hilda to type her notes immediately, to give a copy to Miss Hammerlin and one to me. Hilda bowed and scraped, and fled for her typewriter.

"You need to have everything ready before I leave today so I can review it," Harry said. "I'm meeting my brother first thing in the morning. I don't want him to see anything out of place. Understand?"

"Your brother will be impressed, even if he doesn't want to be."

"Good. Good." He took my arm and stepped closer. "Anything on what we discussed regarding Cutter?"

"All silk."

"Good. Good. I want a full report from you as soon as you can do it, but wait until after the funeral. After my brother goes home." He patted my shoulder and opened the door. "Good work. You and Gallen both. You deserve raises. Unfortunately, as you know, the recent business climate has been...unfavorable. We all of us have to tighten our pants under the present situation. But you certainly do have my award."

The door closed, leaving me alone with Harry's award. I had a gutful of Harry's award.

Harry did another review just before sunset. He pronounced himself very pleased. Then Hilda jotted down a long list of changes he wanted made before morning. The changes kept us busy all night, and we were just finishing when Harry's dark red, black-trimmed Rolls Royce Tourer pulled through the side gate about daylight. Harry wasn't with his brother. He wanted to stop at the studio before meeting Louis at the depot. Sometime during a sleepless night, he had decided on more changes. The last he'd be able to make.

"I want you at the station to keep an eye on things. You can get back here before the funeral starts."

"To keep an eye on things."

"That's what I pay you for."

Harry got to the station about an hour ahead of his brother's train. He had time to move some of the newsreel cameras and give the crew final instructions.

Some reporters and radio people were already there,

but Harry refused to let any of his people speak on the radio.

"This is a sad occasion," Harry told the gathering. "A great motion picture star, a fine gentleman, and upstanding citizen has left us much too soon. While I understand his legend of fans want to deserve his final passing, we must, all of us in the business, along with the many newspaper and radio people, remain decorable."

"Thank God he didn't talk into a microphone," producer Milton Levy said later.

Nor did the newspaper boys quote him. I guess they didn't think it *decorable* to do so.

Most of Harry's top execs waited until the last minute to appear. A lookout, stationed on a tall building down the railroad line, had orders to wave a huge flag that belonged to the prop department when the train bearing Louis York came into view. A few minutes before seven, the flag waved. Several high-priced, fancy cars appeared a few moments later, managing to get up close to where the *Chief* was to stop because they had planned it that way.

I hopped in my Chevy and peeled back to the studio. From the little balcony on the top floor of the main studio building, I got a good view of the funeral procession when it turned off Sunset Boulevard and rolled through the front gates.

A little more than two thousand turned out for Johnny Cutter's going away party. It lasted about three hours from the time Harry's Rolls glided grandly through the gate until the last car in the procession had rolled back onto Sunset.

The services inside the massive Stage Ten began with Harry's chorus girls, all dressed in modest black, singing three hymns chosen by the musical department and approved by Harry.

"Hymns," Theo Stein scoffed. "The only thing those dames know about that is it's the bottom of a dress."

Harry ordered his writers to pen eulogies, calling upon all their skills, and Harry had them passed out to actors to say at the funeral. He wanted the eulogies memorized.

"If they are memorized," he said, "they can speak from the heart. Be more sincere."

Harry didn't trust the clergy, so he hired a stage actor from Canada to deliver the main message. A tall, cadaverous man dressed in flowing robes provided by the prop department, he delivered his lines—compliments of the Wolheim brothers—with impeccable precision. He didn't have to memorize them. He carried a Bible with his lines pasted on six-by-nine cards and glued to several pages. Solemnly, he turned the pages, pulled off his act without a snag, and then was quickly hustled off the lot by Tay Fishback and put on a train. In his inside breast pocket was a long, white envelope thick with U.S. C-notes.

The chorus girls launched into "Whispering Hope" as six of Harry's top male leads carried out the casket. Loudspeakers along the route broadcast the hymn, which ended exactly the moment the hearse eased through the gate, thanks to a simple relay setup.

The long procession started up Sunset Boulevard, an unmarked police car in the front with its lights flashing. Several motorcycle cops rode their iron along both sides of the procession and two followed behind. Traffic cops along the way had been told by the police chief to salute when the hearse went by. I knew those boys well enough to know what some of those salutes would be.

The main gate closed behind the last car in the procession and I turned to leave. Theo was at the door to the balcony, watching the long line of cars disappearing down Sunset. "No rewrites on that script. Print it."

"Didn't hear you come up."

"Just got here." He wiped away a non-existent tear. "I needed solitude after such an emotional experience."

"You'd think Harry would shut down the studio for a day of mourning."

"What mourning? Cutter's picture is a panic. As for its star, there's always another Johnny Cutter. Besides, shutting the studio down midweek would cost a lot of money."

"The studio can stay open, Theo. I'm going home."

"If I ask you a question, will you answer it honestly?"

"I won't lie to you."

"Was Cutter murdered? That's the rumor."

"What does it matter? Harry says it was an accident."

"I'm a big enough cynic not to believe that. And a big enough hypocrite to accept it."

"You and me both."

"Harry said a moth of epic proportions would spring up around the death of Johnny Cutter." I stared at him. Theo grinned. "Harry meant myth."

I went home and collapsed.

I called Lena Landers on Wednesday morning and asked if I could stop by that afternoon. She invited me to brunch.

I rang up Betsy and her relief poured through the line. Harry and Louis were giddy, she said and, for once, were not arguing. The funeral reviews were terrific, the box office for Cutter's final picture blew off the roof, and the Brothers York gleefully discussed re-releasing some of Johnny Cutter's pictures.

All around good times.

CHAPTER 37

Frank Harless knocked on my apartment door as I was getting dressed for Lena Landers.

"We got the guy who killed Jonesy," he said flatly when I opened the door.

Mike and Tank were prophets. Harless stepped into the room and I closed the door. He turned down my offer of coffee or something stronger.

"He was a bell bottom down at San Pedro. Found him on the pier cut up like shark bait. Portuguese named Orestes Jesus Flores. Most called him Orry. He was also known around the docks as the Flower Man."

"How'd you make him?"

"Wharf rat down there saw Flores and another man in a beef last night. Says both of them pulled shivs, and the Flower Man got a Harlem sunset. Perp saw the witness and took off. Witness says the perp was a big guy in a dark flogger, wearing a sailor's cap. Witness didn't see his face. Flores was wearing a dark green sweater with a small piece missing. It matched a sweater piece we found in Jonesy's hand. Flores had a key on him. We tracked it to a lockbox downtown. Inside, we found Jonesy's shield, his service piece, and two rings he was known to wear. And twenty-five one hundred dollar bills."

"That's a neat package."

"Suits the captain."

"Anybody else?"

"Everybody else. Right up to the mayor. The Elmo Jones case is closed."

"But you don't like it."

"Doesn't matter what I like. I do what I'm told." He looked around, went to the kitchen table, hooked his fedora on the back of the chair, and sat down. He lit a Lucky. "Think I'll have that cup of joe, after all. Black, one sugar."

"Same as always."

"Ever cross paths with a squatty torpedo named Carmine Broglio?" he asked as I was filling his cup.

"I know a lot of bimbos. Not all of 'em are squatty."

"This one's squatty. And very dead." Harless touched his throat with his right forefinger. "Took a slug right there."

"Guess he's off my list for bridge."

"Some hikers found him yesterday in a canyon off Mulholland."

"Hell of a place to take a hike."

"Rattles around in my brain."

"What rattles around in your brain?"

"Coincidence. We found Carmine not far from Johnny Cutter's house. Cutter's dead. Carmine's dead close by. Carmine went first. That kind of coincidence rattles around in my brain. Especially if you add Jones to it."

"Glad you sat down." My mind tossed around the thought that if I had known Johnny Cutter was going to get killed, I would have lost Carmine a long way from Cutter's house. "I think the weight on those flat feet is causing that rattling in your brain."

"Carmine was in that canyon about two weeks. Wrapped in a blanket, tied down with strips of another blanket. Obviously moved. No pains to hide that. Looks like the coyotes got to him but we found ID in his wallet. The name rang a loud bell."

"Chewed him up pretty good?"

"Coyotes can gnaw a man. There was enough of one hand left to take fingerprints. We sent them off to the New York boys to confirm the ID."

"New York?"

"Carmine was a trigger man for Joe Masseria. Ever hear of him?"

"I wouldn't invite him to bridge."

"He bowed out back in March. You might have heard? Made most of the papers."

"And Carmine lit out to here? Hiding from the heat?"

"Maybe. Who knows?"

"You got his wallet. What else?"

"Some money, showing he wasn't robbed. Funny thing is no keys. No clue to a place where he might have been staying."

"No map to the stars' houses?"

"You mean was there anything on him to tie him to Cutter? No."

"Could be just a gang hit."

"Not their style. Carmine took a little .32 caliber pill from someone standing right up against him."

"Any leads?"

He shrugged, tasted the joe, and took a drag on the gasper. "Not my case."

"Who pulled it?"

"Steve Entner and Wally Duerson."

"Didn't those two once arrest Murrieta?"

"Oh, they'll dig their heels into this one." Harless took another sip of coffee. "For all of five minutes. They'll cold case it soon as the print match comes back from

New York. Nobody on this force is going to waste time on a dead New York hood."

"And no leads."

"And no leads."

"But it's rattling in your brain."

"It will a bit. Like I said, it's not my case and I won't horn in on Entner and Duerson."

"Might be worth looking into."

"Might."

"You don't sound so sure."

"I told you. No leads. No nothing. Looking into that would be a trip for biscuits."

"But that rattle tells you different."

"Look, even if I could get a search warrant for Cutter's house, just based on that rattle, I wouldn't find anything. Our boys went through that place with a microscope after they dried out Cutter. Didn't miss a corner. You and the rest of Harry's boys did a bang-up palooka. Made my boys grungy. Hope Harry appreciates his help."

"He does. Unfortunately, times are hard. Might not be enough dough in the studio coffers to keep Harry in five dollar cigars. Hear him talk."

"No boost?"

I shook my head. "I just try to keep Harry happy doing little odd jobs for him."

"Those little odd jobs can get a man in trouble."

"Not eating can get a man in bigger trouble."

"Well, unless something falls into our laps, we got nothing. Can't tie Carmine to Cutter, don't know where Carmine's been or how he got there. Don't know where he was staying."

"Take a little legwork."

"Entner and Duerson don't like a lot of legwork on cases like this. Won't be much return on their effort."

"And you?"

"Not my case. Same for Joan Banes."

"Joan Banes?"

"Used to be in pictures. Buried her last week. Trouble is, Sunday night she killed a dirty ex-cop in a house in Beverly Hills owned by a woman named Thomasina Garston."

"Pretty good trick for a corpse."

"You should know. You were there."

"Tommy? Yeah, I was there with her."

"You didn't know her real name was Joan Banes? Actually, Dorothea Gardner."

I shrugged. "She was going by Thomasina Garston."

"You didn't know she was involved with Hiram Strakowsky?"

"I made Hiram."

"He partnered with Elmo Jones once."

"He and Jones busted up a long time ago."

"Maybe, maybe not. They could have kept in touch after Hiram was bounced."

"A shakedown? Jones would do that. Hiram, too. But blackmailing who? And Hiram was killed in self-defense."

Harless blew a smoke ring and found something interesting on the ceiling. "Nobody's denying that. But some questions have come up."

"Such as?"

"Why was Hiram there? When, why, and how did Dorothea Gardner turn into Joan Banes, then Thiele Garsone, which is Thomasina Garston's alias. You get there before or after Hiram got shot?"

"Ask me as a friend and I'll talk about the weather. Ask me as a cop, and I'll tell you to put me on the witness stand if you want an answer."

"There won't be a trial and you know it. Like I said, lot of questions. Answers prove elusive. If it's extortion, who was being bled and over what? You got any answers that don't involve weather?"

"What does the woman say?"

"Said she wants a lawyer."

"Get one?"

"Yeah, a high priced mouthpiece from Beverly Hills. Won't let her talk to us."

"Next step?"

"We might exhume the body supposed to be Joan Banes. It'll turn out to be the Garston dame so we might be able to pin a murder rap on Dorothea."

"Might?"

"If we dig around and get lucky. If she suddenly opens up to us."

"Think she will?"

"Dunno. We might not have her that long. Missouri boys want her on a murder rap from thirteen years ago."

"Missouri? Thirteen years? Mighty quick work."

"We had Dorothea's prints on file. Missouri boys circulated them in 1918 when she fractured her parents with a fireplace poker. Some eager beaver rookie did a routine look at prints yesterday. Didn't take long to match 'em. A Beverly cop called back East. A couple of Missouri bulls caught a train this morning."

"Gonna let them have her?"

"Sounds like it. Might be that nobody around here wants to keep her."

"You might not drag up anything. Just because she took the Garston name doesn't mean she killed her."

"No, it doesn't. I think the BH boys will bundle her off to Missouri and forget about her. Otherwise, they might dig up something to make the Beverly high-hats nervous. That's no way to keep your job up there."

"So you aren't officially involved."

"Not officially, not unofficially. That's BH's worries. Strictly."

"So why did you drop by?"

"Thought I'd invite you to tea. On me. No shop talk."

"Take a rain check? I've got a brunch date."

He smiled the smile of a man slightly tired of his grim and nasty world, but still at ease with it. He ground out the Lucky. "Better looking than me?"

"Nobody's better looking than you."

CHAPTER 38

Brunch wasn't quite ready when I got to Lena's place. She was waiting for me in her spacious back yard, sitting at a little round patio table in the shade of a young Chinese elm. The wooden table and matching wicker chairs shone a brilliant white under fresh paint. The color matched perfectly Lena's impeccably styled hair, done up today with bright little violets pinned just above her left ear by a solid gold hair clip decorated with diamonds that formed her initials in script. A crystal pitcher of iced tea took up the center of the table. Lena raised a tall, cut crystal glass in greeting when her plump Mexican maid announced me.

The warm spell that had settled over Southern California hadn't abated. The bright sun cast harsh shadows, and a faint breeze gently rustled the elm leaves. A bit of sunlight gleamed on the blue water in the rectangular pool and almost made it seem violet. A perfect line of palm trees grew along both sides of the pool. A hammock stretched between two of the palms in the back of the pool near the diving board. A practiced eye had invitingly arranged five patio tables, similar to the one where Lena sat, around the pool. Bright green, head-high shrubbery encircled the yard.

Lena wore a lightweight, silk periwinkle blouse with short sleeves and wide lapels. The blouse color almost perfectly matched her eyes and let the light through nicely. She kept the top two buttons strategically undone, letting me see she was wearing nothing underneath. She had on no makeup, except for a little mascara around her eyes and light, reddish-pink rouge on her cheeks. Her white, silk shorts stopped a couple of inches above her knees, and her supple leather belt was the same color as her blouse. Barefoot, she sat a little sideways at the table, stretching out those eye-grabbing gams for maximum effect. Those long pins could have stopped a locomotive on a dime.

She gave me a friendly hello but didn't stand, instead waving a manicured hand toward the chair opposite her. I sat.

"How's your head?"

"I put a little mortar back there. You can barely see the crack."

"Jimmy Gallen told me you were too hard-headed to let a little thing like a sapping slow you down. Why don't you take off that coat and tie? You look a little silly."

"You might not want me to stay long."

She raised her long, ultra-thin eyebrows, colored to match her ice cream hair. The brows were barely visible against her spotless skin. "Why? I thought we would have a nice brunch and then maybe we'd go for a swim."

"I didn't bring a swimsuit."

"It's a private pool. Why would we need them?"

I poured iced tea into a crystal glass. My hand shook a little. My mind launched flip-flops. "What about the maid?"

Lena smiled, her dazzling white teeth a perfect match for her dazzling white hair. "Elena has the afternoon off, right after she's served us."

Elena must have heard somebody yell action. She came through the patio door with a silver platter holding two fresh salads and six quartered ham salad sandwiches, half on rye and half on wheat. A range of condiments balanced on the platter.

"Joan Banes has been arrested." I helped myself to two sandwiches, both on wheat, and added some mustard and dill pickles.

"I was hoping you came just to see me. Oh, well."

"You've heard?"

"Jimmy Gallen told me."

"You went to the gravesite that day with me to sell me on Joan Banes being buried, not Thiele Garsone."

"I told you I wish I hadn't."

"Who was the driver?"

"One of the crew Jones used on *Sea Venture* whenever we took it out. He said to call him Orry."

"From San Pedro?"

"I don't know. Maybe...yes. That crew Jones used came from around San Pedro."

"Eight of them?"

"Yeah, eight. Who cares?"

"About now, seven of them are caring. Orry's gone beyond it."

She looked at me strangely. "What happens next?"

"We'll wait and see. I told Joan to keep her kisser shut."

"I do have a stake in what happens."

"Keep your kisser shut. If the bulls come around, get a mouthpiece and let him deal with it. Joan hasn't talked yet and she might not. If she does, it's her word against yours. Unless there's some concrete proof I don't know about."

Lena shook her head. Violet eyes could turn mighty cold. "I hope it's that simple, but you know what Jones was making us do. Somebody else could find out."

"My guess is what Jones was making you do won't see the light of day. It's buried even if Joan does talk. And she has nothing to gain there."

"So you think I'm out of it?"

"I don't think Joan can hurt you. Jones and Strakowsky are dead. Cutter and Thiele are dead. You don't even have to worry about Carmine Broglio."

"Who?"

"The bimbo you popped at Johnny Cutter's house."

Her eyebrows arched and her nostrils flared. It was a well practiced take. "The man I killed at—"

"Stow it, sister. You're an okay actress but don't waste your best stuff on me. Carmine, the gent in question, was trying to muscle in on Jonesy's racket. He and Cutter grew up on the same streets in New York. I'm sure you know that."

Her bright violet eyes bore that baby vamp look that sucked men right out of their theater seats and into the movie screen.

"Yes. Johnny told Carmine, hoping he would go after Jones. Turns out Carmine wasn't going to do that. He just wanted a piece of the poke. A big piece."

"Tell me about Carmine."

"What are you going to do?"

"I want to know the full dope. I'm not a cop now and I'm not out to prove anything, but I'm being paid to protect Harry."

"How much is he paying you?"

"Enough that most of my socks don't have holes in them. Tell me about Carmine."

She sipped her tea and looked me over, those violet eyes showing a little moisture. She could turn on the water when she needed to. "I could pay you more than Harry. Along with some very nice fringe benefits."

"Tell me about Carmine. Make it good."

"Sure. Why not? Johnny told Jones about Carmine when he saw his gangster friend wouldn't tackle Jones. Johnny was hoping they'd kill each other. Or at least, one would get rid of the other. Johnny phoned me here that morning you were at his place. Neither of us had the stomach for what Jones was making us do. Johnny was almost hysterical when he called that morning, but Jones got on the phone and threatened him with vile things."

"Jones was here with you?"

Lena nodded, averted her eyes. She suddenly got very interested in the spotlessly manicured grass. "Yes, we were taking the yacht that night. Jones stopped here that morning to tell me what he wanted me to do."

"Jones sleeping with you?"

"You slay me. Some things you don't know from nothing. Sure, I tried to vamp the bastard. I thought if I could get him in a vulnerable position, I could kill him. But Jones was a three-letter man. He liked boys, not girls. And you're supposed to be a dick."

I just stared at her. Her face got a little fuzzy.

"Believe me, Jones kept that secret under wraps. But ol' Lena knew. You bet. All my life I've twisted peckers into knots, but I couldn't even get a blink from Jones. He'd probably have killed me if he knew I was wise to him."

My turn to sip the tea. "Tell me about Carmine."

"Carmine kept telling Johnny he wanted some Holly-wood poon. A chippy who took directions without asking questions. Johnny told him that morning that one was coming to fix him up with nookie for the day. Johnny left for the studio, you driving him. I drove to Johnny's. Jones was with me. When we got there, Jones hid on the floorboard so he wouldn't be seen. I pulled up, went around to the back to let myself in with a key Johnny had

given me a long time ago. Carmine came out and saw me.
He thought I was his quiff. I was wearing my full length
fur. Nothing underneath. I told that fat bum Johnny asked
me to stop by. I stretched the fur coat wide open and the
big slob's peepers almost came out of his skull. He was
easy. He let me get right up to him and I started doing
stuff that made him close his eyes. I had a little gun in the
pocket of the coat. I shot him in the throat. He tried to get
out his gun, but Jones was there, held him down, and
watched him go out. It was awful. I screamed and started
crying, but Jones slapped me so hard I passed out. I
didn't come to until we were almost back at my place."

"Jones give you the gun?"

"Made me buy it a few weeks ago when Carmine
showed. Took me to some store in San Pedro and made
me buy a small gun, registered in my name, with my address. He kept the gun and gave it to me that morning."

"What happened to it?"

"He took it. Said it had my fingerprints on it, was registered to me, and I had better dry up, keep quiet, and
keep doing what I was told if I didn't want to fry for killing that hood."

"Describe the gun."

"A thirty-two I think. That's what Jones said. Small,
silver with a pearl handle."

"Good. That's what I wanted to hear."

She leaned closer to me, giving me a good look at the
promise beneath that periwinkle silk. Her lips parted
slightly and her breath came in little honeyed rasps.
"What about you?"

"The only thing that'll tie you to Carmine is that gun
and Jones. Jones ain't talking. The gat is gone forever."

"What do you mean?"

"I'm thinking it might be buried deep in Laurel Bay,
or maybe way out in the bottom of the ocean. It might be

in a gun case in some highbinder's office. Wherever it is, you won't ever have to worry about it."

"You're certain?"

"Dead certain."

She leaned back in her chair and smiled at me. "All my life, I've been able to twist peckers into knots without even touching them. Now I'm the one twisted in knots." She sipped the tea and made a face. "Elena. Elena."

A figure appeared at the door to the patio. "*Sí*, Mees Landers."

"Bring a bottle of whiskey."

It took Elena all of fifteen seconds to put a bottle of Canadian Club on the patio table and ten seconds to disappear inside the house. Lena poured a generous helping into her glass and took a long slug. She indicated the bottle. "Go ahead. Maybe we can still have that party."

I poured two fingers into the tea. Lena took the bottle and poured a full hand. "How'd you know I killed Carmine?"

"Had to be a woman. Gat in his holster, coat buttoned, shot right under the chin from very close range. Small pill. Only a woman."

"Could have been Joan. After all, she killed Johnny."

"Jones make her do that?"

"Yes. Same as he made me kill that man at Johnny's."

"And those two killings gave him an even stronger hold on you two."

Lena drained her glass, poured more. "Know what? We were really very happy, the four of us, before we went smash. Johnny, Thiele, and I were happy-go-lucky imps having a blast. Old enough to do whatever we wanted, young enough to take to it. We were getting into the pictures. The sugar was big and easy and, we thought, never-ending. Joan was always so shy, so uptight. We kept trying to get her out of her shell, get her to enjoy life. Maybe she was starting to a little, I don't know. But then Pettigrew croaked at that party, and Joan totally dried up. She completely changed her looks. She began drinking heavily, and Thiele helped her. Johnny and I couldn't stop them. Joan was hiding a dark secret, we knew. We just didn't know how dark at the time. Or deep."

She looked at me, almost pleading. "You must understand. I want you to understand. We loved Joan, the three of us, and then she finally broke down and told us her secret."

"She killed her parents."

Lena nodded. There were real tears in her eyes now. "Her father had sexually abused her for years. She tried to tell her mother but her mother wouldn't listen to it. The bitch was afraid of losing her husband. Losing the nice position she had built for herself in the community. Afraid to face facts. She simply didn't believe Joan— Dorothea her name was then. One night an argument started, escalated fiercely. Joan grabbed a poker and killed her father with a blow to the head. Her mother started screaming and Joan panicked and hit her just to keep her quiet. She told us the whole story. We felt sorry for her. None of us would have ever told on her." Lena dabbed at her eyes. "You know, Joan was the original Ice Cream Blonde. Not me. Early on, she dyed her hair white. It really set her apart. Got her career started."

"Then Jones came into the picture."

"Yes, and Joan went to pieces."

"She snowed up?"

Lena shook her head. "No, that was Thiele. Joan never did drugs. Booze wasn't enough for Thiele. She got hooked on coke when she started running with Alma. She began drifting out of our circle and out of pictures. Nobody would use her anymore. She couldn't stay sober.

She couldn't stay off the coke—or the horse. Whatever was handy. Thiele went from young and gorgeous to bloated and old overnight. I don't know how she stayed alive long as she did."

"Well, don't let Carmine pry on your mind. He's good riddance. Joan's fate was always out of your hands. Cutter, you'll have to live with. Most of all, you'll have to live with what happened to all those young girls who went away for keeps on that big white boat."

"I am sorry about them. So sorry, but what could I do? Jones would have killed me."

"You could have gone to the cops. All of you. But your careers came first." I dug Winnie Kamenshek's photo out of my pocket and placed it on the table so Lena could look at it. "Know her?"

"She looks vaguely familiar."

"Cutter took her to the boat and she went out to sea. She's got a baby sister looks a lot like her. A sweet kid who misses her sister and doesn't know what happened to her. People think I went after Jones over what he did to me. Partly so, I guess. I had seven years to brood about that and I always figured Jonesy would sooner or later get what was coming to him. Sooner or later all of us will. But two kids named Winnie and Mary Kamenshek, and I don't know how many others, are doing the suffering. I guess you'll have a long time to think that out. But it's a hell of thing to live with."

I took a slug of the noodle juice and pushed back my chair. I hadn't touched the salad or either sandwich. Ugly red rimmed Lena's moist, violet eyes.

I set my fedora in place. "I can let myself out."

"No party?"

"No party. Gotta see Harry."

"What are you going to tell that bastard?"

"I'm going to tell him he can relax. Cutter and everything else is buried. He has nothing to worry about. He can make his pictures and run the Earth from his marble tower. I think anything else is nothing to him."

"Nothing?"

"Nothing that'll matter."

CHAPTER 39

Now that someone else at least as powerful as Harry had Johnny Cutter's contract, York Brothers Studios got back to the humdrum routine of making motion pictures with quiet efficiency. Or, as Harry would say, sufficiency. Major releases, B pictures, shorts, cartoons, and newsreels rolled out on schedule as the studio battled tightening dollars. Louis York took the *Chief* back East two days after Cutter's send-off, and Harry York clicked his heels in glee and, with unrelenting joy, once again began aggravating everyone who worked for him.

He signed a few new players, re-signed some whose contracts were expiring, exasperated his producers, writers and directors with endless memos, and meddling, wiggled or didn't wiggle his way through daily rushes, and ran his studio with his customary demented tyranny.

A good-looking young actor named Michael Avery inked a seven-year deal, shortly after Harry had landed an exceptionally beautiful New York stage actress named Catherine Holmes. A tall, athletic youngster, who had played football at Southern Cal and had starred in *The Big Trail* for Fox, came in for a screen test, but Harry passed on him.

"He was in *The Big Flop*," Harry said. "Why would I want him?"

Fans flocked to Johnny Cutter's last movie, *Doorway to Heaven*, making it the biggest box-office hit York Brothers ever had. Harry immediately made plans to re-release Cutter's past movies, including several silents with sound effects added.

I took Mary Kamenshek to lunch one day, finally ready to tell her she was never going to see her sister again. I didn't have to.

"I know she's dead. She wouldn't just disappear," she said between sips of her tomato soup and nibbles on a chicken salad sandwich. "I'll probably never know what happened to her."

"Maybe it's better not to."

"Maybe. I don't know."

"Maybe you should go back home. If I hear anything, I can contact you."

"Nothing to go back to."

I had never heard such a forlorn, lost voice.

"Our parents died a year ago. Winnie said let's go to Hollywood and try our luck." She sucked in her breath and choked back tears. The sad bunny folded her hands in her lap and stared at her soup. "Some luck. But there's nothing back in Vincennes, so I'll stay here."

"Doing what?"

"I've got a part-time job at a store downtown, two days a week. Maybe I can find something else. I saw a sign for a dishwasher."

"A pearl diver? You can do better. I can get you on at York. Wardrobe, maybe."

She looked at me and maybe I saw a little hope in her eyes. Her lips quivered. She ran a forefinger lightly across her eye. "That would be nice. I'm very good at sewing. In school, I—"

"Finish your lunch and we'll go down there."

Harriet Walker oversaw Harry's wardrobe department. I didn't know the tall, gaunt, hard-faced Harriet very well, but knew she constantly chewed double-mint gum so I bought her a dozen packs. A couple of girls who worked for her had once told me that, despite her hard-as-nails looks, she had the softest heart of any woman in the world. I took her aside and told Mary Kamenshek's story to her, leaving out the cold truth about her sister.

When I finished, Harriet was on the verge of tears. There was always turnover in her department, she told me. Two girls had just gotten married and turned in their notices. Harriet said she'd give Mary a trial for a week.

Five days later Harriet called me. "I just hired Mary fulltime. She's a very good seamstress. Very conscientious. Thought you might want to know."

"Don't do it as a favor to me."

"I'm not. I'm doing it as a favor to myself. By the way, thanks for the gum, but bribery wasn't necessary."

Later that afternoon, Gallen called me. "Joan's being extradited. Her lawyer tells me he believes they will reduce the Missouri charges. Maybe even manslaughter if she pleads."

"Cutting a deal in Missouri could be the smartest thing she'll ever do."

"I agree. Her lawyer, too, apparently."

I read Theo's police picture. The dirty cop conspired to get the good cop kicked off the force, but in the end—with the help of a smart police captain, a goofy sidekick, and a fine woman—the good cop not only got back on the force, but got a salary boost.

"You ought to take up science fiction writing," I told him.

Theo grinned. "Harry okayed it, and I'm satisfied. Just wanted to run it past you. The audience is going to want the good cop to win out. Otherwise, the box office suf-fers."

"Run with it."

I was at home the next morning trying to put together some bacon and eggs when I got a call from Mack Sang-er. No flunkies, this time. It was Sanger on the line.

"Up for a fight tonight?"

"Who?" I asked, thinking he was talking about prize-fighters.

"You and me and a few friends against an Argentine boat."

"Count me in."

"Dress in black, stuff you'd wear on a boat. I'll pro-vide anything else you'll need. Be here at dusk. You know where my house is?"

I did, but I wouldn't call it a house. Sanger owned a spread as big as Harry's studio lot, sprawled across a point of land overlooking the Pacific Ocean just north of Laurel City. Thousands of tons of stone and brick formed the rambling California ranch, maybe thirty rooms in all. The smallest room was larger than Harry's office. A guard in the gatehouse pushed a button that rolled the gate open and I drove up the winding, paved road that led to a garage big enough to hold three Ford tri-motors without their wings touching. You could have floated *Sea Venture* in the swimming pool. Three tennis courts lay empty but ready, the smooth clay surfaces painted hunter green.

A large expanse of well-groomed lawn sprouted enough flowers and shrubbery to keep three gardeners busy seven days a week. A path led to the Sanger-owned Laurel Country Club just down the way. A veranda cir-cled the house from the left side of the garage to the right, giving a great view of Laurel City to the south and the Pacific Ocean to the west and north.

Sanger waited for me on the south veranda, overlooking his city. He reminded me of Cristo de Redentor standing watch over Rio de Janeiro.

Every paper in LA ran daily photos of the statue as it was going up, workers flocking over it. Dedication was set in less than a week's time.

"Remember those eight names we found on Elmo Jones? The ones listed under SV?"

I nodded. The sun dipped into the Pacific and the far-flung lights to the south twinkled in the soft twilight. I got caught up in the spectacular view as the dark blues and purples began to overtake the soft reds and deep pinks.

"They turned out to be bell bottoms out of San Pedro who had crewed the yacht when Jones took it to sea. At a certain point in our discussion with them, they became very eager to spill. They told us they met a ship at sea called *Viento Justo*, and one of them knew how to contact that ship. Jones worked through that bird when he had girls to move. In short, we contacted *Viento*, and it will be fifteen miles off shore tonight at midnight, expecting another delivery. The Zwi Migdal exists no more, except for those who will be on that ship. They want one more haul and they intend to disappear. Safe from the authorities. Well, they won't get one more haul, but they will disappear. Thought you might like to go along for the ride."

"Just your boys?"

"Mine and some friends of a friend of mine. He also has a stake in this."

"I want a thousand dollars."

Sanger turned away from the beautiful sunset and looked at me several seconds, his face hard and fixed. He nodded.

"All right. I guess you've earned it." His flat voice

burned like Death Valley. "But I didn't expect that from you."

"Not for me."

"Who then?"

I told him. He thought it over and smiled. "Why don't we make that two large?"

I smiled in return.

"Time to go," he said.

We took the veranda to the north side of the house and went down wide, flagstone steps.

"Neil, you could come work for me if you want. You'd fit right in with my boys. I'll take care of you."

"This might sound irrational, but I got kind of attached to Harry York. He gave me a job when I needed one. I'll stick with him. For a while, anyway."

"Fair enough, but the offer's open."

"I'll keep that in mind."

"Say, what about that lovely frail you brought to the Beach House the other night? You put handcuffs on her, yet?"

"I'll keep that in mind, too."

Few private homes had a freight elevator big enough to hold an army half-track, but Sanger had one and we took it down. The door opened onto a walk leading to a boathouse, tucked into a cove along the northern edge of his house and big enough to anchor a couple of dreadnaughts. A forty-foot, teak cruiser hovered near the entrance, its twin diesels throbbing with an excess of power. A big searchlight perched atop a low fly bridge.

"Nice boat."

"Made especially for me. I got two of them. My friend also has two. All the same."

"What'll they do?"

"About twenty, wide open. Plenty enough for what we need."

Eight black-clad, tough-looking brunos lazed on the deck and I recognized Mike and Tank. All eight wore black corduroy pants, black pea jackets, and black knit caps. Sanger boarded and I was right behind him.

"Like night fishing?" Tank asked.

"If they're biting."

"Oh, I think they're biting tonight," Mike said.

"Trouble is," Tank added, "we're just gonna throw 'em all back."

I shrugged into one of several black pea jackets piled on the deck, drew a knit cap out of the pocket, and tugged it over my head. The boat rumbled slowly out of the cove and started for the open sea under cover of darkness, with no running lights. Clouds, quickly closing in, hid the moon. The marine air cast a chilly pall over the boat and made me happy for the pea jacket.

About thirty minutes later, I heard the steady drumming of other powerful diesels and three boats exactly like the one we were in appeared in the thick darkness, all running under a single light in the front and one in the back. Sanger's pilot coordinated with the other three and we turned our direction southwest. The running lights went out on all four boats.

"From here on," Sanger said to me, "we operate on a Sonar QB set. It's based on the British ASDIC system. They're on all four boats, thanks to a mutual friend."

You couldn't exactly buy the ASDIC at the corner marina, but Randall Curtiss could get anything he wanted. And as much of it as he wanted.

We pushed on in the darkness, running at maybe ten knots. The sea roll became more pronounced the farther we got from shore, but we were only going out fifteen miles and these sturdy boats could easily handle anything short of a major storm. I settled in with Sanger in the main cabin under the fly bridge, sitting in padded chairs on opposite ends of a small, round table. Sanger poured about a finger of top-shelf brown into two glasses, just enough to take the edge off. We sipped slowly.

"We'll meet *Sea Venture* in an hour or so and transfer to her. We've got thirty-two men all together. We'll leave a pilot and one other man on each boat and they'll trail along behind the yacht. I doubt *Viento* can echo locate, but if they can, they won't hear those other boats behind *Sea Venture*."

"What's the plan?"

"Simple. One of the ginks Mike and Tank talked with informed us the Argentine ship will keep a steady course at maneuvering speed and *Sea Venture* will close up in the same direction, but slightly faster. When we're along-side, we'll throw over fenders and moor the ships. Spring lines will keep the two ships at the same speed and breast lines will keep 'em as close as possible. That'll ease the heave. They'll throw over a ladder and we'll tie it down. *Viento* is shorter and has a much deeper draft. But free-board's about the same.

"We told 'em we have ten women. All knocked out by drugs. They'll send over ten men. They plan to throw the skirts over their shoulders and hustle up the ladder. While they're doing that another man comes aboard and pays up. If there's other cargo, it'll be sent over by net. Whole thing won't take fifteen minutes, the gink said."

"You trust what he told you?"

"When Mike and Tank do an interview, they get the straight goods. Believe it." Sanger gave me a tight smile. "They talked to all eight of those seamen, separately, and they all gave out the same dope. Last tale any of 'em will ever tell."

"Any of them say where those women went?"

Sanger sipped whiskey. A sour look hardened his pan and he stared blankly at me. "Shanghai merchant named

Wo Shing. From there, mainland China. Then who knows? They'll pump 'em full of dope, chain 'em to a bed, and work 'em around the clock, then throw 'em out with the dishwater. They'll all be dead in a few months, but it's a never-ending supply. Wo Shing, by the way, is Triad, so that's a dead end. There are a million of 'em, faceless and nameless, but if we go prying, they'll know exactly who we are. Those odds are off the charts."

Sanger emptied his glass, but didn't reach for the bottle. The bunny I had seen in Johnny Cutter's dressing room flashed through my mind. I thought of Mary Kamenshek. I thought about the Flower Man—the patsy in the killing of Jonesy, all cut up like shark bait. I said nothing.

"We'll waylay the ten who come aboard for the women. That'll leave six to ten others aboard *Viento*, not counting their bosses. Maybe a dozen of those bastards, at most, based on our sources in Buenos Aires. We'll have twenty-six, with you and me."

Mike stuck his head in the cabin door. "*Sea Venture*, boss."

Sanger nodded. "We'll have Tommy guns, .45s, and hand grenades. They're waiting for us aboard *Venture*. The second those ten men are waylaid below deck, we open up, grenades first, then the choppers. Then up the ladder. Shouldn't take long to clear that boat."

We went up to the teak deck and watched the pilot pull alongside *Sea Venture*. Sanger's men dropped small fenders over the side and tied us up near the Jacob's ladder. It took only a few minutes for us to climb aboard, leaving the pilot and one other man on the smaller boat. He untied us and pulled the fenders.

The boat drifted away and, almost immediately, one of the other three boats took its place. Within twenty minutes, all were aboard *Sea Venture*, except for the two men in each smaller boat. Below deck, in the main cabin, twenty-six Thompson submachine guns and twenty-six .45 semi-automatics covered a dark brown canvas stretched over the rich carpeting. The choppers were fully loaded and two loaded, seven-shot magazines rested beside each .45. The men gathered around Sanger and went over the plan until each was satisfied.

The ten-man crew that operated *Sea Venture* was nowhere in sight. Their job didn't involve guns, and they were under orders to go below deck via the front companionway as soon as those ten men from *Viento Justo* came aboard.

We checked our watches. It was about an hour and a half to our scheduled rendezvous with the remainder of the Zwi Migdal slavers. Most of Sanger's men hung together, talking, telling jokes. I went below and holed up in the captain's cabin, sitting alone in the darkness. At midnight, I went topside. *Sea Venture* was holding a southwest course at about eight knots. I couldn't hear the four boats trailing us, but I knew they were there. Sanger sat quietly in the pilothouse, listening to the sonar.

The boat rolled gently across calm waters and felt spooky with all the lights dark. I leaned against the rail, shivering slightly as the cold, damp air cut through the pea jacket. Suddenly, Sanger materialized out of the dark.

"Okay, we're a mile from the rendezvous point, fifteen miles from shore."

"If *Viento* isn't there?"

"We circle and wait."

"If it doesn't show?"

"Our man in Argentina watched it turn out to sea. It's coming. Ten women will fetch a quarter million dollars. We also told them we'd buy a quarter million in coke. For a half a million they'll come."

We went back to the cabin, sipped on whiskey. A half

hour later, the sonar pinged. Sanger smiled. "That's them."

Fifteen minutes later, *Sea Venture's* two front flood-lights flashed. Off the port bow, we saw an answering flash of lights.

"Everybody but the crew goes below now," Sanger said. He reminded the crew what they were expected to do, then we went below with the others. Some waited in the four guest cabins, others retreated to the bow. I hid with several others, barely out of sight on the stairway that passed the main salon and down to the crew's quarters. *Sea Venture* slowed and the roll picked up. Voices yelled topside and feet scurried around on the deck. A series of bumps told us *Sea Venture* had moved alongside *Viento*, and then the powerful engines shuddered as the big white boat slowed to a couple of knots.

Feet sounded on the stairs and started down, almost running. Ten unarmed seamen flooded into the main cabin. We surged up the stairs and jumped them from behind. They started yelling in a language I didn't understand. The guest cabin doors burst open and Sanger and his men poured out. The ten men threw their hands up and, at a motion from Mike and Tank, dropped to their knees.

Explosions erupted outside as hand grenades tore into *Viento Justo's* decks. The choppers blasted and the entire sea erupted. Four men stayed to guard the ten in the cabin, and the rest of us hustled up the stairs. We broke onto the open deck, firing the choppers, raking *Viento* with a withering volley. Several more grenades went off aboard the Argentine freighter, and then we were pouring up the ladder. A few ineffective gunshots rattled from *Viento* and were quickly silenced. Twenty men poured onto the deck of the freighter, stepping over bodies horribly mangled by the grenades and the submachine guns. Some of us dropped our choppers and pulled out the .45s. Sanger's men chased the few survivors below deck, where they cowered in fear. Five men expecting drugged, defenseless women were facing two dozen hard brunos packing plenty of firepower.

I went through the pilothouse with two others, pulling out the freighter's captain and kicking him down the companionway. Sanger and the others came aboard, leading the ten they had captured in *Sea Venture's* main salon. They took them below deck and jammed them into a guest cabin while the others searched *Viento Justo*. They found a dozen men dressed in suits cowering in two forward cabins. Sanger ordered all *Viento* survivors to be locked inside the forward cargo area.

Two baby grands I didn't know came up the ladder from *Sea Venture* carrying a heavy, metal chest I had never before seen. They shouldered past me, with no word and without looking at me, and went below. Sanger's men, led by Mike and Tank, went through the freighter stern to bow, searching everywhere, but turning up no other survivors. Whatever else was on *Viento Justo* apparently didn't interest Sanger. He left a few men aboard and the rest of us climbed back to the *Sea Venture*, leaving the Tommy guns and .45s on *Viento*. We quickly returned to the smaller boats. Seamen untied the mooring ropes and hauled in the fenders. *Sea Venture's* big diesels throbbed. The huge, white yacht was soon away, heading north.

The three smaller boats drifted away from the freighter, leaving the fourth boat tied to it, waiting for the men Sanger had left aboard. We drifted ten minutes and then the final eight men aboard *Viento* showed on deck and swung easily down the rope to the smaller boat. All four boats fired up and set an easterly course at full speed, heading back to Laurel City fifteen miles away. After a mile or so, each of the four boats set a different course and all were soon separated by open water and caught up in the darkness.

Fifteen minutes later an explosion in the stern of *Viento Justo* blew the freighter almost in half. Great pieces of *Viento* flew in every direction, lit up by a massive ball of fire that rose high into the air, high enough to alert Nebraska. Coast Guard boats would scramble to the site in a matter of minutes.

Sanger grinned at me. "Hundred pounds of dynamite makes a big noise."

CHAPTER 40

York Brothers Studios had to do without me the morning after *Viento Justo* went to the bottom of the ocean with all hands aboard. I rang up Alice Windler and she agreed to lunch. She jumped at my suggestion that we drive up the coast Saturday, maybe all the way to Monterey. A lodge up there served great seafood and offered a romantic view of the ocean. Drive up Saturday, spend Sunday, drive back Monday. She said she could get that day off.

We set the date and I took her back to work, then I checked in at the studio. I wandered around the lot most of the day, trying to give Harry a little of my time, and late that afternoon headed back to my cubbyhole, timing the whole thing so I could run through wardrobe just as that department was wrapping up the day's labor. Harriet Walker and Mary Kamenshek were making notes for tomorrow's work.

When they were finished, hatchet-faced Harriet gave me a hello, a smile, and a goodbye all in one glance. Mary smiled at me and then saw something over my shoulder that made her smile with a lot more intensity. I turned and saw a prop boy I knew as Hal waiting by a collection of women's shoes that covered history from cave days to the present. He sort of nodded at me, sort of tried to hide behind some galoshes.

I handed Mary an envelope stuffed with twenty one hundred dollar bills.

"This is yours. Don't open it until you get home. The studio owes you. Your sister did some special work on screen tests and that's what she's owed."

"I don't understand."

"Harry pays one hundred dollars for anyone who works on a screen test." I hoped my lie sounded authentic. "He doesn't pay until the tests are completed. Your sister, I just found out, did quite a lot of tests for Harry. This is what he owed her. How are you getting along?"

"I really enjoy this work. Thank you so much. You've been very kind to me. I couldn't possibly repay you."

"You repay me every day you come to work."

She turned the envelope over in her hand. "I still don't understand."

I continued my lie. "Your sister probably didn't want to tell you until she finished and got paid. She was in line for a bit in one of Harry's B pictures. I hear she was starting to get noticed."

"Gosh, that would have been wonderful. I miss her—a lot—but it gets a little better every day."

"Who's the fella waiting for you?"

Her cheeks turned a rosy color and she couldn't hide a demure smile. "His name is Harold. He works in props. He's very nice. You should meet him."

I hugged her. "Some other time. It's late. You should run along. If I can ever help you with anything, don't hesitate."

"You've done so much already."

"Part of my job is helping out around here a little."

✺✺✺

Thursday, January 14, 1932:

National News Service

CAPE GIRARDEAU, MO—The packed county courtroom exploded with pent-up emotion yesterday afternoon as the jury in the sensational 14-year-old Dorothea Gardner murder trial returned a verdict of guilty in the first degree against the former star of the silver screen. Miss Gardner stood erect and displayed no affectation as the decision was announced.

The beautiful Cape Girardeau native was convicted in the brutal murders of her father, Delbert Horatio Gardner, and her mother, Ellen Elizabeth Andrews Gardner, at their home in this city in June of 1918. The conclusion of the jury was that Miss Gardner, who was 18 years of age at the time she committed this vicious and heinous crime, battered her poor parents to death with a fireplace poker and fled to Los Angeles, Calif., in an effort to evade authorities.

The jury rendered its decision at 2:38 p.m.

Sentencing has been scheduled for Monday. A high-placed courtroom employee said, on condition of anonymity, that Miss Gardner is expected to receive the maximum sentence of life in prison for her callous and cold-blooded attack on her dear parents.

While in Los Angeles, Miss Gardner began a career in the motion picture industry, appearing in several pictures under the assumed name of Joan Banes. Her true identity became known when she was questioned in the shooting death of a former Los Angeles policeman named Hiram Willard Strakowsky. It is rumored that rep-

resentatives from the Los Angeles Police Department wish to question Miss Gardner in the death of another former screen actress, Thomasina Garston, who performed under the stage name of Thiele Garsone...

❧❦❧

Monday, January 18, 1932:

Los Angeles Morning Journal
HOLMBY HILLS—A shocked and grieving motion picture industry was plunged into the darkness of despair yesterday when the very popular and acclaimed actress Lena Landers was found lifeless in the front seat of her automobile in the garage of her home in this exclusive section of the city.

The official cause of death for the talented and beautiful actress was listed as asphyxiation from carbon monoxide fumes produced by a running engine in an enclosed space. Police say it was apparently an accident, but foul play or suicide has not been ruled out, pending further investigation. Her many friends say the actress had not fully recovered from the September death of her great friend, the former motion picture star John Cutter.

The former actress was found slumped over the wheel of her automobile by her Mexican maid when said maid arrived for work yesterday morning at 8. Police say the electric ignition on Miss Landers' automobile was in the on position and that the gasoline tank was empty. The police theorize the late actress returned home in the early hours of yesterday morning and fell asleep behind the wheel, neglecting to switch off the engine. She had apparently attended a party in Beverly Hills the previous evening, according to police, who are investigating Miss Landers' activities. There is an unsubstantiated rumor that a neighbor walking his dog in the late hours of Saturday night noticed a dark red Chrysler four-door sedan parked outside the gate to Miss Landers' home. Police will neither confirm nor deny that rumor, but a police department spokesman says that matter is also under investigation.

A source close to the ongoing police investigation intimated officials are intrigued by a brief, hand-written note found beside the late star's body. The police have released the note for publication, to wit: I can only hope those poor girls find it in their hearts to forgive me.

The subject matter of that note is, according to police, undetermined at this time.

The gorgeous and stunning Lena Landers, film's Ice Cream Blonde, was...

CHAPTER 41

I stopped reading about Lena Landers. I felt nothing. I was as empty as Johnny Cutter's soul. That afternoon, I drove up to Sawtelle to see Nels. His eyes fluttered when I entered his room and his right hand tried to move. He smiled faintly and tried to speak, but his voice was a hoarse croak. He squeezed my hand. I could barely feel it. Hardly anything remained of him.

I sat beside him the rest of the day, talking as he drifted in and out of sleep. I told him everything that had happened since the morning Jimmy Gallen and I had set out to find Johnny Cutter. I left out nothing. I don't know how much he heard, it just felt good to talk.

Nurse Brownlee brought in his dinner and stayed a few minutes. She couldn't hide the sorrow in her eyes when she started to set up his tray.

I took the tray. "I'll do that." I liked Nurse Brownlee, but just now I didn't want her around.

"He'll need to be fed," she said softly. Tears wet the corners of her eyes.

"I'll do it."

"You eat it," Nels whispered when Nurse Brownlee left. "I'm not hungry." He was immediately asleep again.

The window in his room opened out over the grounds

of the soldiers' home. Elongated shadows from the fading sun darkened the distant orange groves. Behind them, the dark green land shelved down toward the Santa Monica beaches.

I couldn't see the beaches from the window, but I didn't have to.

Two boys played on those white beaches. I could see them clearly in my mind. Two young brothers—twins— dug in the wet sand while a carefree world turned lazily in its worn groove. Two young brothers with no thoughts of tomorrow were building staunch armies the crashing waves would easily wash away, while their proud parents looked on and dreamed of bright futures for their sons.

Where had those futures gone?

Gone west.

About the Author

Ray Dyson first took up eating in Evansville, IN, just long enough ago that not only is the house he was born in no longer there, neither is the street. He attended The Ohio State University School of Journalism, and spent several years as a newspaperman, covering crime and sports. He is a former sports editor and sports columnist, and now lives in Mansfield, OH, with his wife, Pamela, where he works as a freelance journalist. He has a particular interest in American history (especially the Civil War), the American West, and the American cinema.

Dyson is the author of three books: a baseball story *Smokey Joe*, a western novel, *Bannon: The Scavenger Breed*, and his crime story, *The Ice Cream Blonde,* which is set in Hollywood in 1931.